Mortal Designs

Mortal Designs

Reem Bassiouney

Translated by
Melanie Magidow

The American University in Cairo Press
Cairo New York

First published in 2016 by
The American University in Cairo Press
113 Sharia Kasr el Aini, Cairo, Egypt
420 Fifth Avenue, New York, NY 10018
www.aucpress.com

Exclusive distribution outside Egypt and North America by I.B.Tauris & Co Ltd.,
6 Salem Road, London, W4 2BU

Dar el Kutub No. 25538/14
ISBN 978 977 416 714 0

Dar el Kutub Cataloging-in-Publication Data

Bassiouney, Reem
        Mortal Designs: A Novel / Reem Bassiouney.—Cairo: The American
    University in Cairo Press, 2016.
        p.   cm.
        ISBN 978 977 416 714 0
        1. English fiction
        823

1 2 3 4 5   20 19 18 17 16

Designed by Fatiha Bouzidi
Printed in Egypt

To my mother and father

When Carter discovered the tomb of Tutankhamen, he looked in from a small opening he had made in the wall. Lord Carnarvon asked him, full of curiosity and impatience, "What do you see?"

Carter replied, "I see wonderful things."

Author's Note

THE 1919 REVOLUTION WAS LED by Egyptians against the British, leading to partial independence in 1922.

President Nasser led the 1952 Revolution. He called for the end of aristocracy and socialism, and aspired to become the leader of the whole Arab world. He vowed to fight corruption and give rights to peasants, and he nationalized the lands of the aristocracy. But although he fought for social justice, his regime, like those of the next two presidents, would be on the authoritarian side. At the zenith of his popularity, he was defeated by Israel in 1967. The defeat had repercussions in Egypt and across the Arab nation because of the shock and loss of hope. From 1967 to 1973, Egypt fought the War of Attrition with Israel.

When President Sadat took over in 1971 he called for corrective measures and a new revolution, which he termed the "corrective revolution." He began releasing political prisoners and promised a more inclusive regime, reversing the socialist movement of Nasser and starting a capitalist economic movement. However, he still ruled as an authoritarian. In 1973, Egypt regained its pride in the October War against Israel, retaking the entire Sinai Peninsula in 1982. In 1978, there was unrest in Egypt, which came to be called the "bread riots." This unrest resulted from Sadat's measures to cancel some subsidies on basic foods such as bread. Eventually he had to back down and retain subsidies on bread and other basic foods in Egypt. Sadat was assassinated in 1981.

Sadat's capitalist movement was not popular with the masses, and corruption started to increase rapidly during Mubarak's era, in which this novel takes place. The captain refers to the 1952 Revolution and the disillusionment of his generation following the 1967 war. But the novel also predicts a new revolution, termed the "Third Revolution." The novel was published in June 2010, and the January 25 Revolution of the "Arab Spring" took place six months later, calling for liberty, justice, and bread . . . yet again. The 1952 Revolution aimed at eliminating feudalism, narrowing the gaps between rich and poor, and making education free for all. By the beginning of the twenty-first century, and after years of capitalism and corruption, the gap between rich and poor is both wide and visible. Moving between social classes in Egypt remains very difficult; almost impossible.

The references to ancient Egyptian priests as carriers of knowledge form a key part of this novel. In ancient Egypt, knowledge was sacred, and only priests were permitted to acquire certain aspects of scientific and philosophical knowledge. Finally, some Egyptians still build tombs for themselves and their families, an ancient custom not altogether extinct.

From *The Book of the Dead and the Living*

To the First Thief, the one who hastens to take the first step,

I beseech you not to consider tomb robbing, but instead to read the walls.

For on the wall, you would read of the First Revolution, and the Second, and the Third.

From the wall, you would learn how love possesses hearts.

On the wall, a person dies, and is resurrected time after time.

In our land, we do not choose the grave.

We have no way out in our book.

In our land, you read your book with your hands tied, searching for the grave forevermore.

In our land is revealed the wonder of all things.

One

"FORGIVE ME, I KNOW YOU don't make social calls, especially not for a company client. But as you see, I'm on the verge of dying." The captain paused a moment, watching the woman who moved about in front of him. Turning to his guest, he continued: "Let's talk about building a tomb. I've been afraid of the dark my whole life. Nothing can conquer the dark but the fair, tender arms of a woman who wants to enfold you, and makes you shake like an oar in the hand of a drunk. But I know I won't be meeting any woman in the grave, and nothing will be enfolding me but the dirt. No money, no desire, nothing. The end, my friend.

"Look at her, her hips swinging before you, just asking for it. A woman has no flavor before she turns forty. She'll never satisfy you until she's forty. What do we do in this world but eat and be eaten? What could surpass a woman in her forties, like this one, consuming me? That's how she looks, with her bosom just screaming desperation and thighs looking for an ample, lofty, strong sail."

Hazim Shafiq stood in disdain, and said, "I thought you wanted me for something important."

Captain Murad grasped his hand. "Have a seat. There is no greater basis for friendship than exchanging the secrets of love and life. In fact"—Murad leaned in and whispered in his ear—"from my long experience, I can tell you that nothing brings two men together like sharing the love of one woman."

3

Hazim opened his mouth in exasperation, but tried to sound calm. "Sorry, I don't understand."

"Death is on the threshold, and I need your help."

"To have a relationship with this—this—" For the first time, he looked at the woman moving industriously about in front of him. "Is she your maid?"

"Give me some credit. Maids don't do it for me."

Hazim looked again. She was tall and fair, wearing a traditional loose black dress with long, embroidered sleeves and a red silk headscarf, its end flowing past her shoulder. He could not see her face, or even make out the outline of her body under the loose dress.

"Is she your grandchildren's governess?"

The captain laughed. "A fellaha—a village girl! Would I get a peasant to teach my grandchildren? Their teacher speaks three languages, though not Arabic—she doesn't need it."

Looking at his watch, Hazim asked, "What do you need from me?"

Murad surveyed him with big eyes. "You lost interest in her so quickly. You've never pursued a woman, have you? A different generation; an Egypt I don't know. We used to pursue women like sharks in mating season. Seeing a woman's eyes, a woman's lips, even a woman's eyelashes would set us hopelessly on fire! That time has passed—the time when men dreamed of revolution, land, industry, life. The rulers misled us and deceived us. The ship sank. The treasure disappeared. Or maybe there never was any treasure. Who knows?" Murad paused for a moment. "Can I ask you a delicate question?"

"No."

"I have to ask it. Forgive me, 'no' never stopped me before. How did the leader die? The one who raised our hopes so?"

It was a familiar and predictable question for Hazim. So many had asked him the same question when he was a child, and when he was a young man. "I don't know. My father told me nothing about it."

"Come on! Your father was his personal doctor, and we all know how he died. Hope killed him, or perhaps the loss of hope. Or maybe he longed for a lighted tomb like I do now."

"You're very poetic. Do you write poetry?"

"All Egyptians of the revolution write poetry, wandering lost for forty years or more."

"I'm not one of the Egyptians of the revolution, so I don't write poetry."

"You won't tell me how the deliverer of the Arab Nation died?"

"No."

"Then I'll tell you what I want. But tell me the truth, does your sail quiver and straighten for this woman? A fellaha, yes, with the dust of the rich earth, surrounded by the silt of the Nile from before the Aswan Dam was built. You'd be delirious in her arms."

"Who is she? Your relative?"

"No, how would I know her? My wife's taken her under her wing and showers her in generosity."

"Who?"

"I don't know. She'll do anything to please my wife, but she probably won't do the one thing that would make her a queen in Egypt and worthy of everyone's respect."

"Marry you?"

"Enough of marriage, and the weight of its years. Have an affair with me. I could make her dreams come true in a second. You know what they say about honor and dignity and mothers. Anyway, do you want her as much as I do now?"

"No," Hazim answered without hesitation.

"That's too bad. I was hoping we'd become friends."

"I have to go."

"Don't be angry. No doubt you like the other kind of woman—blond, thin, American universities, Western clothes. All right, I don't have long to live; I abhor dark graves and their solitude. I need your help."

"How?"

"I want you to build me a tomb, like the tombs of the ancients."

"The ancients?"

"Our ancestors."

"I don't understand. You . . . what religion are you?"

The captain laughed. "I'm afraid of the grave and its darkness. I want a great big beautiful mausoleum, with space around it where my family can relax, and a tall tower, and a secret door, and lots of openings to the sunshine."

"Who do you think you are? Ahmose? Ramses?"

"Much as Ahmose conquered the Hyksos, so I have withstood seventy years of hopes and dashed hopes, wars both national and international, movements both extremist and opportunist, like diving into dirty, shallow water while claiming it's rich, deep, overflowing with life. I'll pay you whatever you want."

"Money doesn't interest me at all."

"Something else interests you, and I will give it to you."

"What's that?"

"As soon as I saw you, I knew what you were looking for."

"For what?"

"For immortality."

"What do you mean?"

"Build an artistic wonder, and you'll live forever."

"Sorry, but you must be out of your mind."

"Let's just say it's our little secret that no one needs to know. Build me a palace full of light. The whim of a man on the verge of death. Do you want to see the doctors' diagnosis?"

"I won't believe them."

"Can you do it? You're the best architect in Egypt."

"Perhaps."

"I'll give you complete freedom. Design your wonder, build it, and immortalize yourself, and me."

"Captain."

"Hazim."

Hazim straightened his back against the couch. "Let's talk about this tomb."

Captain Murad's house was crammed full of antique furniture and relics, like the Egyptian Museum. As Hazim's eyes roamed the villa, he felt like retching, for nothing irritated him like extravagant taste and flamboyant designs. It seemed to him that the captain had flung gold at his floor as if that would give it value, but the gold was lost amid the junk, dust, and massive furniture that devoured everything like dinosaurs.

Pouring wine into his glass, the captain asked, "Does it bother you if I have a glass before dinner?"

Hazim shook his head.

The captain drained the bottle. "I only drink it to preserve my heart. Red wine is good for the heart." He sighed. "In the seventies, no Egyptian house was without wine. Do you remember? How old were you? You look to me like you're in your forties."

"Fifties."

"Right. In the seventies, a bottle of Black Label whiskey resided in every Egyptian kitchen in the summer, just in case of hard times, and no one got upset or angry about it. What a time! I don't know how to describe it. When I was little, people told me: 'Stay out of politics.' We Egyptians don't interfere in politics, as if our country were run by an unseen magician. Then, when the 1952 Revolution started, they said, 'This is your country, returned to you, but stay out of politics: leave the bread to its baker. You're young and inexperienced, and we're in a state of emergency.' For fifty years, we've been in a state of emergency. It's become a constant state of emergency, and I'm still keeping away from politics and cozying up to women. It's best not to get close to both at once, or you'll kill yourself with perfection. What remains for my generation but dalliance with women? We never matured enough to take things over, and we didn't interfere in politics. They said our country was returned to us. We celebrated. They said justice prevailed. We rejoiced. They said we'd been defeated, and then that we were victorious. They said, 'We'll export, import, and rule.' We said, 'Okay, you're the experts and visionaries. We're the ignorant public.'"

"You like politics?"

"I like Egypt. And all its women. Seriously. Believe me, my loyalty is only to my country. I've seen the world and all its women—white, Asian—and the only thing that satisfies my eyes is a woman like this one before you. Let's eat, and then keep talking."

Hazim looked at Karima, the captain's wife. Her short black hair fell into her eyes. Her sharp features did not give away her age. She was slim, wearing white pants and a blue blouse, looking about uncertainly as if she had not yet settled into this house or this world. Her husky voice betrayed years of smoking cigarettes and the like. The peasant woman looked at Karima, the wife of the captain, with admiration and anticipation, ready to carry out her wishes in record time, faster than the speed of light.

The fellaha sat across from Hazim at the table. She looked quiet and shy, her eyelashes quickly lowering in submission. She neither ate nor spoke.

Karima, Murad's wife, gushed: "Eat, Asma dear. Don't worry. Don't think about them. God bless you, dear."

Then she looked at her husband, saying, "The poor thing is wasting away. Murad, please find a buyer for her land. You can't imagine how her husband's family takes advantage of her since his passing. And what did she ever do to anyone? It's just not fair!" She leaned toward Asma, whispering, "Honey, why aren't you eating?"

Asma replied in a hoarse voice, "Thank you, ma—"

"Asma, honey. Murad, see here, she wants to send her youngest son to school in Cairo. And her eldest is in the

8

Faculty of Economics and Political Science! Can you imagine? With my friend Leila's son. That's how we met. Seriously, the fellaheen still have all the talent. Eat, Asma, don't be shy."

Looking her over as if she were a new boat he was about to buy, Murad asked, "Where's your land?"

"In Benha." She spoke like a Cairene, with only a slight lilt giving away her Delta origins.

To Hazim, he said, "What do you think of her land? Maybe it would work for our project."

For the first time, Asma looked at Hazim. Her eyes focused on him for a moment as if she were looking at a man from another planet. Then she bowed her head. "My land has been zoned for building. You won't find any better."

Without looking at her, he said, "I'd have to see it first."

Suddenly Karima whispered, "I forgot the salt, and the maid didn't come today. They're just no use anymore. You wouldn't know of someone from the fellaheen, would you, Asma?"

Asma rose quickly and fetched the salt and the water pitcher. "I can bring you a maid, or two or three. Just tell me—"

"Asma, now we're really friends! Do you know Hazim?"

She shook her head without meeting his eyes.

Karima laughed. "No one in Egypt doesn't know him! Where have you been living? Hazim is a university professor, or he was, at the School of Engineering. Now he has his own company. His father was the most famous doctor in Egypt, Dr. Samih Shafiq. Have you heard of him?"

She lied smoothly: "Of course. It's an honor."

Then she rose abruptly, having capably taken on the roles of maid, friend, and cook. She cleared the dishes and put them in the dishwasher, while Karima looked on in pleased surprise.

She prepared tea before saying hopefully, "I have one request, madam."

"Anything."

"I would like for you to be my guests at the farm. The grandchildren would really love it, and it would be a chance for you to see the land. Please say you'll come, madam. Please."

Karima smiled and looked at her husband, who quickly said, "Of course."

The day that Hazim settled his agreement to build the tomb was one of the most beautiful days of his life. If it was not the most beautiful of all, it was still the day Captain Murad gave him a chance at immortality and creation, and he could ask no more of life. As an innovator, he loved designing artistic wonders and lofty edifices. He had grown bored with designing hotels, banks, clubs, and movie theaters. He needed a new challenge to fill his days and nights.

It was a crazy idea, but it was viable. The tomb complex, including both the mausoleum and the plaza surrounding it, began to take shape in his mind even before he left the captain's villa and headed to his gray BMW, where the driver had been waiting patiently for him for hours. As soon as the driver saw him, he sprang from his seat. He silently opened the car door, closed it, returned to his seat, and began to drive. Hazim's car had tinted windows, designed to separate the rabble from those in charge. Hazim did not need such windows so he could have sex with a teenager who quivered with desire, or even with beautiful women, as the captain did in his Mercedes. He needed these windows to separate himself from noise, pollution, poverty, noxious odors, uncoordinated clothing, and the buildings that dominated the landscape like eruptions of ugliness and futility. Hazim needed to spend his time in complete concentration to work seriously like his father and grandfather. And on this day especially, Hazim needed to work.

Gaber, Hazim's driver, would wring his hands daily, and say to his wife as he smoked his shisha in the evening: "The man is insane—he's so detached from everyone! He's never spoken more than three or four words to me in a month. What drove him to such bitterness?"

Actually Hazim avoided talking with all commoners, not wanting to waste his time with them. When Gaber would begin complaining about the present age or would talk about his wife, Dr. Hazim would say firmly, "Gaber . . ."

Gaber understood what he meant, closing his mouth in irritation, and muttering, "Damn your arrogance. You're crazy!"

When a car would come near to Hazim's car, and Gaber would honk the horn with all his might and curse the other driver's ancestors, Hazim would say calmly, "If you do that one more time, I don't want to see your face again. Do you hear me?" Gaber would start to defend himself and blame the other driver, but Hazim would interrupt: "Don't talk. Close the window, and don't talk."

When Gaber would open the window to put out his forearm and smell the life-filled dust, Hazim would take off his glasses and say, "Close the window. I'm trying to read."

If Gaber tried to oppose him, as was his nature, saying, "The weather is lovely," Hazim would whisper to himself, "Idiot . . ."

Hazim's rituals were certainly eccentric. His home in Zamalek, in its most famous old building, was nearly bare of furniture. He believed in the beauty of simplicity, emptiness, and white spaces left blank except for a painting of a calm, blue ocean in another reality. A shining life; a country of spaciousness, emptiness, and inhumanity. Every Thursday morning when he woke, he took three hundred-pound banknotes from his pocket, and put them in his right desk drawer. Then he prepared his decaffeinated Nescafé, read his papers, and opened the door for Umm Ayman, greeting her with closed mouth and a nod of the head before he left for work.

He knew that Umm Ayman would open the drawer on the right side, and find there three hundred pounds. She would steal only one hundred pounds, and then continue working vigorously. When he returned, she would try to talk with him and confide in him to elicit his sympathy. She would talk about her sluggish husband who hit her on a daily basis, and perhaps she would point to her head or to the scar on her forehead from one of her husband's beatings. She would talk about her son and his friends, and how they were "the wrong crowd." She would be the victim of a world without mercy. And while she spoke, he would read his architecture book silently, offering no indication that he heard her words at all. Hazim was no fool. He knew that Umm Ayman's eyes glistened with tears on the days that she stole one hundred pounds. She always stole it on Thursday, and never more than just one hundred pounds. He always knew, and he always put the hundred in place.

It did not worry him that Umm Ayman stole from him, for he expected no more from her type. Common people did not have the luxury of easy living, stability, and natural intelligence. We do not expect good from common people. As long as he controlled the situation, he did not mind. As long as Umm Ayman stole in a regular way, she could be studied as a statistic, and the time and amount could be anticipated without difficulty.

She had worked for him for seven years. In the beginning, he thought she needed more money, so he raised her salary. Gradually he realized that she needed to come across one hundred pounds every Thursday, and she had to take it. She *needed* to steal the money, so he did not confront her or pay it any mind. And when Gaber took Hazim's luxury car to meet with his disreputable friends for coffee in plain sight every Friday, claiming that the car needed maintenance, Hazim looked the other way. As long as Gaber returned the car and carried out his instructions, and as long as Gaber enjoyed the idea of deceiving his benefactor like a slave betraying his sultan by seducing his wife, Hazim paid no mind. He did not expect much from common people; ignorance and greed held sway over them all. As long as there was a regular system that the common people maintained, he paid no mind. He appreciated order, the expectation of results, and the fact that risks had consequences.

From *The Book of the Dead and the Living*

First Thief, the one who hastened to take the first step, accomplished impossibility, shook off the dust, and discovered the treasure.

Forgive my lamentable language. I did not study in the Egyptian schools that the revolution produced. I have no objection to the revolution, for revolutions are the result of anger. Anger leads to ease, and ease leads to thieves like yourself. Ours is a country of little ease and much anger. When we get angry, we shout. When we shout, we cry. When we cry, we entrust our concerns to the Creator, and we live in patience and resignation. In any case, I am not a product of the First, Second, or Third Revolutions. I am not a product of the Marxist, Nasserist, capitalist, religious, Arab, Hebrew, thieving, or feudalist movements. Neither the conscious school nor the unconscious school. I do not come from the working classes. I come from a select group, of which I will speak shortly.

O perseverant Thief who endeavored to reach the goal, and arrived at last. When you read these words on the wall of the tomb, then you will learn who I am and where my country is. She is an unfaithful, hard, deceitful, authentic, patient, or widowed woman with whom destiny plays. You will know who she is. Forgive me, for my language is very pitiful. Why did I learn Arabic anyway, since I am an unusual Egyptian, like my father and grandfather. A scholar. A priest in whose hands lie the keys to life and death, and the secret of immortality. An Egyptian determined for glory, from the line that controlled the pharaohs and ruled over kings. My father used to say, "Every land has just one king, who lives in luxury while the rest toil. And every land has a scholar who controls the king." As for my country, there are many kings, and innumerable servants. In my country, you can live as a king within the wonderful walls of your tomb, and forget all about poverty, indigence, the people, destiny, the stars. My father said, "Most thieves are kings, and most kings are walled in by leadership and an entourage. But my son, you are neither king nor slave. You belong to the children of the pyramids, part of the fabric of civilization amid the sun and moon, your status severed from the tyrant dragons. You are a scholar. In your hands are secrets and knowledge. Knowledge is not for the masses or slaves or thieves. Knowledge is for the priest. The priest is born into pride. I, your father, was a priest. I lived better than kings, and I died better than kings. My name was immortalized on the wall of time like the pyramids. You are my son."

Forgive me, Thief. My written Arabic does not fully enable me to inscribe walls, for I am a designer, a builder, and a thinker. I work, but I do not write professionally. I did not graduate from the factories of the revolution, and I do not believe in equal opportunity in a country in which there are many kings and leaders, and the slave is fettered from the day of his birth until the day he is buried, without a tomb.

Two

Asma al-Sharqawi was a first-rate politician, and she excelled at diplomacy; at even the craftiest stratagems. Lying was the most efficient route to her objective. Viciousness, cunning, skirting the facts time after time, until the facts themselves surrendered, leaving Asma holding the victory flag—all were harmless means to reach noble ends.

Like any woman, Asma had a weakness. She had not loved her late husband, although she had respected him, perhaps more since he passed away. For then he had given her the chance to love him without having to put up with his stupid behavior or failure to use his brain, as she had to while he was alive. A stupid man can become the smartest of men when he is dead, but a smart man only oppresses a woman after his death. Nevertheless, Asma's one weakness was her children.

She protected them, stifled them, used them, and pushed them to fly through the air without wings. Since she had given birth to her first son, she had believed that he would become Egypt's ambassador to the United States. Since she had given birth to the youngest boy, she had believed that he would become a prominent police officer, and then the First Assistant to the Minister of the Interior. When she had her daughter, she never doubted that she would become the first of the Abid family to go to medical school, the first to build a private hospital, and the first to discover a cure for hepatitis C. Asma thought nothing of the obstacles she would face to realize her dreams. She did not think of the greatest obstacle until quite a bit of time had passed. Asma's children may have been geniuses, as she claimed, more intelligent than anyone, Egyptian or not. They may have memorized all their schoolwork, studying scrutinizing their books into the night and gulping down arithmetic, logic, and chemistry like a bitter daily medicine. They may have studied nonstop for hours. However, poor Asma forgot about the most important thing needed to realize her dreams. Poor Asma did not think through how things would turn out. Poor Asma forgot that she was completely unknown!

Who was Asma? Who was her husband, Muhammad Abid? They had several acres in Benha, a large house, and one agricultural employee to maintain the land. Asma was, unfortunately, an utterly unknown woman. No one knew her but civil officers and the local mayor. Our country does not respect those without connections. Her children's opportunities were few and limited. Perhaps the eldest son could teach in a country school, like his father. Her daughter, like herself, would end up married at eighteen to a teacher who had a little land, and who would build her a big house and set up a satellite dish for her. As for her youngest son, if he was lucky he would work as a cell phone salesman. His would be the best position of them all, and he would maintain his own land.

When the world weighed on her, she went to the town mayor in her black clothing, tears in her eyes. The end of her headscarf had many uses: wiping her eyes or her nose, and covering her mouth as she whispered, "May God keep you for us, Mayor. I went to the commissioner yesterday, and I commended you to him, telling him about your graciousness and kindness; what you do for us, and for everyone."

The same day, she went to the commissioner and told him the same thing, except that she ended by cursing the corrupt mayor, who had failed to graduate from high school and had inherited his position from his father without any rightful claim. And she cursed the government and the depths to which it stooped. She invited the commissioner to lunch, informing everyone of the plan. She cooked for three weeks, irritating her sister-in-law, her brother, the neighbors, and all of her husband's family. When the commissioner left, she put three more ducks in his car, as well as a country-style leg of lamb, three cooking pots full of food, and homemade pastries and cookies. She repeated blessings over him, and saw to the cooking herself, as if he had come to open the Suez Canal after the Tripartite Aggression. No sooner had he left than she spit on her left hand, saying "May God ruin your house and the mayor's on the same day."

Since her husband's death, she took on new roles every day. She was at times a lonely, widowed woman with no man, surrounded by unjust thieves, and relying only on God. At other times, she was wildly desperate and careless. A shame-less woman is capable of killing if she must. She fears no one but God.

She did not care for her son's driving, and she did not like his constant worrying about everything. But today she had to invite Hazim herself. Clearly Asma had become an upper-class woman, one of those who have plenty of freedom and very little patience. For people can be categorized as those who are patient by nature and those who are patient by necessity, and she refused to wait around when she could take action. The image of Hazim lingered in her imagination. If she became one of his followers, she would have a presence everywhere: the government, the university, the street. The time had come to filter out the temporary friends and utilize the friends she planned to keep. As a respectable lady, a mother, and a hagga who never ceased uttering prayers, she wanted an honorable and decent friendship, perhaps with his wife or daughter, his sister, or a female cousin. The whole way she was thinking of who to mention to Hazim. What if he was not even at his office? What if he did not recognize her? What if he would not meet with her? Looking at her son's face, she resolved to overcome any obstacle. She patted his hand and drew a breath, sitting up in her seat.

"Tomorrow you'll outdo them all. My son!"

He smiled proudly, and did not answer.

She waited for the secretary to admit her to meet with Hazim. As soon as he gave permission, she entered, pulling her son behind her. Today she was wearing a white blouse and three gold chains. One of them her husband had bought her; its pendant was a gold coin. The second chain had a tiny Quran on it, and the third said "Mashallah"—whatever God wills. She wore her long black skirt and her red headscarf, with a tight black border outlining her face. Kohl lined her wide eyes. Her fine features and her bright face stood out from the headscarf.

As she extended her hand, she said warmly: "Hello sir, peace be upon you. It's an honor to visit you. My son so wanted to meet you."

He shook her hand without feigning any interest. She could not tell if he remembered her or not. Across from him sat a woman who seemed Asma's age. She had short black hair and a slender figure, and wore strange clothing: wide pants and a sleeveless blouse. The blouse was long and loose. The woman was small, and looked as if she had just come off the set of an American film, playing the role of a guerilla leader. Asma did not know if she was attractive; her taste in women differed so much from the media.

"Do you remember me? You promised me on Friday that I could visit you. Please don't disappoint me! We came all this way, Taha and I, so I could invite you myself. The place is going to light up with you there!"

She patted Taha's hand again. He was several.centimeters taller than her, and looked like a strong young man. "This is my son, Dr. Hazim," she told him with enthusiasm.

"Welcome," Hazim replied, smiling. "Yes, I remember you, but I don't remember making you any promises. I'm sorry, but I work every day, even Friday. What would you like to drink?"

She felt confused, and was not sure why. Why was she shy of him, and angry with him for refusing her invitation? She found herself accusing him of arrogance and being difficult, even though the captain and his wife were far more arrogant and difficult. She did not understand her reaction. But she answered sweetly, "I won't drink anything until you change your mind. You must come, or I will be very disappointed. Please don't let Taha down."

She looked at the woman across from him, so he gestured to the woman and said, "Dr. Rasha, professor of philosophy at Cairo University."

Before he had even said her name, Asma had already greeted her with four kisses on her cheeks and patted her back until she was nearly bowing to Rasha.

"It's such a pleasure to meet you. Praise be to God—you and your beauty! I hope that you'll honor us with your presence on Friday. I've wanted to meet you for so long."

Rasha looked at her in astonishment. "Meet *me*?"

Asma replied with warmth and enthusiasm: "I would be so honored for Dr. Hazim's wife to be my guest. May God bless you and your children."

"I'm not Hazim's wife," Rasha spluttered.

Asma looked at her in puzzlement. She had called him "Hazim," by his first name. Then what was her relationship to him? She put the thought out of her mind.

Standing, and moving her head and her whole body for emphasis, she said, "You must come Friday with Dr. Hazim. Please, don't let me down!"

Smiling, Hazim asked her son, "What do you study?"

"I'm in the second year at the School of Economics and Political Science," Taha answered.

Rasha interjected: "Egyptian universities have become terrible. I work in them, and I'm aware of the radicalism and stagnation. We worshipped knowledge in my day, but now . . . now ignorance is rampant. I don't know how to do my job anymore, but at least I have some open-minded colleagues. What do you think . . . sorry, what was your name?"

Asma had come for a specific purpose that was beginning to look hopeless and she said, a little impatiently, "I'm Asma, Taha's mother."

"Do you have radicalism in your area? Where are you from?"

"From Egypt, Mother of the World!"

"Right, I mean where in Egypt?"

"From Benha. Radicalism . . . maybe. I don't worry myself about it. When your husband leaves you with three small children upon his passing, one can't think about that; about politics and extremism and . . . I'm sure you understand. Religion is God's affair, and our only recourse is the Lord."

Rasha asked, intrigued, "Are you religious?"

Asma looked at her with discomfort, as this line of conversation did not interest her. "Of course. I told you, I have nothing else."

Rasha opened her mouth, but Hazim cut her off.

"Uh, Umm Taha? Or Hagga, or madam? What would you like to be called?"

Once again, she felt hurt and aggravated after all her efforts, but she said smoothly, "Umm Taha or Hagga, as you like. Will you be coming on Friday to see the land?"

He smiled. "Perhaps. Give me the address."

"And Dr. Rasha, of course," she exclaimed joyfully.

He looked at Rasha, who replied, "Sure, why not?"

As she left Hazim's office, Asma felt a strange sense of unease. She began comparing herself with Rasha. She had never completed her education, and had never even set foot in a college. She had married after high school. They must think of her as a nobody. But why should that bother her? Everyone—all her relatives and acquaintances—thought her insignificant. So what? She did not want him to think her insignificant, or to have to put on airs in front of him. Not even sometimes. Who was she to him? Who was she to any of them? She should just think about the lunch invitation.

Asma's entrance into the circle of polite society was not sheer coincidence. Asma had not decided, in premeditation and through careful observation, to pursue money. When she married Abid, she was eighteen and full of life. Abid had been a young man of twenty-four, and he had loved her since the first time he met her, when she was visiting her father in the school where he worked. Abid had been a geography teacher, with his own property, and his family was known for its prosperity. He had been a man for whom any young woman in Benha might hope. Her life with him lasted ten years, spent in a calm that approached happiness. Then he came down with an illness from which he never recovered. She remained at his side the last year, steady and uncomplaining, waiting determinedly and expectantly for her future. When he died, Taha was nine, Salma six, and Ahmed only one month old. Her life began to change, but not because of her husband's death. That was a common, natural occurrence. She was neither the first nor the last widow. She had been administering her husband's land from the beginning, and he had trusted her intelligence.

Asma's life began to change when her son started college, her daughter became a teenager, and her youngest son began asking for expensive toys. When Salma started to withdraw into her room and refused to go out, and when she claimed to be sick whenever her mother asked her to visit relatives, especially her father's sister, then Asma entered a period of questioning and reflection. She knew that the motivation for her daughter's withdrawal into herself was that Salma did not know English or study at the American University like her cousin, who had married a prominent car dealer. Her lifestyle was different, her clothes were different, her way of speaking and even her jewelry were different. It was Salma's outburst that finally moved her mother: "Mama! We're fellaheen. They think of us as nobody, all the time. I don't understand half of what my cousin says. I don't know anything about her friends. I don't spend the summer on the North Coast. The last time I saw the sea was when Dad rented an apartment in Sidi Bishr in Alexandria for the summer two years before he died. I'm not a member of any club. I live in a village in Benha!"

Asma began knocking her head against her daughter's strange ideas. But even more motivating for her to serve in the army of the elite was her eldest son's lack of humility and his desire to study, pass his exams, and then change the world—unlike his father, who had resigned his fate to God. When she tried to encourage him in reaching his dreams, he would reply resignedly, "Who am I anyway? You want me to get a hundred-pound-a-week job? I could never be more than that. You don't know anything about the others at university."

The tone of desperation that settled over Asma's children was more than she could bear. The straw that broke the camel's back was her youngest son Ahmed. When he came home from school with his fingers swollen and his eyes red from weeping, his mother asked what was wrong. He said that his social studies teacher told him to hold out his hand so he could rap his knuckles with a big stick. When he could not keep his hand out after one blow, he hid it behind his back, and so the teacher hit him four times instead of just two. Her heart blazed with anger. She did not merely lament her fate. Indeed, the next morning she went to the school in her black dress and shouted in the teacher's face. The teacher shouted back and stood by his methods. When she threatened him, he said indifferently, "If you don't like it, sister, then take him to a private school."

She shut her mouth and went home. She vowed that her son Ahmed must attend private school and speak English, and live in dignity and honor like the children of the wealthy. When she went to the school to submit her son's forms, and requested to meet with the principal, the secretary looked at her disdainfully, and said, "We only accept those who already know English, and the children of a certain class."

Asma persevered: "We are the best of people."

The secretary replied coldly, "The principal does not have time to meet with you."

It was clear just by looking at Asma that she had no connections. She needed friends. The time had come to look for assistance and guidance. Karima, the captain's wife, seemed most suitable for her objective. The first thing Asma did was buy her eldest son a car with an installment plan. Thus began her plan for growth, happiness, and advancement through Egyptian society. The secret plan started a new revolution. She crowed over her children in the face of her own mother's confusion: "Asma's children are the best in Egypt. Asma's children are the best in Egypt." At first, her children looked at her in exasperation and disbelief. But as the revolution started to take shape, everyone began to believe in Asma's ability to realize the impossible.

Asma had decided that Friday—the day of her lunch invitation for Captain Murad and his family, and for Hazim and his family—would be a fateful day on which Egypt would be delivered of its afflictions. Dignity would be restored to the lowly. Stability would be restored to the working class. From Friday forward, Asma and her family would rise above their trials and misfortunes. She would sing out, "Stop, O Creation, see how I build up the rules of nobility all by myself." Nobility, in our country, has clear and indisputable rules: an invitation to lunch, an invitation for a Nile trip, cell phones, a gift, a smile from a gorgeous woman, a shortcut to the top, joining a political party. Because Asma was ambitious and wanted to climb the Egyptian social ladder, taking a hundred steps a day; and because Asma wanted to advocate for equality and workers' liberation; and because Asma dared to dream of a better future for her children—the diplomat, the doctor, and the officer; and because Asma was by nature motivated and a bit unbalanced, not believing in fate like other Egyptians, wanting instead to redistribute the wealth all over again and dispossess all private property, Friday was a fateful day indeed.

Her mother, seated in her favorite chair, sucked on her lips. She was a small, self-absorbed woman. She wore only loose black clothing by day. In the evening, she wore whatever was at hand: kids' socks, her deceased husband's socks, both boys' and girls' socks. Pure cotton sweaters, layered one over the other—and this because she believed that Benha winters tracked down the soul before the body. Asma's mother would say, "You'll be sorry, girl. You've lost your sense, spending money right and left. You'll end up bankrupt. Who do you think you are? Leave the creation to the Creator. Your ambition is going to ruin us all. Your husband's family, who you distanced from us over land; your siblings, who you blame for not standing by you. Like I said, you've finally lost your mind. 'Run, Son of Adam, as much as you like, but you can't outrun your future.' What do you want? Aren't we happy here (thanks be to God)? You want the kids to all be royalty? Seriously, how? Everyone gets their own lot in life. You got yours. What is life, girl, but good food, comfortable furnishings, a TV and satellite, and a Turkish soap opera?"

Asma answered with difficulty: "You'll see what Asma's kids are going to do! They're going to be the best of people. They're going to run this country!"

"Girl, think! Who do you think you are? Who's your father and your husband? Whose daughter are you? This is Egypt, you dolt! Daughter of Muhammad, employee of the

24

governorate of al-Qalyubiya! Who knows Muhammad, in order for his offspring to become 'the best of people'?"

"Soon everyone will know of him."

"Asma, they're just lording it over you. They're playing with you. You're like the festival lamb. They're going to butcher you just like the Eid sheep. Don't you get it? Life is all about giving and taking. What do you have to give them? Money? You're a widow with three kids. They don't need your two cents. They have money and prestige. Or are you going to give them something else?"

She said angrily, "What are you implying?"

"I'm worried about you. You're a very pretty girl, and I'm worried about you. Raise your children and walk near the wall. They're all playing with you, and you can say your superstitious mother said so!"

Asma rose in distress, and began to prepare lunch, as she usually did when her mother's speeches irritated and frightened her. That day she hired a maid just for the Friday lunch. For the captain's grandchildren she arranged not just two donkeys, but three, for them to ride around the area. She made fiteer pancakes and cookies for Lady Karima to take back with her to Cairo. Everything would be ready for the great victory within six hours, not the six days that it would take anyone else!

Asma had to make all the arrangements and assess the losses. She estimated that she would spend nearly a thousand pounds on this lunch visit. That meant that she must succeed by any means to reach her goal. It also meant that her children would be eating fried eggplant and potatoes cooked with rice for the rest of the month. Plus, she would have to budget carefully for months in order to pay for her daughter's private tutoring to enable her to get a high score in the high school final exam. However, she did not think through this all at once. After all, if the captain bought the land, that would solve everything; and if the captain's wife helped to vouch for her son, then he could enter the diplomatic track. Her daughter could enroll in the

American University, and her youngest in private school. All her dreams would be realized. The lunch visit would have to be perfect, run as well as schools in developed countries, or better. She had been cooking for three days, not letting her children taste the stuffed vegetables or try the duck that glistened on the table like a welcoming mother. Her heart fluttered when she heard the captain's car approaching, with Hazim's car behind it. Her campaign to eliminate the paralysis of being disadvantaged and the disease of weakness had begun.

Asma's house was painted dark green. She had repainted the walls three years earlier because her daughter was approaching marriageable age. It was a single-story house with three bedrooms, a small kitchen, and a wide-open living space containing a fine dark-wood table that her father had bought for her when she got married, a Persian carpet that saw the light of day only on special occasions like this one, and a golden couch covered at all times by a yellow sheet. Today the room was fit to host presidents and ministers. Asma herself had washed the chandeliers. She had scrubbed the bathtub with every kind of imported cleaner. She had pasted new wallpaper over the spot that had been discolored by humidity, and that would have been fully visible to anyone sitting on the toilet to do his or her business.

She spun like a top amid everyone, tending to needs, kissing the children, and admonishing her children to be nice to the captain's grandchildren. She served fresh juice, then the crisp qaraqish cookies that she had perfected, and finally a lavish lunch. Most of those present did not eat. Asma loaded food onto everyone's plate as if she were distributing Solomon's treasures among her own children. Rasha was trying to eat the duck breast without fork or knife, and could not figure out how to cut it with a spoon. As for the captain, he was eating heartily, saying, "What great food! I haven't eaten like this in years."

His children and grandchildren touched nothing, disgusted by everything—the smells, the dishes, the modest furnishings, the old table. Karima asked Asma loudly and without thinking: "Did you wash your hands before you cooked, Asma?"

Asma replied without a trace of annoyance: "Indeed I did, my dear. And I cooked everything myself. Try it! Our food is clean and delicious."

Asma took a piece of duck and put it on Karima's plate.

"Is there no knife for cutting the duck?" Karima mumbled. "I can't eat like this."

Asma cheerfully went to the kitchen, saying, "In just a second you'll have a knife. I'm at your service. We're so glad you could come today."

Rasha looked at Hazim and whispered in his ear, "The captain's wife is horrible. He's much better than her. Do you see what poor Asma is dealing with? And why aren't you eating? Oh, of course you wouldn't eat."

She looked at him, tried again to cut the breast meat with her spoon, gave up, and started eating just the rice.

Asma gave Karima a knife, saying, "Cut what you like, my dear. It's such an honor to have you here today." Karima began cutting into the duck, and she started to eat. Asma smiled victoriously. She did not engage anyone in conversation or sit with anyone; she was overseeing everything.

After lunch, it was time to entertain the grandchildren. Asma had three of the farm workers lead the children on the donkeys around the irrigation canal area. The children enjoyed it. Every time she heard their laughter, she sighed comfortably. She clasped her hands in front of her, gazing at the sun and the canal, and smiling. Rasha watched her all the while, until the canal caught her attention. It was broad and surrounded by trees. Not one of the captain's daughters tried to speak with Asma. Even the captain's wife was busy with the grandchildren.

Rasha came closer and, pointing to the canal, asked, "What is that cord?"

Asma answered unconcernedly, "It's been there for a month, and no one pays it any attention—neither the government nor the mayor."

In the canal there was a dead black water buffalo with open, shining eyes, its whole body floating on the surface. In front of the water buffalo an electric cord had fallen into the water, where it lay slack.

"That cord could kill someone!" Rasha exclaimed. "Does anyone use the canal?"

"No," Asma answered, her eyes on the captain's grandchildren. "No one uses the canal. Everyone is afraid. They are afraid of the water buffalo too, not trusting water in which their animals have perished."

"The water buffalo obviously died from the cord."

"Who knows?" replied Asma noncommittally. Then she looked at Rasha and patted her hand. "It's an honor having you here today."

Asma looked at the tiny white shorts that Rasha wore, and the loose green blouse. To Asma, Rasha's legs seemed very unattractive, short and skinny; but every man had his own taste, or so it seemed.

Rasha, as though reading her thoughts, asked, "Does it bother you that I wear shorts?"

Asma patted her hand again, and assured her: "Not at all, my dear. It's so good of you to come. You should wear whatever you like."

Rasha replied assertively, "I certainly do wear whatever I like. The restraints on free liberated women in Egypt really bother me. These conservative ideas come from abroad, and they want to bring us all down with them. I do this because I want to challenge these restrictions. I have complete freedom in what I wear. Right?"

"Of course!" Asma exclaimed. "Wear what you want. You're strong, and a professor. You know better than anyone."

Rasha smiled and seemed more interested in the conversation. "You feel the coercion too? I mean, pressure on you from every direction?"

"It's as if you can read my thoughts," Asma said.

"There's such oppression of Egyptian women."

Asma was quiet. She did not understand the point of this conversation.

Rasha said, "For example, don't you want to wear shorts one day?"

"No. You'll have to excuse me, but I'm not used to such clothes."

"That's because—"

But before Rasha could finish, she heard the screams of the grandson from on the donkey. Asma's heart nearly stopped, and she asked breathlessly, "What happened?" She could see the child before her, so she was reassured that he was living. A second later everyone came out, following the child's screams, but she could not understand why he was screaming. Was he afraid of the donkey? The Malaysian nanny picked him up and handed him to his mother. He said, through his tears, that the ball that he loved and kept with him had fallen into the canal while he was on the donkey's back.

Asma said quickly, "I'll buy you another one today."

But the child looked at her with loathing, and told his mother that the donkey and the donkey's owner were the reason he'd lost the ball he loved. The mother shot Asma a look of blame. Karima's face changed, and she told the nanny, "Go down and get the ball for him."

The nanny faltered in her broken Arabic: "The canal is dangerous, and has dead animals and an electrical cord in it."

"Asma," Karima ordered, "tell that worker to go down and get the ball. Can't you see how upset the boy is?"

Asma restrained herself, and said carefully, "No one is going near the canal, but I will buy a better ball today. Now."

Asma's answer startled Karima. She could not believe that Asma would oppose her after she had introduced her to members of high society.

"Then we're going now," she said.

Asma's son Taha intervened at this point, saying to his mother, "I'll try to get the ball from the canal."

Asma opened her mouth to speak, but Karima interjected, "All right, great. What are you waiting for?"

But Asma said sharply, "No. You will not go down to the canal."

Before her son could argue, and without thinking, she headed to the canal in full sight of everyone, saying, "I will return with the ball for your grandson, Madam Karima. We have better ones, though."

Hazim was standing at the door of the house, watching the situation from afar, as was his wont. His eyes widened in astonishment, and some apprehension, but he did not move. Rasha, however, shouted, "No! Don't go! You'll die. Please, someone say something."

Tears glittered in the eyes of Asma's daughter Salma, as she hung on to her little brother Ahmed's hand. Silence fell over the group. There was only the sound of the sticky mud that clung to Asma's legs as she walked cautiously, closing her eyes as she neared the ball and the cord. She was whispering all the Quranic verses she knew. The water reached her chest as she grasped the ball, only steps from the cord. The people of the area surrounded her, watching in wonder this brave woman whose story would become legend in a matter of seconds, when she would be struck down dead. But Asma slowly moved to exit the canal. It was a miracle, of course, or perhaps the electricity was cut off, or the cord itself was faulty. In any case, her story would not become legend after all.

Hazim had come down to watch. Beside him were the captain, his grandson, and Asma's children.

The captain smiled, and whispered in Hazim's ear, "Seriously, how would a woman like that be in the arms of a man she wanted? And don't tell me you don't want her now. A woman worth a hundred men. My God, I feel like a teenager in her presence."

Asma rested her hand on a small stone to climb out of the water. The captain reached out, saying, "Take my hand."

But her son had also extended his hand for her. She grasped her son's hand, coming out of the water with her black gilbab robe stuck to her body.

The captain gulped as he took in Asma's body, the damp dress clinging to it spectacularly, making her ready to be devoured like the duck on the table. His eyes fondled her behind shamelessly. The captain shuddered as he watched her hand the ball to the child and go inside. The child took the ball and laughed, and then threw it back into the canal.

Karima looked at him in rebuke. "Again! This time I'm not going to ask anyone to get it. This time there will be consequences, and you can wait for me to buy you a new ball."

Asma was breathless from fear. She had feared dying, leaving her children with no family and no future. But risk had been inevitable, and the risk had brought about the expected outcome. The situation left an impression on Karima, and she decided to give Asma the key to an apartment in Marina, an exclusive resort on the North Coast. She sometimes gave the key to someone from whom she wanted something, or to someone she wanted to be rid of.

She said proudly, "A week in Marina, Asma, with your children. But take care of the house. See to it that nothing gets stolen."

When the sunset call to prayer rang out, Asma asked the men if they would like a room for prayer. No one responded but her son. After she had served the baklava, kunafa pastry, and crème caramel, the captain asked her to accompany him to the bathroom, as he did not know where it was. No sooner had the captain reached the bathroom than he looked around, and then pushed her into the room on his left. She knew that look of hunger and desire, and it did not frighten her. When she saw it in the captain's eyes, she was dazzled for a moment, and then disregarded it. But when he closed the door, put his hand on hers, and breathed "You're beautiful, Asma," she backed up, opened the door, and said, "God bless you, Captain. I'm flattered."

"What do you want? Tell me. Anything. Your son can go to a private foreign-language school. Taha will be a diplomat. I'll buy your land for a half million. What do you say?"

He came up and put a hand on her chest. She pushed it away firmly but calmly, and said graciously, "A widow raising kids. Bless your heart, what a gallant man. I've no one but the Lord. I couldn't anger him. Where would I go with the kids? God keep us, Murad, sir, and bless you for your sympathy. I swear, I've had no one since the day my husband died."

He kept the door shut with his foot. He could not understand her refusal, or anything she said.

His hand moved toward her thigh as he whispered, "You want a legitimate marriage?"

She caught his hand and said, a little stiffly, "I'm flattered, but I wouldn't dream of it. If only I could. My family would cut me off. I couldn't. My son is taller than I am! I want your sympathy and noble character. It will be to your credit. I've devoted myself to my children."

He recoiled in distaste. "You're insane!"

She placated him: "I beg you, don't be mad at me. Promise me you won't be mad at me. Take the land, Murad, sir, just for the honor of your visit. It's not worth a half million."

His eyes widened in surprise.

She continued: "I'm raising my kids, Murad, sir. How much would you sell it for? Land with the sun from every angle. I'll give it to you for six hundred thousand in thanks for your visit today."

He opened his mouth, dismayed. Not even a hair of hers had trembled when he touched her. She was neither fearful nor submissive. When he proposed marriage, she ignored it. She started in on the price of her land! What a truly vile fellaha, such lowly people. Why had he talked with her in the first place? But she was a woman like a lion. No, a river crocodile, leading you on and playing with you.

In the voice of a businessman, he said, "Marry me, and I'll give you a million for the land."

"Give me six hundred, and we'll call it even."

"Don't make me angry, Asma. I'm not accustomed to it."

"You think I'm playing? I couldn't be more serious if my life depended on it. You can ask for anything, but don't belittle me in front of my children. We're fellaheen . . . I can't. Anything but that."

"Anything?"

"Honor is the Lord's, and I've been the Lord's my whole life. I've got no one else. I swear the land is worth more than that."

"I'm not buying it."

"I'm banking on your generosity and your morals."

He did not answer.

She whispered, a little hopefully, "I'm banking on your sympathy for a lady in my position. I know of your generosity, and I've heard of your morals. You fought in the 1973 War, didn't you? Or was it in the War of Attrition? You were a diver, and you destroyed an enemy ship, right?"

Turning to leave the room, he said, "You're insane."

"So you'll buy it then? You wouldn't disappoint a poor woman like me."

He left the room in a rage, colliding with Hazim, who was on his way to the bathroom to wash his hands. Hazim raised his eyebrows questioningly as he looked at the captain and Asma together, and the door that had been closed seconds ago. Was he looking at her with surprise? Or lack of surprise? In judgment? Or without any expression at all?

Her eyes met Hazim's for a moment. She lowered her eyes, and walked mechanically to the garden. She did not know why she desperately wanted to tell him that she was innocent. Hazim seemed more important than the captain. He seemed honest. He never smiled, and did not look around for ways to manipulate others. As if the world meant nothing to him. What about his friend Rasha? What was their relationship, anyway? No doubt she was his partner in more ways than one.

After that, Asma looked rather distracted. While she was trying to behave naturally, she was wondering why she wanted to clear her reputation in Hazim's presence. As everyone was preparing to leave, she went back to her usual habit of bustling around.

Putting cookies in Hazim's car, she said, "Please, I insist."

He did not answer. He looked at her, and she whispered, "I need your help. Could I talk with you, just for a minute?"

"Sure," he said, sounding a little bored.

She looked around, saying, "Let's take a quick walk, if you don't mind."

She walked at his side, and suddenly trembled at the sight of his hands. She had never seen a man like him before. And she had never trembled for a man before either. He was radiant, as if in a dream.

She walked at his side silently, and then whispered, "Do you like the land?"

"Yes," he said nonchalantly.

"What's the plan? An apartment building?"

He did not answer.

She said, "I hope that you'll consider my son your protégé, as if he were your own. I hope that you enjoyed today, and that you'll come visit us again. And, from my heart, I hope that you'll help my son get into the diplomatic corps. We're good people, really. We don't have any political agenda. No one would represent Egypt better in America than Taha. He's a pure Egyptian man, smart, and—"

He looked into her face and said calmly, "You have high hopes."

"Can you help me?"

"Why?"

"Charity. I'm alone, and . . ."

He examined her face without speaking.

She resumed: "Help me. God bless you, you and your children."

"How?"

"I want to sell the land, to change all our lives."

He looked at his watch, and then stopped. Looking into her eyes, at once smitten and repelled, he said, "You almost killed yourself today."

She said, her heart pounding without her knowing why, "I risk my life thousands of times every day for trivial things."

"So you're willing to do anything to sell the land?"

"Not at all," she replied quickly. "Of course not. I'll never go against God."

He nodded, and said, "I'll see what I can do." He turned to go back to his car.

"Is the captain your friend?" she burst out.

He did not answer.

"I'm not a woman of Cairo. No one can buy me."

Suddenly he stopped, and said innocently, "I don't understand."

"Please understand me. May God protect you. I'm grateful for everything. And I know that you'll help me. Because you're very kind. And you understand me, right?"

He smiled courteously, and held out his hand to shake hands with her. "Thank you for a lovely day."

No sooner had Rasha gotten into the car next to Hazim than she began talking nonstop, cursing the captain and his wife, then the government and its negligence, bilharzia, canal water, the high cost of living, and the pollution of the Nile, the Nile Valley, and the residents of the Nile Valley. She spoke with enthusiasm, anger, and a great deal of resentment for the wealthy and the elite.

"The poor thing would have died to appease the captain and his wife. Did you see the neglect? Did you see the poverty? Just seeing that place makes one want to call for revolution. The French Revolution started over less! Yet we Egyptians allow the injustice. Now you know why I support the opposition party. Because they're tired of injustice. It's time the scholars and the educated intervened. Don't you think so?"

He did not answer.

She continued: "What about that Asma? Crazy, huh? She's really beautiful, though. Her clothes are more colorful than necessary, and all her gold is not very tasteful, but she has fine features and a well-proportioned body. She's not as graceful as I am, but she is quite slender. She must not eat much of the food she cooks. She seems pretty intelligent. You know, female circumcision is so prevalent in the Delta region. I wonder if she was yet another victim of it. Of course she was—why am I even asking? Can you believe she didn't know the meaning of 'ecstasy with a man'? Actually, it's better that way. The men in our country—"

He interrupted her: "Stop talking."

"You're different. I told you, it's about time scholars got involved. You should join us in the opposition party."

He did not answer.

So she continued: "What a weird day. Does that fellaha feel what we do? Is she concerned about different things? I don't understand her. I may have studied in French schools, but I did still study in Egypt, to some extent. I should ask her about these things. What do you think?"

He lowered his gaze so that he would not see the naked children around him, bathing in the canal. The tinted glass could not hide them, as if they were phosphorescent frogs, glowing in the dark, or jinn of the netherworld, escaping every which way.

"She's not a subject in an experimental piece of fieldwork," he said. "Think, Rasha."

"I'm concerned about human rights in Egypt. Rights! Egyptians don't even know the word. Do you understand? Hazim . . . ?"

"The land is fertile, good for agriculture. Did you notice?"

She was quiet for a moment. Then she said, "There's a lot of loneliness around us. Me and you, and that fellaha. Each of us is alone, in his or her own way. Me, because I'm different, but I love Egypt. Who loves Egypt anymore? I don't know, but we'd probably throw him in the desolate Sahara to die of thirst. You, because you don't know Egypt at all. And her, because she is all of Egypt."

"Always a philosopher."

"You used to love me. Do you remember?"

He said calmly, his eyes widening, "I still love you." He looked at Gaber, the driver, and tried to make his face impassive as he listened to her chatter. Then she whispered in Hazim's ear, "There was a time when you loved me like a man loves a woman. Not like a friend loves a friend."

He placed a kiss on her cheek, and said, "Ten years ago."

She smiled and said, "In our Egypt, we can still be friends. In the Egypt of that fellaha, we'd probably be killed for our actions. What if I told her that I had a relationship with you ten years ago, and that you were not just my friend, but my lover? What would she say? Like I said, they know nothing about personal freedom, about rights. As long as I'm not hurting anyone, what's the problem?"

"There is no problem."

"You only love educated, philosophical women. Yet you married Shereen."

"I was young and stupid."

"I learned a lot today, my friend. I think we should divide Egypt into emirates. I'd belong to the French emirate. You'd belong to the, I don't know, the scholars' emirate. The captain would belong to the American or British emirate. He has characteristics of both of them. Asma—or should I say Umm Taha—would be in, I don't know, the Arab–Egyptian emirate, the Nile Valley emirate, the emirate of the pharaohs. Oh, I have so many ideas today. I'm going to write an article about all this for *Le Monde*."

When Hazim had taken up with Rasha, the relationship had been clear and mutually beneficial. Rasha's first marriage had failed, as had his. They were friends, spending a lot of time together. After their first kiss, they continued to live in happiness for five years with no restrictions. When the physical relationship began to dry up, they remained friends. She was his closest female friend. He had met others after her, and she too had gotten to know others after him, but their friendship had remained.

When Asma went to sleep after the lunch visit, her back hurting as if she were about to give birth, there came to her a vision of her husband. She still remembered his face. He was always calm and smiling in her imagination. Asma had been a good wife, most of the time. Sometimes she would fight with her husband for a day, or two or three, until he would swear that he was going to marry someone else. Then she would give in, and open the bedroom door for him. She had not enjoyed sex, but she had seen it as a tool in her hands, and she used it with him often. When her husband died, she was thirty. She decided with her common sense to give up her femininity. She was a widow. A widow is vulnerable, and so no one could deny her anything. In our country, mothers are celebrated, and all stand before them in fear and awe. She decided to emphasize the mother image, and forget her image as a woman. She would always say, "I'm a mother raising her kids; a single mother raising her children." She had never analyzed her feelings toward her husband. She had no time during either his life or his death to do so. He was a man. Every woman needs a man, alive if possible, and dead if necessary.

She knew that she was pretty. When her husband died, she had noticed the looks of lust from men as she never had before. Most of the village men had tried either to seduce her or marry her. Thus she needed her loose black abaya to cover her femininity and protect herself. Since she was a child, doted on by her father, who wished for her a splendid future, she had been trusting. The captain's looks and gestures meant nothing to her. What was new was that they came from a man completely outside of Benha; a wealthy and reputable man. But she knew her place. She would ignore him, and walk her own path.

She moaned as she held her back. Her daughter, lying next to her, asked, "Are you all right? Mom, why did we invite them? I don't like any of them. That captain's wife is conceited and shameless."

Her mother reprimanded her: "Don't say that. She's kind and generous. Her circumstances are a bit difficult, but she's very nice. There are hardly any like her these days. She helps us and asks for nothing in return."

"She treats us like monkeys and belittles us," her daughter grumbled.

Asma sighed and said with finality, "Let's not talk nonsense. We're going to Marina! Can you believe it? Marina that we hear about in the movies! Has your cousin been there? Tomorrow morning, call her and tell her."

Three

NEWS OF THE VILLA IN MARINA, in which Asma and her children would spend their summer vacation, spread from al-Qalyubiya to Tanta, the coast, Greater Cairo, and Giza. Asma boasted that she was the first person from al-Qalyubiya to spend her annual vacation in Marina, and her children would be the vanguard in building the nation and its glorious future for generations to come. She would waft incense through the house to prevent jealousy, but it would only increase when her son went to a private foreign-language school, her daughter enrolled in the American University, and she herself won the Nobel Peace Prize for gathering Egypt together, cross and crescent, king and servant, and all classes, the crushed and the crusher. She would accomplish that which America and the Arab world had not, uniting friends and foes.

Preparation for traveling to Marina started a month in advance. It called for buying new clothing, making qaraqish, storing up all manner of mangoes, jams, juices, and meats. For Asma would be going as a lady, not as a fellaha. Asma even went so far as to buy a whole box of bottled water, and set it in the window for the neighbors to see. The excitement began to spread among the children, as they came to know their mother's abilities to work magic and accomplish the impossible. Yet Asma's mother still sucked her lips, accusing her daughter of insanity. She continued to watch her favorite shows on TV— religious programs and Turkish soap operas—and to turn the house upside down searching for her glasses. Asma's mother could not see without her glasses. She could hardly lift a finger without leaning on her walking stick. It seemed to everyone that just as Asma's mother confused objects, so her daughter confused social roles.

When the old white Peugeot neared the entrance of the illustrious Marina, Asma trembled like a bride on her wedding night.

She announced, "We've arrived at Marina, Mama."

"More like we've arrived on the moon, girl!" her mother groused.

But Marina was more beautiful than the moon, and it was farther away. One nearly floated in it, through the wide, clean streets; the villas surrounding green spaces, trees, palms, and blue and purple flowers; luxury cars more luscious than mulid festival sweets or rich water-buffalo butter. The Marina employees worked silently, disappearing from sight. The young people of Marina surpassed all others around the world in their happiness and ease of living. At times, it seemed to Asma that she had died and gone to heaven. She would probably see her husband presently, wearing all white, driving a RAV 4, with a girl at his side in tight shorts, with long, smooth hair and blue eyes.

She asked her son apprehensively, "Do you know the address of the villa?"

"We'll just ask for directions," he answered, smiling as if he had just met five of the very richest girls of Marina.

That night she dreamed again that her son had married a politician's daughter, and her daughter had a maid from Ethiopia and another from Argentina, and her new house in Zamalek was prepared to receive all her grandchildren, equipped with laptops, TVs, modern red and white furniture, chamois rugs, a kitchen with wide windows, and a dining room table of pure marble. She slept, feeling victory in every limb. She had succeeded in changing the present and the future. The government should enlist Asma to break the opposition movements.

After breakfast, her mother declined to go out with them, complaining that the sea for her was just a bother, a mess, and a lot of black sand. Asma told her son to carry the umbrella, her daughter to carry the chairs, and her youngest son to carry the bag of food and drinks. She stepped out toward the beach confidently. She passed through the street and the beachside villas, and walked onto the sand. As she neared the waves, she decided to stake her umbrella in the front row. She looked over at a large family that had set up a giant umbrella. Then she sat in her chair and said encouragingly, "All right, kids, go get in the water!"

Her daughter looked at their neighbors, the girls all wearing bikinis. They seemed utterly carefree and happy, drinking fresh mango juice. The boys were eating American chips from big red canisters and drinking beer from green glass bottles. They shouted and laughed. One boy was putting sunscreen on his girlfriend's back, whispering in her ear.

Salma turned to her mother in dismay, saying, "I can't go in the water in my clothes. What would people say?"

Asma looked piercingly at her daughter. "Why would you care what they say? Salma, like your mother, you don't oppose God and you do what you want with confidence. Why do you think I waste my time being around these people? To see you turn out better than any of them."

Salma knew her mother's words by heart. She nodded, but said with finality, "I don't want to swim."

The two boys needed no encouragement to swim, diving in with enthusiasm.

Asma got out the qaraqish, offering one to Salma. She did not take it. Silence prevailed. Asma did not know what to say to her daughter, or how to convince her. Her firmness intimidated her son, and her weakness horrified him. With her daughter,

43

neither weakness nor strength had any effect. Asma gazed at her neighbor's hands and French-manicured nails, their white tips shining like the floor of a butcher shop just cleaned by a seventeen-year-old boy in the bloom of youth. The woman stretched a piece of chewing gum between her fingertips, and the maid took it from her straightaway, disposing of it in an unmarked bin. Then the rich woman stretched out her other hand to indicate a cherry bag, empty but for the pits, and it too disappeared into the bin. Even Umm al-Madamir, who communicated with spirits back in al-Qalyubiya, would not treat a genie so haughtily!

Her neighbor pointed with a substantial hand, dripping with gold, and called to the umbrella man, "I want to add another umbrella here."

She pointed to where Asma sat, as if she did not even notice Asma herself. She did not look at her. The umbrella man brought another umbrella, and timidly asked Asma to scoot back.

Asma looked startled, and said sternly, "This is my place. I'm not moving."

Only at this did the lady look at her, astonished and dis-gusted, as if she had just seen her . She looked at her husband, asleep at her side, a gold towel covering his face. "Marina is changing. Have you seen this view? Enough gilbabs, fellaheen, and haggas to make you sick!"

Asma took a second to control herself, and then said to the umbrella man, "I'm not moving, brother. Find something else to do."

Her daughter said softly, "Come on, Mom, let's move."

"They think they own God's land and ocean," she retorted. "We have a villa just like they do. Don't you worry."

At this, the woman shouted at the worker: "Get that lady out of here, and that's final! I'm going to close my eyes, and when I open them again, I'd better not find her in front of me! Get it?"

44

Her husband, turning his face toward the worker, added, "She's getting upset. What are you waiting for?"

In a second, two more workers joined the first. "Please move, Hagga," they said, their request mixed with sternness. "Please."

"I won't move until the police come!" Asma shouted, as her children surrounded her looking concerned.

The worker replied, "We can get the police. But why don't you just move without causing any problems?"

The argument continued for about five minutes, until the woman raised her cell phone to her ear. Was she calling the police, or perhaps a private guard? They didn't know, but the worker started to remove the umbrella, saying roughly, "Leave, or we'll carry you away!"

Asma would not move until her eldest son grasped her hand, saying, "Please Mama, let's go. Please."

Asma did not know what happened after that. Her face was burning with embarrassment, anger, and shame. And more important, with helplessness in front of her children. The tears, imprisoned in her eyes, blocked her vision. She walked quickly, her children behind her, and saw only the woman's nails scratching her face and her eyes. Or so she imagined.

On her return, her mother asked why she was back so early, but she did not answer. She went into her room, closed the door, and remembered her father's words: "You're going to be great, Asma. A girl worth a hundred men."

Her daughter knocked on the door. The sight of her mother could have helped to soften her heart. Her mother's helplessness raised Asma exponentially in her estimation. But Asma did not open the door. She rested her head in her palms, and one or two tears dropped from her eyes.

Ahmed told his grandmother what had happened, and his grandmother blamed his mother. She shouted through the door: "Didn't I tell you? Life is made up of different social classes. What do we have to do with those people?"

Asma did not emerge from her room all day. She did not want to face her children in her helplessness and lack of a plan. She did not know whether she should go to the police, and return to the beach. The police these days were an unpredictable, gelatinous organism. No one knew who they supported, or for whom they worked. She would go home tomorrow. Enough of this shame and disgrace!

As was her way, her daughter opened the door quietly and lay down beside her on the bed. Then her young son did the same. She relaxed her back against the bed, stretched out her arms to her children, and closed her eyes. She did not fall asleep until morning.

Hearing a knock at the door, she roused from her slumber and shouted, "Yes? Who is it?"

No one answered.

She opened the door, expecting almost anything. The police supporting her. The police blaming her and evicting her. The lady come to box her ears. The lady wanting to apologize to her. Anything goes in Egypt. Especially in Marina, nothing was impossible.

She gazed at the young man standing before her. He reminded her of someone. Such a beautiful face, such an enchanting smile . . .

The boy smiled politely and said, "Auntie Asma."

"Yes, come in," she said warmly.

"My father wants to invite you and your children to the beach today."

Her heart skipped a beat.

He continued: "I'm Dr. Hazim's son. He heard you were in Marina, and wants to invite you to join him for lunch at the beach today."

She smiled and asked, "Which beach?"

The boy looked at her as if he knew everything. "The beach you were at yesterday. The very same place. There is an umbrella ready, and a table and everything set up. We're waiting for you there."

"Come in, son," she said enthusiastically.

He politely declined. "I'm a little busy. I'll see you soon. Goodbye."

She closed the door, audibly thanking God. Her mother shouted from the next room: "Who was it, Asma?"

Happily waking her children, she said, "Come on, we're going to the beach."

The children replied as one: "No."

"Today will be different," she said proudly.

Together, they asked: "Why?"

"Because Dr. Hazim has invited us. Mother, are you coming with us? Please come along."

She shook her head. Looking at her daughter, she said, "You look like a festival lamb that the butcher decided to keep because it turned out to be a ewe!"

"Mother—"

"Fellaha, girl. Your mom's a fellaha, not a lady like you. God forgive your father for turning your head."

She did not know why she wanted to apply so much kohl and lipstick today. She looked at herself in the mirror, her cheeks as rosy as if she were sixteen. She closed her eyes a moment. Had he been there yesterday? Did he know everything?

As it happened, Hazim had a large villa overlooking the sea. He had been sitting on the balcony with his son the day before, and was startled, for a second, to see Asma. He looked up from his architecture book to observe her, as if she were a lab rat. He was fascinated by the situation. When the battle began between Asma and his next-door neighbors, whom he called the "thieves of Egypt" and "idiots of the Arab Nation," he sympathized with the poor fellaha. He ordinarily came to Marina in the winter, to get away from people. This summer, however, his son was adamant about going to Marina because he was in love with the neighbors' daughter. He did not try to convince his son that their neighbors' daughter had no taste in clothing, perfume, or villa design. He left his son to discover it on his own, over time. In this love story, innumerable text and Facebook messages were sent between their swanky cell phones and new laptops. He trusted his son to be smarter than he was, and not choose the glamorous beauty that ran after him, only to drop him on the ground like a handful of sand.

It was a beautiful sunny day. He put up his big umbrella and sat by the water, reading his book with headphones on to drown out the sounds of the barbarians around him. The lady with the white-tipped fingernails was sitting a few steps away. The nearer she got to Hazim, the more he ignored her, as usual. She had dreamed of herself and her husband winning his friendship, to no avail, and so had decided that he was a snob with no sense of humor.

No sooner did Asma reach the beach than the workers hastened to her, apologizing and explaining that they had not known she was Hazim's guest.

As soon as she saw Hazim, she felt her body trembling. "We are honored by your invitation," she said.

He smiled at her, shook her hand mechanically, and sat, saying, "I would like you to consider this your umbrella and your sea. Pardon me. I will not be able to stay with you much."

Her eyes looked over at the neighbor woman. Their eyes met. Victory shone in the eyes of Asma and her children, and annoyance in the eyes of the neighbor. She turned her face away disdainfully.

Asma said happily, "Ahmed, honey, go swim with your brother. Just not too deep." Then she gently pushed her daughter forward. "Go ahead, Salma. Today you're wearing a bathing suit just like everyone else. It's a modest suit and shows you're a respectable girl."

This time Salma smiled confidently and said, "Well, I'll just try it out."

Asma inclined her head, and there was silence for a time. Hazim read his book, and she looked at nothing. Then she looked at him, as a woman looks at a man. She looked at the fine, black hairs on his arm. She could see some on his chest, through the opening of his fitted shirt. She looked at his firm mouth, and his small eyes behind his glasses. She took in his scent, his flavor. He was different from her husband. She remembered him for a few moments, and her face fell. It seemed to her that Hazim did not see her or notice her attention. That set her heart free. What could it hurt for her to look at him, since she did not know him well, and never would? What harm was there in seeing him and getting close to him with merely her eyes?

After a while, he asked, "What will you have to drink? May I call you by your first name?"

"Of course," she said, smiling. "It's an honor."

He looked at her and said, "I'm going to ask for an orange juice. Shall I ask for orange juice for you as well?"

Flustered, she said, "Thank you, but I don't want anything to drink. I'm just hoping that you'll do us the favor of visiting again."

"Of course," he told her, looking at his book. "The cook made chicken and fish today. I didn't know what the kids would like. He'll be here in a few minutes. Ask him for whatever you like. Please, Asma, consider everything here your own."

Their eyes met, but she was unsure whether he was really looking at her. He had called her by her name. This in and of itself was sufficient to stir her, as if she were a girl of sixteen.

"God bless you," she said. "I respect and esteem you highly, as do my children. Taha aspires to be like you one day."

He smiled without answering, so she continued: "If the captain buys the land, I'll be able to put Salma through the American University, and enroll Ahmed in a private school. Our life would change. I want my children to become the best of people."

He replied logically: "So if Ahmed enrolls in private school, and Salma goes to the American University, then they will be the best of people?" Looking around, he added, "Everyone around you now, are they the best of people?"

She said without understanding, "A good education gives you a better chance. That's what my father used to say."

"A good education does give a better chance to those who take advantage of it. Those who really learn."

"Can you try to influence the captain? Everyone respects and admires you. It's an honor to ask this of you."

He gave her a long look that she did not understand. Then he said suddenly, "I'm afraid I must return to Cairo today, but I hope you and your children enjoy your vacation here. If you need anything, tell the employees here or in the villa. The neighbors won't bother you. I promise."

Then he stood, extending his hand. She shook his hand reluctantly, and he left.

To a large degree, a woman's reaction to a given situation can be predicted. Even if the woman were Asma. Even if the woman claimed to be just a mother; a saint focused on her mission with all the popular sayings that honor mothers. When the saint is faced with a priest who is rescuing her from the fangs of a ferocious predator—a wild beast half woman and half jackal, cowardly and quick to flee—then such a woman must be dazzled. Rescuing a woman from a situation like this ensures a woman's loyalty for at least seven days—probably eight in Asma's case, since she was known for her sincerity.

Since Asma had met Hazim, frightening emotions had been flickering within her, her heart quaking with new feelings. He was a man different from her husband, or Captain Murad, or all other men. By his nature, he had not looked at her once with desire in his eyes. She felt no deception in his palm when he shook her hand. She had seen nothing from him but goodness and kindness. Her heart was bound to throb for him. His elegant clothing, neat hair, firm features, calm speech . . . and his superior mind. What does a saint do when faced with a monk who holds the keys to life and the awesomeness of magic, damnation, and complete power and strength?

Asma was naturally smitten. She closed her eyes, and felt his hand on her face, wiping away her tears. This is not to say that Asma had become a teenager again, or that she had any intention of leaving the temple to throw herself at the river crocodiles like the Nile brides. It is only to say that Asma loved in silence, without hope. She had grown accustomed, from the beginning, to living patiently, seriously, silently. What frightened her was that she was in her forties, and dreaming of a man at night, a man who would warm her. It was simply an impossible dream. She saw his eyes smiling at her. She felt his mouth approach her neck, clinging there for all eternity. He was neither jackal nor wolf. He was a lion ravishing her. She shut her eyes tighter, breathing a prayer of protection. She tried to remember the image of her husband, and could not.

In Asma's more pragmatic moments, she followed the progression of life in the Nile's wildflowers, the chatter of warm animals, the birth of young mice in both smoothness and pain, the mating of cattle in the light of the sun. And because Asma feared neither life nor death, she knew that it was useless to fight her feelings. Battling her body, which she had long restrained, would not work. For someone in her state, negotiations were the best option. She determined to see him whenever she could. She would watch him as her mother watched men in movies, admiring them from afar. She would watch and enjoy, merely seeing him from time to time. Perhaps she would even exchange words with him. It would be enough. Practicality is the most preferable, most efficient path to peace and safety.

From *The Book of the Dead and the Living*

RECORD THIS PIECE OF ADVICE *from my father in your story, Thief. . . .*

My country, sometimes harsh, sometimes suffering, has remained lofty amid all its setbacks. In the end, ages of darkness and light do not overcome it. This is because of people like us, who have abundant knowledge. My father was a scholar and a philosopher. He would always say: Shafiq's family does not leave its homeland. In Egypt everyone knows us, and outside of Egypt we are like penguins in an African jungle, alien and helpless. We understand the Egyptians, and they understand us. They are from us, and we are from them, with all their various classes. Don't worry about the differences of their classes, son. In the end, we know one another like a gazelle knows her children from afar, by their scent and sound. No one leaves his country but the one who cannot live in it. Because he has no refuge—he's a desperate refugee. We know this.

He was an ideal man. To be my father, you would have to be ideal. In any case, Thief, his words had a simple, clear structure. On them, I build all the resolutions of my life. There appears in my memory, from time to time, the face of my father, and our villa in Giza. It was spacious, with a carefully designed garden. In it were all kinds of toys, mine and my sister's. My father never lost his temper in front of us. We had many parties, attended by important people. My country was full of flowers; French gâteaux and rich Turkish dishes made by our talented cook; books of history, heritage, engineering, and medicine. It was filled with trees that changed color with the four seasons of the year. When I was a child, there were four seasons in a year. When I turned fifty, I learned that the year has only two seasons. The books and flowers vanished into nothingness; the trees remained, only to laugh at me and blame me. For not understanding, and for not knowing.

Four

LUCK PLAYS AN IMPORTANT ROLE in the life of every Egyptian. There are those born as nobles, and there are those born as children of Egyptians. Unfortunately, Hazim was born the son of a scholar–priest, virtually a sultan. Why unfortunately? Because Hazim's life was very difficult. Fate did not afford him hours to wait in a breadline, having fought his way there. Nor did it allow him to go to the traffic office to spend a day suffering and sweating, pleading with a police officer, and then a military officer, to speed things up. Instead, he got his driver's license when he was sixteen, while sitting on the balcony of his father's villa admiring the flowers. It was two more years before he learned to drive, and he had not visited the traffic office to this day. Fate did not allow Hazim to experience the wrath of a physics teacher who gave him a blow that stayed with him forever, reminding him that taking orders was the best survival strategy. Unfortunately, his whole school trembled before him, son of Dr. Shafiq, the most famous cardiologist in Egypt. Dr. Shafiq had been the personal physician of the late president, and was the director of his own hospital and clinic. All of Egypt knew of him, respected him, and revered him. His father had been one of the few men who, with a gesture of the hand, could make dreams come true, parting rivers and launching boats.

Unfortunately, Hazim did not have the fortune of undergoing the experience of any young Egyptian man, slammed by helplessness in college when he meets the girl of his dreams, only for her to leave him for a better dowry. His dreams were not wrapped up in the nearly impossible task of setting up his own home. He had not ridden in a bus or a microbus, or even a taxi. Ever.

Hazim's life had been carefully and neatly laid out before he was born. Everyone rushed to serve him, and to ask for his blessing. When he passed the high school exams, he received letters from seven college deans, asking him to choose their school. When he graduated from the American University and declined entrance to medical school, the Egyptian State Department opened its arms to accept him as an ambassador and representative of his beautiful, pure country. He was the culmination of scholars and scholarship.

The pressure increased until his life grew truly wearisome: a professor inviting him to dinner, an ambassador inviting him to lunch, and everyone plotting a grand future for him. When he traveled to Holland with a diplomatic delegation, he felt very bored. Everyone worked for him, serving him and respecting him, and standing when he entered a room. So when he was twenty-five, he told his father that he wanted to go to the College of Engineering, Department of Architecture, and become an architect. Everyone present was shocked. Hazim was able to experiment with every technique, and to experience every kind of innovation in his field, before he earned his doctorate in architecture. And everyone praised him for his intelligence and his upright character. An angel of angels. He raised neither his voice nor his hand. A paragon of ethics, honor, and intelligence.

The job opportunities raining down on him were like an iron hammer pounding on an innocent child. The tightening of the noose prompted his mother to say, "My poor son withstands so many pressures."

When Hazim opened his architecture firm, he did not have to concern himself with obtaining permits. He never lectured an employee. He never met with a tax-assessment officer. There were others who did all of that for him. He was his father's best friend, carrying the banner of knowledge in his country. When his father died, he cried silently, hugging his younger sister. She was thirty at the time.

Hazim cried only twice in his life. The day his father died and the day his wife tore his son from his arms, shouting angrily, "I hate you, Hazim. I hate you. I love another man. Do you hear me? You smothered me. You killed me. You are bereft of feelings. Of life! You think the world is a ball in your hands, and you are its master. No sir. I am not your slave!"

He did not understand her words at all.

He had been twenty-five when he fell in love with Shereen. She was studying engineering, and she was gorgeous. Her father was a famous businessman. She chased him around day after day, and when he saw her in a crowd he smiled at her. So she melted in his arms, and loved him. She whispered that he was her life. He could not wait for marriage. She did not wait, but dissolved in him in a reckless, youthful outburst.

When he married her, she was in her second month of pregnancy. She told him, "I love you. I would do anything for you." But their relationship could not continue in peace amid the greatest test he had ever faced.

When he began building a villa in the Alexandria suburb of King Maryut for his wife and son, he designed it without consulting her. He built a high fence, painted it a blue that he liked, and installed some Greek statues. He did not ask her what she wanted. So when she went to the villa, she decided to change it according to her own taste. She began the alterations without informing him, changing the color of the fence to orange, and removing the Greek statues. When he learned of the alterations, he said sternly, "How could you? Tomorrow I will change it back. Everything has its order."

"Yes, an order to everything!" she shouted in his face. "Do you know what you are? You are nothing but a spoiled child.

No one discusses anything with you, or has to live with you except me. Everything is the way you want it, as if I were just a doll. The color of the house, the furniture, my son's name, even when you make love with me."

He looked at her angrily, so she forged ahead: "Yes, I won't take it back. I enjoy you, but you always have to be the one in charge, the one who knows everything. You never ask me. Don't you get it? You're a machine, not a human being. Believe me, life with you is like life with that fence, before it was orange."

He said firmly, "It's my house, and my design. I will change it back."

"If you change the color of the fence, I'm leaving you."

He said carelessly, "If I had to live with this color, I'd leave life altogether. I can't. My eyes can't stand common taste."

"My taste? Are you saying that I am common?"

"That's the way it seems to me now."

Shereen did not speak with him for a whole month. When he returned from work, she would quickly go to her room, sending her son out to sit with his father. He would stay with his son through the night, the boy asleep in his arms. After a month had passed, Shereen left the door of her room open. Her husband entered and slept next to her, and it seemed that everything had returned to the way it was. But the reconciliation was not equitable, and the weapons were merely hidden.

Two months after the fence incident, Hazim returned home one night to find his wife and son gone. That was the day he cried because he thought he might never see his son again. He knew Shereen. She seemed to him changed and ruined. When he did not find her in Egypt, he knew that she had fled with his son to Europe. Europe was large, and impossible to search.

At the age of thirty, Hazim passed the most difficult days of his life, and it is possible he never got over them. The feelings of helplessness were new and frightening. The search for his son continued for an entire year. He poured money and energy into it. Even pressuring his wife's family did not work. All his father's influence did not work. All his intelligence, authority, possessions, and knowledge did not work. When he located her by way of international police, and went to her sorrowfully, she stood in front of him in her apartment in Paris, and said forcefully, "You would have taken him from me."

He did not hear her. He held his child in his arms, and whispered, "We'll come to an understanding."

"Don't take him from me. There's no understanding with you anyway! I'm married here, and I'm going to live here with my son."

Money did not entice her, and threats did not budge her. She hated Hazim as a woman wounded in her dignity, a hate near to the folly of love. When she saw Hazim before her, his eyes full of helplessness, she felt a joy beyond the joy of deceiving him. Following two months of negotiations, she decided to return with him to Egypt, after he promised that he would not take their child from her. When she returned, he reassured her and lavished on her affection and forgiveness until he won her over, and she thought he had changed and become the husband for whom she had always hoped. But Hazim, or rather Hazim's lawyer, unsheathed every legal and illegal weapon in three sessions, gaining a judge's verdict to grant him custody of the child. The mother could see him only two hours per week, under strict supervision. Throughout the child's suffering, as he was being taken from country to country and through the courts, his father flooded him with love, and was his whole life.

Now Hazim's son Khalid had just graduated from university. He visited his mother regularly, and his life revolved around his father, but he had recently decided to take up a kind of work that no one in the Shafiq family had ever done. It was sad, treacherous, and very necessary. Hazim's son had decided to move to America to study and settle down. When he revealed his desire to his father, trembling, his father ignored him and started talking about the changing quality of mutton in Egypt. When Khalid persevered, talking about opportunities, the future, education, and so on, Hazim ignored him again, so Khalid said softly, "It's my life, Dad."

His father replied, sitting at the table, "We should change this breakfast table. White is taking over everything."

"Dad, did you hear a word of what I said?"

"When you say something useful, I'll listen."

"Dad, this is my dream."

"You're always talking about your dreams, as if you sleep all winter long like a hibernating bear. Perhaps you had better wake up."

Khalid said resignedly, "We'll talk some other time. I guess you're busy right now."

"I am. Very."

"Do I have to go with you to visit the captain?" asked Asma's son in annoyance.

"Yes," she answered firmly. "Would you leave your mother in a man's office all alone? You are my man now. You must come with me."

Taha walked beside her as she requested a meeting with the captain, in the hope of closing the land deal that day.

The secretary asked her to enter, looking at her with a mix of envy and contempt, which confirmed for Asma that this woman was more than just his secretary. As soon as the captain saw her, he stood to greet her and her son. Before she could say anything, he looked at Taha and said, "Wait for us outside, Taha."

Taha's face fell. His mother looked at him for a moment, undecided. Then she said, "Wait outside a few minutes."

As soon as he went out, the captain shouted at her as if he were about to loose a chandelier on her head: "You brought your son here to protect yourself from me? Are you an imbecile? I thought you were smart!"

"Not at all," she said innocently. "He wanted to come with me. He misses his father since he died. Would I lie to you? You are our only hope. I came seeking your kindness."

Trying to control himself, he replied: "That's what you said before."

"The land is yours. It's enough that you honored us with a visit in our home."

He sat back in his chair. He was more aggravated today than she had anticipated, but at least he would not try to touch her.

"Let's talk another time," he said.

She persevered: "I'm hoping for your generosity."

"You already said that!" he shouted in her face. "Enough. Enough talking. I'll think about it."

"Are we agreed then?" she asked shakily.

He sighed in exasperation. "Go on, get out of here. I said I'd think about it. Go on."

She swallowed in frustration, opened the door, and went out. When her son asked her about the meeting, she said, "God willing, he'll buy the land. He wanted to discuss the details."

After Asma returned to Benha, and was preparing dinner for her children, her mother stared at her as usual.

"I see you circling around yourself like a buzzard, Asma," her mother said. "You'll go crazy in the end, my dear. Leave the bread to its baker. You weren't born a man, and you'll never be one. Your brother is still alive and could provide for you and your children. You love being self-sufficient, but you can barely manage to eat or drink. When was the last time you bought me baklava? Am I not your mother? You're busy thinking about Marina and all this nonsense. God forbid! I'm afraid you'll lose your mind."

Asma's mind was wandering a bit. Her husband's image no longer came to her often, although his name did not leave her tongue. This feeling of constriction in the throat, headache, and fever would not be cured. It was neither swine flu nor dog flu, not hyena or jackal, but lion . . . the lion who had recently rescued her.

When she woke one day feeling pain throughout her whole body and a rasping in her voice, she whispered to her maid, "I want to go to Umm al-Madamir."

Umm al-Madamir was the best at getting things accomplished, reversing ill luck, hitching a man, and opposing the jinn. The maid looked astonished and said, "For who, Hagga?"

Asma said resignedly, "I don't know yet."

When she went to Umm al-Madamir, she whispered to her, "I want you to help me."

Umm al-Madamir smiled and said, "I'd be honored, Hagga Asma."

"What can you do?" Asma asked desperately.

Examining her, she replied, "I'll make her go crazy, that damn girl who's bothering you!"

"No. I want something else."

"For him to love you and become like a ring on your finger, following you around everywhere?"

Without any surprise, for she trusted Umm al-Madamir and her outstanding ability, she said, "I want something else."

"Shall I bind him? So he won't be able to have sex with you, or with anyone else?"

She said quickly, "I want something else. I want to . . . can you change the feelings of a woman in love? Could you?"

Umm al-Madamir looked at Asma searchingly and said, "Your secret is safe with me."

"It's not me."

"Of course I can, if he enchanted her. Did he use magic on you?"

"No."

"He doesn't have feelings for you?"

"I don't want him to have feelings for me."

"I thought you knew better than that, Asma. How could I control someone's heart? I can hurt him if you like."

"I don't want that."

"Girl, my heart goes out to you. Leave it to fate. You'll be back."

"Why?"

"To ask me to bind him, of course."

It is natural for a mother to manipulate her children emotionally, and for them to do the same to her in turn. In this blessed country, we live on emotions and manipulation, sometimes together and sometimes separately. Asma, like every mother, knew how to manipulate her children. Her status as a widow granted her total power over them. Everyone knew of her excessive love for her children, and her complete control over them. She had a unique parenting philosophy that could have been recorded in those expensive academic books that no one buys. Asma's tears were the most important tools for maintaining her power. Second was her health, which she sacrificed for the sake of her children. Third, her competence and influence.

She was the mother, and the mother is to be obeyed. The mother does not err. The mother sacrifices herself. She is half human and half angel. And a widowed mother is a saint, her sins washed away in a sea of hardships. Thus Asma was considered fit for the highest of positions, even if only among Egyptians. With all her wisdom, patience, and stubbornness—and, most important, her unbounded dictatorial inclinations—she could have been head of the government and all the ministries.

When her eldest son entered the Faculty of Economics and Political Science, she said, "You are our hope. I'm selling everything for your sake."

Her soft words ignited guilt in Taha's heart. So he studied day and night. He called her every day from Cairo to report on his day at school. On the weekends, he threw himself into her arms, leaving her on Saturday morning with tears in his eyes.

When he was late returning home once, Asma crept into his room to wait for him to arrive. With her mother's heart, which knows the recesses of all things and is capable of curing epidemics and parasites, she felt that her son was on the brink of doing something disastrous, even if he had not actually done any such thing yet. He was still at the start of his college years.

After the dawn prayer, which Asma prayed in her angelic white gown, she sat on her son's bed awaiting him. Would he return with some floozy he had met on the street? Would he return with a bottle of wine, weaving right and left, oscillating between madness and happiness, as they did in the movies? Would he return stoned, after smoking a smooth block of weed? Or would he return with a beard, having joined a terrorist group? In any case, his fate would be worse than that of homeless children or those growing up in shantytowns. Not only would he have done something dangerous, but his punishment would be coming to him no matter what!

One of Asma's predictions proved true. Her son returned stoned, having smoked a pack of weed that he had bought from a trusted friend. No sooner had he crept into his room and turned on the light than he received his surprise: his mother in her white hijab, sitting on the bed, neither crying nor sleeping. She looked at him with eyes wide, flooded with all the rage of the people of the Nile Valley.

"Mama?" he whispered in fright. "Glad to see you're well."

His mother's sandals interrupted him, landing on his face and neck as she screamed: "You son of a dog! You come here blasted when I'm killing myself for you! No more university. Come work the land if you think you're such a big man!"

There was no end to her insults of his manhood, his character, and all he had. Her screams woke the whole house, and the neighbors of the nearby streets, but no one ran to enter the room. After hurling the sandals, Asma was panting from exhaustion. Blood appeared on Taha's face, head, and neck. Tears flowed from his eyes, and he whispered, "Enough, Mama . . ."

She collapsed, crying and saying prayers, bemoaning her fortune, beseeching all the angels and prophets, and leaving her fate to God.

He sat next to her on the bed in shock, unspeaking. His emotions were a mixture of anger, embarrassment, sorrow, and a great deal of guilt.

When she had calmed down, she said severely, "You will stop your studies entirely."

He spoke without thinking: "No. It's Dad's money, not yours. And it's my right."

He expected her to lash out. His hand even instinctively covered his face to shield it from any further blows from the dilapidated sandals. But his mother replied calmly, "Yes, you're right. Of course. Tomorrow, come take your right. Work the land, interact with the village people, buy and sell. I will wait at home for you to bring me the income every day. You, sir, will shoulder the responsibility of your siblings in your father's absence. Another solution that will make us all happier is for me to marry, after depriving myself of all things for your sake, mister. You who speak of rights. I'll get married and leave your siblings for you to raise and support. What do you think of that?"

He did not answer.

She shook him, demanding: "Speak!"

He bowed his head, and whispered, "I'm sorry, Mama."

"No studying," she said firmly.

"It won't happen again. I promise you."

But he knew his mother and her stubbornness. He began going with her on her rounds on the land, and sadness hung over him. He tried to reconcile with her for three days, crying and begging: "Just forgive me and don't be angry with me. I'll do whatever you want. I promise."

After two weeks, she permitted him to return to Cairo and the university. He had to give her a full daily report to end this state of blockade and restore an atmosphere of trust. After three weeks, he would kiss her hand in the morning, and she would pat his head. Like a tribal chief, she would bestow her blessings upon him, and say in her firm way, "You are my support, and the man of the family. Do not forsake me." From that time forward, Taha resolved to obey his mother, and to cut off all his friends, both good and otherwise.

From *The Book of the Dead and the Living*

Dear First Thief,

Plunderer of tombs, resurrector of the dead and their dreams,

Forgive me for my unsophisticated Arabic. But I am Egyptian, entirely like you.

Or perhaps not entirely like you.

Anyway, our language is not fluent.

My father always used to say that there are three things in life that a man can never control, and no scholar can explain the reasons for this scientifically. That's what my father said, and my father knew everything. A man has no control over: a nation that both ignores and adores him; a woman he desires, but before whom his body falls apart; and history that is rewritten every day by friends, enemies, businesspeople, scholars, soldiers, kings, nations, congregations, the East, the West, and all that is between them.

Five

NOW THAT ASMA HAD ENTERED high society, she would visit Karima, the captain's wife, every three days. She brought traditional Egyptian sweets and sat with her, listening sometimes to her praises, at other times to her complaints, and generally to her drivel. Karima did a lot of senseless talking, and she was moody. Sometimes she was sympathetic to the maid, suddenly hugging and kissing her in concern. Other times she slapped her violently. She often spoke of her husband, complaining about his deception, his self-centered delusions, and so on. Karima loved all things traditional. They reminded her of the greatness of Egyptians. Homemade ghee, hand-embroidered sashes, kohl eyeliner, henna, the small, dark eggs of rare, valuable hens, and cottage cheese from sleek, pretty cows. Sometimes Karima's mood would alter in less than a minute, and she would stand abruptly, saying, "I have to go to sleep now, Asma." Or, "I'm busy now."

Although Asma felt put out, and cursed the time that forced her to depend on this crazy woman, she persevered patiently. Sometimes the maid would open the door for Asma, and ask her not to enter. Karima would call from within: "Who's at the door?"

The maid would answer, "It's Madam Asma."

"Tell her I'm busy. Have her come another time."

Asma's patience was limitless. Especially when she was listening to Karima's promises to talk with her friend and move little Ahmed to a private school for half the regular cost. She also promised to persuade her husband to buy Asma's land. In her moments of generosity, she made many promises.

Asma discovered that Karima's favorite pastime was smoking a shisha on the roof of the villa at night. She would sit beside her, listening to her foolish stories, liking neither smoking nor the scent of the smoke.

The news that Asma was joining the circles of influential people was bound to make headlines. The first to inform her of her newly public status was the mayor's wife. When Asma hosted her for lunch, the mayor's wife began criticizing the food, telling her that she did not know how to cook and that she should learn the authentic way to cook from her.

Asma said proudly, "How strange! Karima, the captain's wife, loves my cooking."

"Asma, stop putting on airs!" the mayor's wife said. "She doesn't even know you. She came to visit you once, and you've never seen her since."

Picking up the phone, Asma said, "She's my friend. Shall I call her now? I'm not putting on airs."

"No, don't call her, you wily fox. What does her house look like?"

"Like a palace."

"Does she have a kitchen like in the movies? With chairs all around, and a high sideboard for breakfast?"

Asma answered proudly, "I've had breakfast with her, and sat on the high chairs. Do you want to come with me on Thursday?"

"No, sister! I'm not like you. I have a husband and children. You have no man to keep you in line."

"I don't need a man to keep me in line, dear. God takes care of that."

"You've always been so sure of yourself!"

"And you're my best friend. Want some tea?"

Once when her son Taha was sitting next to her, reading a book as she patted his back, he said shyly, "Mama . . . I want to tell you something."

Looking at him closely and discerning the topic, she said, "You're in love?"

"She's my classmate, and she comes from a big family."

"Rich and from a good family?" she said happily.

"Yes, and a member of the Ahli Club too. She understands our situation—I talked with her."

"What situation?" she said angrily. "You're better than she is!"

Averting his eyes, he said, "Yes of course, but I spoke with her and explained that I'm the man of the house. So if we got married, she'd be marrying a man whose first responsibility is his mother and siblings. His mother first, before anything else. She's my age, twenty I mean, and we agreed to be engaged until graduation. Then, if we both get into the Diplomatic Institute, maybe we wouldn't need to worry about finding an apartment."

Something in what Taha said drove the smile from his mother's face, and revealed the depth of anger that he had so long feared.

So he said quickly, "What's wrong, Mama?"

"You agreed! You and who? Are you an orphan with neither father nor mother? Is she a girl who does not ask her parents? And you? You agree with her without me knowing! I'm the one who devoted her life to you. You were just a bit of flesh in my arms at age nine. Do you remember? I fought both friend and foe for your sake. And now you make an agreement without me, and you're only twenty."

"No, you misunderstand. I mean—"

"So your mother is stupid and ignorant too. What exactly did you agree to, mister?"

Terrified by the noose tightening around him, he quickly said, "Whatever you decide first. You meet her, then decide, of course. When would you like to meet her?"

"Did you tell her this shameless mother of yours would meet her? I'm not meeting anyone. Forget about this topic until after your sister marries. You want to get married so badly, but do you think a girl like that would live with me?"

For hours, he asked her to reconsider. He asked his sister to intervene on his behalf, as well as his grandmother and anyone else who would listen. When his mother finally agreed to meet her, she was ready to see that this girl would not suit her son. For if she dared to settle an agreement without consulting the mother, then she would not do. It was as if she was agreeing to a man as an individual, without a family.

When the girl came to visit them, Asma's instinctive dislike for her increased from the first moment—she was especially offended by the girl's lack of courtesy when she greeted her, as if she had not even wanted to meet her. She did not like the way she carried the dishes or helped with the lunch. The girl did not even attempt to talk with Ahmed and Salma. Later, Asma and Salma agreed wholeheartedly that this marriage was definitely off.

But her son asked excitedly, "What did you think?"

"Pretty," she said tepidly, "but everything is down to fate, Taha. I don't like her, and I don't agree to her. How would she live with us, son? Forget about her."

Taha did not try to discuss it further with his mother, but neither did he forget about his girlfriend.

Asma's mother sucked on her lips and muttered, "When a lady cries over the least thing, and shakes and laughs, throwing her weight around, and losing her cool like you do . . ."

"Shut up!" Asma snapped.

"So hardhearted."

"My heart's for my kids."

"That's exactly what I'm talking about. May God preserve them for you." She looked closely at Asma, "You're still pretty and graceful as a movie star. It must be your husband's death. A man tires a woman out, and she ages as a result. He died, and saved you from aging. Your heart's for your kids, right?"

She would have continued, but Asma cut her off, saying, "I have to go pick up my husband's pension."

It was Saturday, the day that Asma collected her husband's monthly pension. She put on her loose black dress and black headscarf. She did not wear any makeup, not even the eyeliner that was always in her bag. She gave her youngest son a vacation from school and they walked to the post office. As soon as she entered, she pushed herself through the throng of people, pulling her son behind her. She stretched out her hand, and shouted at the top of her voice to the employee: "God keep you. I must get back soon. My son has school and we haven't paid his fees yet."

The clerk usually ignored her for a couple of hours, until her shouting annoyed him and she had nearly lost her voice. Then he would say contemptuously, "Take your ticket."

She did so quickly. Before she could give it back, someone else took her place, and the hand withdrew. She might have used her elbow to shove her neighbor's hand aside. Then she threw the ticket in front of him, where he left it for another hour. Then he looked at her foolishly, as if it were the first time he had seen a ticket. He left her again, and Asma started saying prayers both for and against him. Her son began grumbling, shrieking, and occasionally crying. Due to the added pressure, the employee took out the three hundred pounds and gave it to her. She took it and ran outside in the greatest haste, cursing the day her husband died, as well as the day that she was born. Then she looked at her watch, and realized that she had been there seven hours. Yet she was lucky. Anyone else would not have managed to collect anything in a single day.

Her sister often asked her why she went to pick up her husband's pension since she owned land. She would answer firmly, "It's my children's right. I must collect it."

Then her sister would whisper something to her mother that Asma could only guess at.

From *The Book of the Dead and the Living*

FIRST THIEF,

I want to inform you of something important.

Don't you dare—are you listening to me? Don't you dare criticize the design of my tomb. I mean this tomb. For it is mine, and it is of me.

I grew tired living in the shadow of the ancient ones. I was wearied by the comparison of myself, my father, and my ancestors. Don't tell me that I have not and will not reach their level of greatness.

Don't take my measure according to the past that has passed away, and the present that is upon us. Leave me the dignity of creativity. I have nothing else left. Nothing in my era that makes me proud will ever return, except history. I write it, and rewrite it. Until the ink in my pen dries and my paper disintegrates. Give me the chance to create, for it does not occur often.

Six

Today the captain was wearing a gold necklace and three rings. The first ring had a blue stone, the second a black stone, and the third a red stone. Hazim was looking at the stones, searching in vain for a pattern in the choice of colors. He found no order, and that disturbed him. The captain was jumping, as usual, from one topic to another every minute, scattering Hazim's thoughts.

"There are many things that I want with me in the tomb," the captain said. "Actually, maybe it's not that many. The light brown leather suitcase that my father bought for me when I was ten. It looked like the briefcase of a successful leader. I valued it more than anything else. It made me hopeful for the future. It has five pockets. They're worn out now. But it makes me feel safe. The past is safest, because it contains no surprises.

"I have a photo from the battlefield, with my buddies. Most of them have died. I was thin, with black hair and piercing eyes. Behind me is a submarine on the surface of the sea. The sea is so beautiful. There you are completely free, and yet a helpless slave.

"And I want to take a tray of flatbread, smelling of the country ghee my mother used to make. She was a stern woman, and didn't cook often.

"And I want to take my soft mattress, my navy uniform, the scent of old boat wood, and a history book. I'm writing the book myself, start to finish, and I'm the hero, the army, and the culmination of high hopes."

Hazim looked at him sarcastically. "I just design. You can put in it whatever you want."

The captain smiled innocently from his chair. "Did I ever tell you about India, and the women of India?"

"Excuse me, I thought we were discussing the design."

"I want to tell you about my experience with women while I was traveling. Do you want to hear?"

Hazim smiled, "Of course. All your experiences are very interesting."

"I hope you're not making fun of me now."

"I'm not making fun of you. What did you find in India?"

"Listen, friend. The British outlawed dogs and Indians from their clubs, restaurants, hotels, and places of relaxation and recreation. The Indians outlawed one another from the same places. The rulers of our country permitted dogs in their clubs, restaurants, and hotels, but not the populace. So the fellaheen, workers, teachers, and white-collar employees decried the injustice, being as they were the Rising Generation in the First Revolution, which fell by chance on their shoulders. Then came peace, factories, land, and schools. After the Second Revolution, the Rising Generation stopped rising. The staircase came to an end. Order and peace returned to the region, and our country became a country for rulers again. As for what we mistakenly call 'the people,' it never existed, neither before the revolution, nor after it."

Hazim whistled. "When you talk like that, I feel like I'm with nationalist Ahmed Orabi. In your view of the revolution, what's the fate of the servants and the underdogs?"

"I haven't decided their fate yet, but that doesn't mean that I don't care about them."

"We could sit and talk for hours about history, the Setback, the Shock, and so on, but I'm surprised at all this bitterness and oppression in you."

"They always come together, and when you're a captain, you become accustomed to every kind of woman. When you need a woman and you're at sea, you don't remember your wife and her gracious smile. You don't need an innocent smile; you just need a woman. At the first port, you erase the memory of your wife from your mind. Do you understand?"

"I'm trying."

"We're business partners." He leaned toward Hazim and whispered, "If a sailor ever tells you that he's never cheated on his wife, don't believe him. Years on the sea make you lose your mind. You feel like you're in the belly of a tyrannical whale, and you need light."

Hazim replied, "I don't think I will ever meet another sailor like you. You constantly contradict yourself."

"We all do that, but I know myself. I don't fool myself. Life is full of stations and levels. We all have our own class. Even the fisherman sorts his fish, the small ones from the big ones, the expensive from the cheap, the superior from the inferior. People are like fish."

"You're contradicting yourself again," Hazim said wearily. "You were saying that all people are equal!"

The captain looked around before saying, "All men are equal in front of the woman they want. They are all alike in her arms, no matter who she is. When a man buries his head in her breasts, he forgets what class he comes from. He remembers only the softness of her breasts in his hands."

Hazim waved his hand in distaste. "Spare me your poetry today. Let's focus on the topic of the tomb."

The captain smiled victoriously. "My words shock you."

Hazim gave him a long look. "You want to shock me, don't you?"

"You don't know a man until he loses his temper."

"We were talking about the tomb."

"We were talking about a woman and her breasts."

Hazim spoke determinedly, as if he had not heard. "Look at this design," he said, and handed him some papers.

The captain found the papers captivating. He said slowly, "The feel of it is like a fresh tilapia shuddering in your hands. Almost white, soft, and firm. It doesn't give in to your fingers. It must be strong, not skinny. And its colors—"

Hazim interrupted him. "Excuse me, are we talking about the tomb or fish now?"

"We're talking about a woman's breast. You sense the texture before you see it. It should be momentarily round when you squeeze it, like an egg."

"Do you want me to explain the tomb design to you?"

"Of course."

As if he had not heard a word the captain was saying, Hazim began explaining the design of the tomb, the grounds, and the mausoleum with the enthusiasm of a man laying out the lines of time and destiny. The captain was listening with all his attention, and did not interrupt Hazim even once. His young second wife, whom he had married in secret a year ago, walked in wearing jeans, her hair soft and her shirt tight. She approached the captain softly, whispering something in his ear. The captain indicated that she should be quiet. She obeyed him.

When Hazim finished the explanation, the captain said wholeheartedly, "Brilliant!"

His wife whispered in his ear again, and he said urgently, "Go away, go on."

Then he came closer to Hazim, whispering, "She was my secretary, and I liked her coffee. She makes the best coffee in the world. What does a man of my age need other than someone skilled at making coffee? Nothing else interests me. Here, taste her coffee."

Somewhat curious, Hazim said, "You married her?"

"Just an urfi marriage, not a registered marriage. She understands me and knows my needs. I visit her sometimes, not often. I had to marry her, if for no other reason than to annoy Karima. It's awful being married to a woman like Karima—like handcuffs or life imprisonment with no mercy. If I hadn't married again, she would have stuck to me like an unforgiven sin. A woman's got to keep longing for you, be ready to fight for you. You've got to keep her busy too so you do not experience the evil that wells up from her roots. Believe me, I don't feel at all content in a woman's lap, just as I wouldn't feel comfortable in the arms of the Nile! You understand?"

Hazim smiled. "I don't understand you. Are you a talented politician or a womanizer?"

"I fought in the War of Attrition in the sixties, and all my mental resources were drained. They said, 'We're fighting Israel.' They said, 'We recognize Israel.' They said, 'We're forgetting Israel,' and so on. They had all the expertise. Today you can buy anything—land, a house, a woman, power if you want it. Even democracy is bought and sold from its original producer, America the Inventor. But there's one thing you can't buy."

"What's that?"

"Light in a dark tomb. I'm so afraid of death. If my life remains as it is . . . oh, the worry could make you lose your mind. What truly saddens me is that the fighter and the killer are still fighting and killing in an internal battle, and who knows who the enemy is." The captain smiled and continued: "You think I'm a womanizer. But really, I prefer a cup of dark, spiced coffee, and conversation about Egypt and the future, more than sex with any woman."

Hazim replied, mocking and fully engaged in the conversation: "Yet you're still a womanizer."

"Only because with a woman, you naturally come. But in conversations about the future of Egypt, you remain miserable as a dog pulled away from his mate at the moment of satiation! You'll have to excuse me, but I feel at ease with you."

"No problem. But I still feel that you are . . ."

"A hypocrite?"

"You talk about Egypt while you take advantage of it. Sorry, I tend to be frank. They say you bought your first boat after you left the navy to transport marijuana. And that you made enough out of just one trip. Is that true?"

"Even if it was true, do you think I'd tell you?"

"No, but I had to ask."

"Because you don't want to work with a criminal? And you won't take dirty money?"

Hazim said nonchalantly, "That doesn't matter to me. I'm a designer. I'm designing a timeless work. I don't care who for."

"I'm impressed."

They fell silent for a moment. Then Hazim said abruptly, "The Benha land will do."

The captain looked at him slyly. "Asma's land?"

"Yeah," he answered with seeming carelessness.

"All right, then I'll buy it from her. Let's start the project today."

Hazim searched his face. "Why?"

The captain replied craftily: "The fellaha arouses your interest, doesn't she? Are you asking me if I've had a relationship with her? You want her now like I do? I told you before—"

Hazim cut him off disdainfully. "No. Who do you think I am?"

"She's not good enough for you?"

"She's not from the same planet as me."

"So what keeps you from wanting her, even so?"

"If I wanted her, you'd leave her to me?"

"I don't think so."

Hazim smiled. "No, I don't want her. And I don't think she's that kind of woman. She has her own ideas about what she wants. Leave her be."

The captain whistled. "My God, you're used to giving orders and being obeyed, aren't you? There's no harm in trying. A man can't force a woman into anything anyway."

Hazim, seeming to believe him fully, said, "So you won't take advantage of people's circumstances and coerce them, right?"

"No, I'd never take advantage of people's circumstances. But don't blame me if I take advantage of their greed. We all do that."

"Whatever," Hazim replied coolly. "It's none of my business. As for the colors of the tomb, these are the colors I've chosen. Look at the openings through which light will enter, day and night. You will never be in the dark. And no one will notice the openings, or even where the light is coming from."

The captain scrutinized the design. Then he pointed with his thumb. "Can you change this color? I don't like red."

"We need it to reflect the light. Do you not like red, or do you not like darkness?"

The captain looked at him in surprise. "Okay, we all love Egypt. But you've got to change this color. I'm afraid of death as a matter of course, but colors of hell terrify me!"

Hazim scrutinized him for a moment. "Captain."

"Yes."

"I left my wife because she changed the color of the fence at my villa without my knowledge."

"I heard that infamous story. Didn't I warn you about women?"

"Am I in charge of colors?"

"I told you you're used to commanding and being obeyed! I'm the one in charge of the colors of my tomb, and the colors of my life. You design and take your money."

Hazim stood calmly. "Money? I don't need money, my friend. What you will give me is not even enough to buy Eid presents for my son." He grasped Hazim's hand urgently. "Sit down. Don't get mad at me. Believe me, we'll work something out."

But Hazim replied, on his way to the door: "Perhaps, but not now. Another time."

Trying to stand, the captain called out, "Come back. Listen to me."

"I heard you, and that's the end of it. Let me think about it."

"You never learned to negotiate. But why would you? I feel sorry for your wife. What color did she want?"

"Orange."

"So she was crazy. But I didn't ask for orange. And no one can build the tomb but you."

Hazim looked at him suspiciously, so the captain continued. "You're the best architect in Egypt, but don't forget I could get an architect from Norway, like the one who designed the Alexandria Library. It has underground floors built with tremendous precision."

As he opened the door, his face downcast, Hazim said, "Now we're done talking."

Unfortunately, the tomb project was the most important thing to Hazim now, after his son. The idea of immortality, building the mausoleum, designing Time, and writing *The Book of the Dead and the Living* completely overwhelmed him. After he had spent a month working day and night on the design, he could not just throw it out. He had never done that in his career. He drew up designs like Shahryar and his virgin wives. If a client did not accept him, then he terminated the contract.

He was too angry to sleep that night. His mind worked constantly. It was now impossible to build the tomb for the captain. What he considered criminal humiliation could not be forgiven. Was he overreacting? Why all this anger? Because he hated the captain? Because he despised his actions? Or because he was set against the color red? The reason did not matter. He was not one to analyze his feelings. What he felt now was that his legacy project had been destroyed, and now that he was in his fifties the chance to build a tomb would not come to him again.

What had he accomplished? How had he immortalized his name? What did he possess?

Lots of money.

The esteem and respect of everyone. His pick of the women.

A son who was educated and intelligent.

He had designed banks, factories, and hotels.

He had failed in his marriage, and in all his relationships. Sometimes because he tired of a woman, and sometimes because he focused on minute details—women hate details. And sometimes because they accused him of arrogance, conceitedness, domination, and selfishness. All these accusations did not necessarily mean much, except that women did not trust enough in his success and strength.

He had no friends, but had many acquaintances. How was it that his only friend was a crazy woman like Rasha? He did not have the patience to listen to frivolous stories. He did not have time for dallying in restaurants and hotels, smoking water pipes and talking politics.

His work was his life and his country. It was all he possessed and desired. So to reach fifty without having designed a single tomb naturally worried him. His life would come to an end, and no one would remember him. No one would recognize him as having a share in immortality or in a mausoleum. That would not do.

Enough of money and influence. The time had come to work by and for himself. Why was he building the tomb for the captain anyway? A man with no morals or conscience did not deserve immortality. Tomb building was for pharaohs and great people. Tomb building was his job, and he would start today, not tomorrow. He would build the tomb first, and then decide who deserved it. Immortality does not wait. Like life, it passes on as quickly as one can draw a square with a pen.

Asma's land would work.

He called his secretary, and asked him to invite Asma and her family to lunch on his behalf, and to reserve a table at a swanky seafood restaurant in Cairo.

She was seeking strength from the image of her son, so that she could turn to Hazim casually. She patted her son's hand beside her, unable to touch the food because of the butterflies in her stomach.

Hazim smiled at her as he put a crab on her plate, saying "Eat. Why aren't you eating?"

Her daughter said excitedly to her younger brother, "Have you ever seen a crab? Look at its underside!" Asma gave her a look, but she said, "We don't eat fish much. We have tilapia and mullet from the river, but not farmed fish."

Looking at Taha, Hazim asked, "Do you speak English or French? You should learn both to get into the Diplomatic Institute, and you should start now."

"Thank you for the advice," Taha's mother gushed. "Taha will start tomorrow. What do you think? Wouldn't he be a good diplomat? He's calm, and can handle responsibility . . ."

She fell silent, gazing into his eyes as they held hers. She lowered her head, having forgotten what she was saying, and began to pick at her food. Her feelings were weirdly mixed, like the colors of a surrealist painting: a thrilling mélange of fear, joy, longing, excitement, and a great desire to stare at him for hours. She reprimanded and cursed herself, accusing her heart of adolescent stupidity. Nothing worked. Emotions overwhelmed her with every fine word he spoke; with the glory that surrounded him; with the looks he gave, full of solidity, trustworthiness, and knowledge of all things; with the compassion hidden in his heart, along with kindness, generosity, strength, and all beautiful traits.

"And Salma wants to go to the American University?" he asked.

Salma opened her mouth to speak, but her mother answered for her. "She's not interested in the American University—she wants to go to the Faculty of Commerce! Can you believe that? And there are so many graduates each year from the Faculty of Commerce! If she went to the American University, she would be sure to find gainful employment, and to marry a man of her standing, and of her father's standing."

Curious, he asked, "And what did her father do?"

"He was a geography teacher, but he didn't work for a living. He was a landowner, from a prominent family."

"May he rest in peace. Salma, do you like English?"

"I hate it," she said dully.

Her mother gave her a look of reproof, saying, "I'll see to it that she learns, of course. And Ahmed has an even greater ability to learn at his age."

He smiled, his eyes moving from Asma to her children. In a serious tone, he said, "I want to talk with you about the land. Did you agree to sell to the captain?"

She answered with the shrewdness that had become part of her personality: "I don't understand. Do you mean did we agree on a price?"

He smiled again, as if he understood her cunning. "Did you agree on a price, on the sale, on everything, or didn't you?"

"Kind of."

"Kind of what?"

"God willing."

"Of course, 'God willing.' But if you didn't agree with him on a price, then we need to talk. The value of the land is not a half million pounds, and it would be a shame for you to throw your children's fortune to the wind."

It grew silent. She looked at him, forgetting her feelings for a moment, and focused on his words. "Then how much is it worth?"

"You must have made inquiries—" he fell silent momentarily. "Hagga. Or should I say Madam?"

She wished that he would call her by name, as he had in Marina, but he did not. She brushed his question aside.

"It's not worth more than that. I asked. Besides, the captain will pay in cash."

"What would you say to a hundred thousand more than the price the captain wants to pay you? In cash."

She thought for a second, then answered uncertainly: "I gave him my word."

He did not speak.

"You want to buy it to build some project? What's the project, anyway?"

"I want to buy it for myself."

She replied spontaneously, in complete trust: "It's yours. Without any money. It's yours."

He laughed. "Why?"

"Because you are, by God, the kind of man who, if put on a wound, would heal it."

"Is it mine for a half million, or for six hundred thousand?"

"Whatever your conscience dictates. I won't take issue with it."

"What about your agreement with the captain?"

"Just a helpless woman going back on her word."

He laughed. "Let's eat."

"Will you buy the land?"

"I'd like to see it again first."

She blurted out: "Forgive me. If it was just my land, I would give it to you for free, but for the children here. I have broken my promise to the captain for you. Don't leave me hanging between heaven and earth."

He replied in surprise and warmth, "Leave you hanging?"

"My feet are in the air. Let's say the Fatiha, and sign a contract tomorrow."

"Tomorrow?"

"I was going to sign the contract with the captain the day after tomorrow."

He laughed. "No, you were not going to sign the contract with the captain. I'll be ready to sign a contract in one month. Give me a month to get to know the land better."

"Sorry, but why do you need to get to know it better? It's not like it's a bride."

"Mama, let him think about it," Taha interjected.

"Of course," she said quickly. "Have lunch with us tomorrow, and see the land."

Hazim said, "Let's meet in a week, and talk then."

No sooner had she left the restaurant than Asma sighed happily, and began talking enthusiastically and nonstop with her children. Her joy was twofold. First was the joy of seeing him: she had convinced herself that seeing him was enough for her heart. Second was the joy of the land now becoming an object for which two of the richest men were competing. She would gain either way.

As soon as they had left, she said, "Taha, tomorrow go to the captain."

He looked at her, perplexed. Holding up her skirt as she got in the car, she went on: "You know the new Swiss chocolate we saw in the captain's house?"

"What do you mean, Mother?"

"Listen to me son, carefully. Take one hundred pounds, and buy a kilo of that miserable good-for-nothing Swiss chocolate that they sell for thousands. Go visit the captain in his office. When you go in, give him the chocolate. Flatter him and butter him up for a quarter of an hour. Then tell him that you're learning English, and that you study day and night."

"Why?"

"Then tell him you want to know when exactly he will buy the land, because we have another buyer who is willing to pay a much higher price. Tell him that if he still wants it, then you'll give it to him because you are the man of the house and you respect him, and because your mother was going to finalize the sale with the other buyer. But you stopped her. And she talked to you, and told you to go. Understand?"

"I don't understand anything."

"Because you're hopeless, just like your father. God have mercy on him, he was good. He was good like you are good."

"But we promised Hazim."

"We promised no one, and no one has bought the land. They're all playing with us, like we're pawns in a chess game, son. Whoever buys the land first, it's his. We've got to sell it soon, before your sister finishes high school and your father's family learns that she went into the Faculty of Commerce because we could not afford the American University. Now do you understand?"

He nodded.

She sighed, saying, "Oh, how I'd like to see you turn out like Dr. Hazim. My God, he has such presence! I've never seen anything like it in a man before."

From *The Book of the Dead and the Living*

DO YOU FEAR THE DARK TOO, Thief?

I do not know what it is about darkness that makes people afraid. In the dark, the world widens and colors disintegrate. Time melts away, leaving eternity typical, predictable, and constant.

It must be the fear of losing freedom and hope. For in the dark, there is no difference between the jailer and the jailed, or between a bird and a prisoner.

I told you, Thief, I'm not one of the Egyptians of the Revolution, and I don't write poetry. I'm not sure if I fear the dark. Sometimes, but not much. What about you? Do you feel guilty now? Or do you think that the darkness is something that only happens to others, and that it will never fall over your eyes?

Seven

ASMA DID NOT FEEL COMFORTABLE with her daughter accompanying her to visit Karima. Her children were for her a treasure to keep hidden in the middle of a desert. No one must know of them, or see them. But Karima was determined to meet Salma. Salma found the visit very annoying, and she had no idea what exactly her mother wanted. To some degree, perhaps, she envied the time and attention her mother lavished on Karima, who Salma considered a pretentious, silly lady. Worse yet, she had no sense of humor. Salma remained silent, her mother speaking excitedly about her. Karima looked at her appraisingly, and offered her mango and orange juice.

When Karima's cell phone rang, Asma whispered to her daughter, "Someday you will have a house bigger than this one, a mansion, a husband who loves you, a maid, a cook . . . you'll see."

"I don't want all that," Salma replied.

Before her mother could scold her, Karima returned and said warmly, "Your daughter is beautiful, Asma. I have a husband for her."

Salma smiled interestedly, and inclined her head.

"Salma will not marry now," Asma said automatically. "She's going to go to college and start working first."

Salma looked sorrowful, so Karima said in surprise, "She *wants* to get married, doesn't she?"

Smiling a little stiffly, Asma answered: "She would not dare to oppose her mother. But we are honored that you thought of us. You are so kind and generous, and full of every virtue."

"Asma, don't you want to know what he does? He's a doctor."

"Really, she's still young," Asma insisted.

"He's my driver's son. Can you believe he ended up a doctor? Times are changing. He's really a good guy."

"My daughter Salma is smart, and not thinking of marriage yet. When she marries, she's going to marry the son of a pasha."

Karima smiled wickedly. "And the son of a pasha is going to marry her for the acre of land you have? You fool! Think, Asma. Are you going senile, or were you already stupid?"

Salma opened her mouth in anger. She had never seen her mother belittled in such a calm, careless manner.

Smiling, Asma replied, "Oh well . . . everyone thinks his or her own children are the best of people."

Karima appeared agitated. She had not expected this rejection from Asma, after she had shown such kindness and interest in her daughter's life. Turning to the maid she called out, "Prepare the bath. I have an appointment in an hour." She left the room without another word.

Asma did not look at her daughter. She merely spoke mechanically: "Let's go."

The whole way, her daughter grumbled and complained. "Mama, she's rude. Mama, promise me you won't visit her again. Why do you see her, anyway? I don't want to go to the American University. Mama . . ."

The heat of Cairo that day was melting even the dust. Asma sat on her seat in the small open space, waiting for the train to Benha. She said nothing.

"Mama, do you hear me? I'm not going to the American University. I hate all that shallowness."

Her mother replied in a soft voice, looking in the direction of the train. "Sit next to me, Salma."

Salma rallied herself at her mother's side, amid the crowds. "Yes?"

"Karima is crazy," Asma said helplessly, "but she means well."

"Why do we have to put up with her?"

"Salma, you will go to the school I choose. You will succeed, and you will do what I tell you to do. You will not marry before graduating, like I did. Salma, listen to me—no one chooses their life or destiny. Fate decreed that I spend my life for your sake. Therefore, it is natural that I choose for you. You obey me because, if I had remarried, I would leave you to do what you wanted. But I have no one but you—you and your brothers. Don't you dare oppose me, or I will be mad at you until Judgment Day. The world belittles us, my girl, day in and day out. I have borne the contempt of the world, but I will not bear the contempt of my children. Do you understand?"

Salma opened her mouth, but her mother covered it, saying, "Be quiet. Enough already. Don't bicker with me. You know better than anyone how the world has treated me. Neither friend nor foe helped me. Your father's family abandoned you when you were seven. They would have put you out on the street if necessary. I don't want to hear another word on the way home."

Not a day passed before Asma called Karima, gushing and apologizing: "Forgive me, Karima, you're so good to me. I'm lucky just to sit in the same room as you."

Karima invited her to come visit again.

Asma was sitting next to Karima one day when Karima, smoking her water pipe, began to speak with her about jinn and spirits. She said gravely, with a shiver, "I want to find someone knowledgeable about such things."

"Just for fun? Or do you have a job for them?"

"Point me toward a woman I can trust."

The next day, Asma brought Umm al-Madamir to Karima, taking along Asma's little sister, Fawziya. Fawziya was known for talking nonstop, taking on the roles of the hero, the villain, and the referee in conversations.

Umm al-Madamir commanded awe and reverence. Slender and petite, she wore only white clothing, making those around her feel as though she were a genie or a pure spirit, drifting about the earth and the heavens. When Umm al-Madamir decided to light a wood fire on the roof of the villa, it seemed to Karima that she must be able to commune with demons and angels. Asma's sister, in contrast, talked without pausing, never thinking of the consequences. She asked questions, only to hang her head in dismay when she received no answer. As the four women gathered around the fire, truth and falsehood were made clear to each of them. Umm al-Madamir certainly had remarkable abilities.

Karima was the happiest, speaking with Umm al-Madamir and asking her advice. The woman replied slowly, as if she were receiving the answers from another world. Karima shivered, thanking Asma, and continuing to ask questions. While Karima smoked her water pipe, Asma sat in silence, listening, her eyes clouded with darkness. Her sister continued talking without respite.

Drawing near Umm al-Madamir, Fawziya asked, "Tell me, Auntie, how do I curb a man's desires?"

Silence fell. Karima looked at her, mildly horrified and jealous. "Your husband? You mean your husband, right?"

Fawziya said rapidly, in her high voice, "Two or three times a day, until he leaves me like a lifeless corpse. I want him to give me a break."

Karima opened her mouth to answer, then laughed nervously. She gestured at Asma next to her, "Where is this sister of yours from? Why do you want him to give you a break? Do you not love him, or just not enjoy him?"

She said thoughtlessly, "Of course I love him. I don't enjoy it, and I don't need to, but if a husband wants his wife like that, then what's she to do? Do you refuse?"

Umm al-Madamir hastened to answer: "Don't refuse your husband. Ever. I have a recipe for you that will decrease the frequency."

Karima looked at Asma, a little disconcerted, and said, "And you, Asma? How was your husband?"

"May he rest in peace. Let's not speak of the dead."

Karima persisted, "No, let's talk. Don't you . . . miss the arms of men? You sleep alone every day? I don't love my husband at all. I don't love him, but I don't like to sleep alone every day. You've slept alone for ten years, and you're in the flower of your youth!"

"I don't sleep alone," Asma answered lightly. "If only I did sleep alone! My son Ahmed sleeps on one arm, and my daughter Salma sleeps on the other."

"And after Ahmed and Salma get married? Then you'll sleep alone. Poor Asma, you'll sleep alone the rest of your life. What if you die, and no one misses you? That's why I put up with my husband: I want someone next to me at night."

Asma did not answer. She looked at the fire, and the smoke that surrounded them. Tears glittered in her eyes as she tried to summon the image of her late husband. She could not, and bit her lip. The tears increased, and one image overtook her: another man she saw herself kissing, embracing, and melting within. A tear fell from her eyes, and she did not hear the remainder of the conversation.

"Asma!" Karima shouted. "Do you hear me? That sister of yours is a wonder! Go on, Fawziya. What happens when your husband kisses you? What's wrong, Asma? Are you crying?"

"Not at all," she answered hastily. "I was just remembering my husband."

Karima winked at her. "He's dead, honey. There are plenty of living men. Asma dear, there are girls your age who haven't yet married. Why don't you get married? Haven't you found a man you like?"

"God forbid," Asma said mournfully. She wiped away her tears with the palm of her hand and said again, "God forbid."

Karima took no heed of her. She continued speaking with Umm al-Madamir and Fawziya.

Umm al-Madamir said, "I see you, Karima . . . Karima . . . with a pure heart . . . but I see a red jinni controlling you now. . . ."

Karima asked in wonder, "How do you see all that?"

"They tell me, Karima . . . your husband . . . in a navy uniform . . . a handsome young man . . . you liked him . . . but he loved something more than you?"

"The sea," Karima murmured. "It took him from me. An adventure, a voyage for months. Will I ever see him again?"

"Maybe you never really knew him. He grows bored easily, like all men. He has a girl in every port. The more he sails the Egyptian sea, the more his eyes drown in tears. He reads and writes poetry. . . ."

Karima replied bitterly: "He stole sleep from my eyes. He defeated me. For forty years, I've been wandering in the wilderness. The problem, Umm al-Madamir, is that I hate him. For a while now, I've just hated him. I stay with him, not for the sake of the children, and not for companionship, but because I'm afraid. How could I leave all his wealth to some bimbo who will just make a fool of him in his old age? I feel like my heart has crumbled. I hate everything. Hate is difficult. Seeing him every day and interacting with him. I hate myself. I despise myself. Three months after our wedding, he returned from his voyage. I watched him approach, and saw this smile on his face. I'll never forget it. He was smiling with ease, satisfaction, I don't know how to describe it. He wasn't impatient to be with me. For the first time ever. And I knew. Or perhaps I didn't know then, but now I know."

Asma patted her hand without speaking.

Karima opened her bag, took out two capsules of antidepressants, and downed them. Then she asked, "How will you help me, Umm al-Madamir?"

The silence grew. Then Umm al-Madamir replied calmly, "What do you want from me, exactly?"

She waved her hand dismissively. "How should I know? Why were you brought here? I'll kill him. I'll butcher him."

"He will die on his own."

"And until then?"

With her customary slowness, Umm al-Madamir said, "Shall I make him rue the day he was born? I can make him wander among people, not knowing who he is or what he wants."

"Then do it!" Karima said forcefully. She took a puff from the water pipe, and said to Asma's sister, "You love your husband, right?"

Fawziya said tepidly, "We all love our husbands, at least at first."

As if she did not hear her, Karima said, "I hate men. I hate marriage, and I wish I could die."

Fawziya patted her hand, and began discussing the details of lovemaking, giving her advice on men.

When the session came to an end, Karima embraced Asma, saying, "You are my best friend."

Asma patted her on the back and smiled. "It's an honor to be a friend of yours."

In the morning, Asma called to check on Karima. Karima exhaled in exasperation. "Asma," she said, "please don't call me again. I'm busy these days. When I have the time, I'll call you."

"Why?" Asma asked quickly. "Are you all right? Is everything okay?"

"Damn you!" Karima muttered. Then she said stiffly, "I told you not to call again."

She hung up, leaving Asma openmouthed, her graciousness in disarray. It seemed that Karima had tired of her, and

99

had decided to drop her. Her opportunities to climb upward had just narrowed significantly. Her progress up the ladder had slipped at least four steps. But she would not despair. With strategy and truly Egyptian patience, gathering her tattered dignity from the wreckage, she left her house a week later to visit Karima. She rode the train to Cairo in the luxury of a second-class seat, and knocked on the door, only to hear from the maid: "She doesn't want to see you, Umm Taha."

Asma held out a box of cookies and homemade ghee. The maid said quickly, "Madam Karima is on a diet now, and doesn't eat such things."

Asma whispered imploringly, "I just want to meet with her to find out why she is angry with me."

The maid sighed in exasperation, and went to call Karima. Karima came from her bedroom in embroidered pajamas, and when she saw Asma before her, she said angrily, "What do you want? Why do you disturb me from my sleep? Don't you understand, I don't want to see your face ever again. What stupidity! Why can't you get that?"

The image became clear. The political reality came into focus. Riding the train home, Asma's eyes glistened with tears. She whispered, "May you die by drowning, Karima. You're a bitch."

Then she spit three times, and muttered to herself, "How did she end up like this?"

Although Asma always wore her loose gilbab and black head-scarf in the village, one day she put on a white blouse and a long black skirt. That day, nervously expecting Hazim, she also applied extra kohl eyeliner. Her mother examined her as usual, saying, "Why do you kohl your eyes like you just inherited a charcoal mine?"

"Mom, there's no such thing as a charcoal mine."

"There is now. Today. It's right in front of me. Are you meeting with the mayor or with the commissioner?"

"I'm meeting with Hazim, who wants to buy the land."

"I thought it was the captain."

"It's Hazim now."

"I don't understand. It changes every day. You meet with a lot of men. You should think of your reputation, girl. A widow meeting with all sorts—doctors, farmers, the mayor. Your brother has every right to cut you off."

Asma answered angrily: "Did I choose to be a widow? Plus, my son is always with me. He is a man, and protects me."

Her mother sucked her lips, and did not answer.

Hazim did not arrive until two o'clock. Asma had been waiting since ten that morning. She called his office. The secretary answered, saying that he did not know where he was. She persisted, asking for his mobile number. The secretary said he could not give it to her.

She said angrily, "I had an appointment with him today."

The secretary replied with finality: "Even if I gave you the number, he wouldn't answer. He doesn't answer calls from unknown numbers. Sorry, I can't."

She hung up and waited, partly angry and partly concerned.

When she heard Hazim's car, she told her daughter to open the door. Then she called her son, and tried to appear natural.

She greeted him warmly and invited him in, but he said calmly that he would like to see the land first.

She called her son and asked him to come with her and Hazim.

Taha came with them, walking in front of them. "I was worried about you," Asma told Hazim graciously. "I thought you would come in the morning."

He looked at her in surprise. "I'm sorry. I believe our appointment was for the afternoon."

"You must have lunch with us," she said warmly. "Could you also give Taha your mobile number? The secretary refused to give it to us. Can you believe it?"

He looked at Taha for a moment. Asma thought that perhaps he was going to refuse, and did not know why the thought pained her. Then he said, "Yes, of course."

His eyes moved toward Taha. There was a small scar on his forehead. It seemed to Hazim that it was not from a bite, but from a strong blow. When the land supervisor called for Taha, Taha looked to his mother. She nodded, and he excused himself and went with the manager.

As soon as Taha disappeared, they were quiet for several minutes. Then, as Asma walked beside Hazim, he asked her with his customary calm, "Your son Taha does not seem aggressive. Does he fight much with the people of the village?"

She looked at him in surprise. "No, not at all."

Suddenly he said, "Did you do that to your son, Umm Taha?"

"Do what?" she asked uncomfortably.

"That scar on his head."

Resignedly, not knowing how to clarify, she said, "If his father was living, he would have done more."

Astonished, he focused his eyes on a cow walking aimlessly. "He is a man, and you must treat him like a man, deliberating with him and convincing him."

"Deliberating with him? The world doesn't deliberate with anyone. If the police had gotten him, they wouldn't deliberate with him, and no one would deliberate with me either. Our fates are written for us; we don't choose them. Forgive me. Don't think ill of me."

He smiled, then stopped, saying, "This area—do you use it to grow corn?"

"Yes."

"If I buy the land, where will you grow corn?"

"I won't need to, will I?"

He nodded, then looked at her face searchingly.

She lowered her eyes in embarrassment. "Do you need anything from me?"

His eyes went suddenly to the few freckles scattered on her nose and cheeks. They made her appear young and innocent. He saw the tiny lines at the corners of her eyes when she looked toward the sun, as if she had just stepped out of a magazine on the geography of Egypt.

He smiled. "Thank you."

She returned with him in silence, her face solemn. As they neared the house, she said, "Dr. Rasha—God bless her—is a relative of yours?"

"No," he answered shortly.

She said urgently, "And Khalid's mother is living?"

"Yes."

She gestured firmly for him to enter, but he was more determined. "You can't stand our food, can you?" she said sadly. "You ate almost nothing before. We are country people, but we know hospitality, believe me. I swear everything is washed with water at least three times. I know you see country women washing everything in dirty water, but I don't do that. We're not like you think. My father was educated, and I hope you will honor us with a visit."

He smiled. "Another time, perhaps."

"You don't like our food. Is that it? I'll cook in front of you if you want. I swear . . ."

"Another time," he said, a little stiffly. "You'll have to excuse me today; I'm very busy."

"Dr. Hazim, on your son's life—"

He interrupted her: "Another time, Umm Taha." Then he disappeared.

She went in, feeling both disheartened and resigned.

She prepared lunch for her children mechanically, her face downcast, tension showing in her eyes. Not one of the children dared to ask what was wrong, lest she get angry with one of them. After lunch, she sat in the open area of the house, watching the television in silence. As usual, she clasped the hand of her youngest son. Her eyes saw neither the screen nor its pictures. When the doorbell rang, and her sister Fawziya came to visit, Asma smiled at her listlessly, and began preparing her something to eat.

Fawziya was completely different from Asma. Her husband was a low-level employee, and her aspirations did not exceed eating harisa with pistachios on holidays, and buying a basket of mangos in the summer. Some summers she would go to Alexandria, and her pleasure there was to sit on the sea wall in the evening at the great Raml Station square, her back to the sea, to watch the ice-cream carts and haggle with the seller of cotton candy. She had a cheerful face and a great laugh. She never stopped talking.

Entering the kitchen to help her sister, she said excitedly, "You have so much food. You always have so much food."

Asma quietly recited the two short Quranic verses against ill fortune, and said, "Fawziya . . . this is your house, sister. Take whatever you want."

Fawziya said sourly, "Why didn't Father marry me to a rich man like your husband? It's my fate."

"He died. My husband died, remember?"

"And left you with a house and land. You're so lucky!"

Asma recited the two verses again.

When Fawziya asked innocently about the reason for her irritation, Asma did not answer at once. Fawziya began talking about the visit to Karima's, and land, and Asma's rich friends.

Asma said, seemingly casual, "Did you hear about Dr. Hazim?"

Her sister replied excitedly: "You didn't tell me about him, but I've heard of him, of course, and my husband says that his father was famous. I don't know how my husband knew that. Of course he reads the newspapers. Maybe he heard of his father from the news. He watches it every day."

"He will likely buy the land," Asma said gruffly. "We still don't know the details, but he's certainly sure of himself."

She paused, searching for the right words. "He's conceited, and thinks he's better than everyone. To him, we are peasants whom he pities. I don't like that. I'm not comfortable with that kind of man."

In disbelief, Fawziya replied, "You prefer Karima and her husband?"

Asma answered uncertainly, as if she had not heard. "I don't know. Those people are shameless. A guy can bring his girlfriend to visit a family, as if that was normal."

"Are you talking about the captain, Karima's husband?"

"I'm talking about Hazim. In front of his son. How could he maintain that sort of relationship in front of his son? He's kind and generous, and can you believe that he had us over for lunch in Marina? And another time, in Cairo. But he looks at us as if we are nothing. He just feels sorry for us. He can't stand our food. Shall I tell him?"

Fawziya looked confused. "Tell him what?"

"I don't know," Asma said sorrowfully.

"You've been talking about him since I got here," Fawziya told her comfortingly. "Do you hate him that much? He must be an unbearable man."

Asma lifted the dish of food from the stove and put it on the table. Her sister looked at her in astonishment. "Asma, the dish is hot as hell. How did you not burn your fingers?"

Asma put her hand on her chest absentmindedly, and said nothing.

Thrusting her hand carefully into the dish of stuffed vegetables, Fawziya said, "If you hate him so much, then don't sell the land to him."

"He could have eaten something," Asma said irritably. "I cooked for him all day. Would that have been so hard? Just to eat something? Being nice to people is done for God's sake."

Fawziya lifted her hand from the dish, glistening with oil and bits of food. "He's unlucky. His whole life, he's never enjoyed stuffed vegetables like this."

"He'll be sorry."

"Of course he will! Nobody makes better stuffed vegetables."

"He could have just sat with us," Asma said bitterly. "Just sit with us. What's wrong with that?"

When Hazim asked her to come to his office, and to bring her lawyer, Asma could hardly believe it. She could not sleep, not one wink.

The captain showed no interest in her son's visit. Not only did he not appear ready to buy the land anytime soon, he did not even deign to see her son. His secretary accepted the chocolates, and said she would give them to him. From that day, the wasted money had gnawed at Asma's heart. When she begged Karima to talk with her husband, Karima completely ignored her, as if she had not heard her. Asma's lost hope in the captain came as something of a relief. It seemed that her wish to see more of Hazim would come true as soon as the project began. He would be close enough for her to see him like shining silver, and that was all she wanted or desired.

She stood before Hazim, her hands folded in front of her like an obedient student. Eyes downcast, she said, "God bless you."

He took out his glasses and a sheaf of papers. Looking at the lawyer, he said, "This is the owner of the land. I want you to prepare the contract as soon as possible."

"We didn't agree on a price," she said quickly.

He looked at her suspiciously. Then he said harshly, "We agreed, Umm Taha."

"Six hundred thousand."

"I have no time for bargaining. I will pay five hundred thousand. No more."

"I told you—"

He cut her off. "It is the lawyer who decides, and this is the price he advised."

She said smoothly, "Of course. We're just honored that you're buying it. I will carry out whatever you say. You are very important to us."

He looked at the lawyer again, and said, "The land is zoned for building?

She swallowed. "Yes, of course."

"Is it in your name, or your husband's name?"

She replied quickly: "He put the deed in my name. It is my land. He put it in my name before he died."

"Do you have the deed?"

"When do you need it?" she asked hesitantly.

He looked in her eyes, and repeated his question sharply, as if he did not believe her. "Do you have the deed?"

"Yes," she replied quickly.

He smiled. "Good. The lawyer will do whatever is necessary, and we will commence tomorrow, for there is no time to lose."

He looked at the wood, iron, and clay around him, as if he were a dazed child looking at a basket of sweets after fasting for years. "That's how civilizations are built," he said.

Asma asked in concern, "Do you need anything?"

He did not hear her. He approached the heavy pieces of iron, and looked at the workers as they placed the pieces on the ground indifferently, some sighing from the labor, and others shouting unnecessarily, calling back to one another needlessly.

He said, in a clear voice, "Give me a piece of iron, and I will give you immortality."

Asma said, a little surprised and completely spontaneously, "What is the iron for? When the time comes, we don't take anything with us into the grave. We're all buried no matter what."

He replied excitedly, his eyes never leaving the workers: "In this you are mistaken. For graves differ. Have you bought a gravesite yet? If you were to buy one, where would it be? Would it be among flowers and mango trees, or among animal dung and droppings of beasts?"

She did not understand, but she said, "Yes. You're right, of course."

He turned to the lumber, took hold of a long plank, and passed an eye along it. "Some graves are for paupers, and others for princes."

"But all are alike to God. So it doesn't matter where we are buried. The angels will come take account of us regardless."

He paused in silence a moment. "You are a believer."

"Nothing but."

"Do you not fear death?"

"Of course I fear death. Without me, my children would be lost and destitute. But I don't think that I will fear death when my children are grown up."

"You do not fear the darkness of the tomb?"

"God is with me."

He nodded, saying, "Sometimes people fear the unknown, the darkness and absence of being. You are fortunate, Umm Taha, because you have faith. There are those who have no faith, and do not know what awaits them." Then he looked at her, scrutinizing her. "You want to know what project I am undertaking on this land?"

"It doesn't matter," she said instantly.

He looked again at the wood in his hand, passing his fingers along its surface, sensing its texture, its strength, and its weak spots.

"I'm building a tomb."

She swallowed, her eyes following his fingers on the wood, imagining her body in its place, his fingers moving carefully from her head to her feet, and then from her right arm to her left, utterly dominating her chest. Her body began to come to life and tremble as she stared at the wood, and at his hand resting on the heart of the wood.

There was a moment's silence. Then he asked, "Umm Taha? Did you hear me?"

"Y–yes," she stammered. "What were you saying?"

"I was saying that I intend to build a tomb. I will begin today."

Dazed, her mouth opened, and she said, "Sorry, I don't understand. You're building what?"

"A tomb, Umm Taha, with a grand mausoleum, and a plaza here." He gestured to indicate the locations.

Stunned, she asked, "For yourself?"

"The end product is ultimately for myself, but the tomb is not necessarily for me."

She shrugged, seemingly disinterested. "As you like. But it's a beautiful piece of good land, more suitable for the living than the dead."

"The dead will pay more for it, so the living must be patient."

"I don't entirely understand. Pardon me, but you are buying the land, right?"

"Isn't that what we agreed? I'm not violating any contract to which I agreed."

"I'm sorry. I didn't mean . . ."

He turned toward the iron. "Then I'll get started."

Her eyes feasted on him as he worked. She was enchanted by everything about him: his movements; his passion; the clean, refined air that surrounded him; and a sort of radiance of greatness. She did not see him interacting with the workers at all. It seemed to her that he did not even see them. He saw stones and wood, his gaze taking them in. He talked with more than one engineer at once, and it was the engineers who interacted with the workers and carried out the instructions. He seemed to see everything, yet his eyes had long ago accustomed themselves to focusing only on what he wanted to see, disregarding any ugliness or disorder.

Whenever their eyes met, her eyes dropped in shyness, and she asked him about something else. She looked at her watch. She tried to leave, but could not. So she rested her chin on her hand, sitting and watching him.

Who was this madwoman, who would give up such a man? Doubtless there were many women who wanted him, who sought to see him or talk with him. Young women, rich women, educated women, ladies like Karima and her children, and better than Karima and her children. Life was like that—like different serving dishes. For every kind of food, there was a dish. Each dish had its own life. And every life has its end.

When he noticed her presence, he would smile at her sometimes. She didn't know whether he smiled out of sympathy, or pride, or something else. And other times he ignored her. She should return to her life, and forget about the dead. She had lives entrusted to her.

Before long, the total sum was in Asma's bank account, and she was looking ahead to when she might see her dreams come true. There was no avoiding the enthusiasm, for the sum would likely provide for them for the rest of their lives. What remained of her husband's property, four feddans, would continue as agricultural land. It was not a great deal of land, but Asma needed to continue working it to provide a regular income. She also needed to contemplate the future of three children. Of course the future would be better. What would ensure the brighter future was the presence of Hazim throughout the building process, as she watched him from afar. For that was all she hoped for and desired.

As Hazim was on the way to work in the morning, his cell phone rang. It was the captain, and today he was prepared to talk. He had been anticipating it for three months.

In an ancient, rattling voice, the captain said, "I heard you're building the tomb without the corpse! Is that wise?"

He smiled. "It was your idea. I don't deny it."

"And it's still my idea. Don't talk about it like you've finished already."

"I've made a good start."

"You may not be used to people opposing you, but I am also not used to people challenging me."

"I don't understand."

110

"Well, listen up. You're building the tomb? On Asma's land! I introduced you to both the fellaha and the tomb! Is that fair?"

"Really, I don't know what the object of this call is. Did you like my design? If not, then why are we having this conversation?"

"Yes, no doubt you do not know the object of this call. I'm going to crush her with my own hands, in a matter of seconds. That fellaha means nothing to me. I'm going to crush her like a cockroach. Her land will disappear from the surface of the earth. She dares to sell the land without my permission! The world has gone to the dogs!"

The line went dead, leaving Hazim frowning and a little unsettled. Of course there was no need to worry; there was nothing the captain could do. Nevertheless, he did not trust the social circle of the captain, and he did not like even interacting with them. It was better this way: now he would not need to interact with the captain and his like.

Walking with his son in the grounds of his posh club at six in the morning on Wednesdays was one of the things that Hazim found most enjoyable. Although his son lived with him most of the time, he did not see him much. For his son had begun to work, and he worked day and night. Usually Hazim walked to the club. Walking in Cairo in the morning, filled as it was with beautiful trees and flowers, lengthened one's life. This was his Cairo that he knew and loved. The daily schedule was routine.

After walking with his son, he returned home, and then went to work. He had lunch with his sister in the Giza villa that she had inherited from their father. His sister did not have much time for cooking, she and her husband both being doctors. She had three nannies, each from a different country. One was from a European country, one from an African country, and one from an Asian country. She wanted to

111

introduce her children to the continents with the oldest civilizations. Hazim's sister had married when she was forty, and with the help of in vitro fertilization, had twins—a son and a daughter. Khalid and his father loved them. She asked the cook to prepare spinach with crème fraîche, Italian cheese, and the tomato soup that her brother loved, and to serve with it smoked salmon and German bread made with bran and imported flour. These foods were what Hazim was used to. He was not familiar with Egyptian dishes such as mulukhiya soup, qulqas stew, mimbar sausages, kirsha tripe, or stuffed pigeon. He had tried them a couple of times when he was a teenager. At that time, he had been adventurous, wanting to try new things and be daring.

In the morning, the uptown area of Zamalek was quite empty, decorated by signs in English and mixtures of English and Arabic. A foreign woman ran in front of them every morning, in denim shorts and a white shirt wet with sweat. In her hand, she carried a plastic bottle of water. Listening to music from her earphones, she focused on her tight legs and strong arms.

At work, Hazim was sometimes indefinable, like Zamalek in the early morning. Although he was generous with the employees, he sought control over everything, interfering and inquiring about every detail. The other architects did not feel comfortable in his presence, especially if he asked one of them to design something. His criticism was harsh (though calmly delivered), and at times entirely unnecessary. Sometimes the employees secretly accused him of smothering them, so that he could be the only designer, and his name the only one visible to the public. His closed office door was more of a wall. He only opened it in dire necessity, and got annoyed if he heard a complaint or anything personal from an employee. Hazim's reputation for attention to detail and order in his life preceded him everywhere.

Eight

AT THREE IN THE MORNING, when the doorbell rang, Asma opened her eyes in horror, certain that her mother had died. Then she remembered that her mother lived with her, and that if she had died, then she herself would be the first to know. She rose wearily to answer the door, her daughter asking, "Is anything wrong, Mama?"

"Go to sleep, Salma," she replied reassuringly.

She put her abaya cloak on over her white nightshirt, tied a scarf on her head, and headed toward the door. She opened it nervously, and looked out at the police officer who stood before her, along with four guards and all the neighbors.

Before she could speak, the officer said coolly, "Are you Asma Muhammad al-Sharqawi?"

Looking around at the neighbors, some of whom gave her taunting, insinuating looks, and some of whom looked frightened for her, she answered, "Yes."

No sooner had she said it than a guard took hold of her roughly and said, "All right, come with me. Let's go."

Her youngest son, holding her hand, was asking, "Mama? What's going on?"

She heard many voices: her daughter shouting, her eldest son coming out with her, her mother calling from her room, asking what was happening.

"What happened?" she asked the officer.

The guard gripped her arm, and she shook off his hand. "I will walk by myself. Don't touch me."

In the middle of the square, with all the neighbors and the young men who were out at night gathered around as if she were in a wrestling match, the guard raised his hand and slapped Asma's face with all his strength, saying, "You whore! Let's go, slut!"

She lost her balance and fell to the ground. A high-pitched ringing filled her ears.

Her son yelled and moved toward the guard. The guard pointed his gun at him. Asma shouted, raising a hand to Taha and holding her nose with her other hand to stop the bleeding. "Shut up, Taha! Don't do anything. Don't do anything."

Taha stepped back, his face awash with anger. Her daughter put her hand on her mouth in fear. Taha bowed his head in defeat. Asma turned her head, cursing the bystanders. The guard, holding her arm and forcing her up off the ground, said, "You're making things very difficult for yourself!"

He pushed her into a police car. She closed her eyes, and tried to register what had just happened. So much blood poured out that she wished she could dispose of her nose altogether to be rid of the troublesome bleeding that came at times of duress. Her nose was unable to withstand a little pressure. The car smelled like armpits and decay, and her nose bled nonstop. She put her hand gingerly to her nose, as if she could halt the onslaught. Her eyes did not meet those of the guard, who stared at her.

When she arrived at the station, the guard ordered her to exit the car, and pushed her roughly. She fell, hit her head, and lay still for a few moments. Then a new officer's hand grasped her. "I'm sorry," he whispered, in what seemed to her a regretful tone.

She looked at his face. He looked like he was in his early twenties. He shouted at the guard, "Leave off, you goon!"

"She's a difficult one, sir!" the guard said.

"I know. And this is my job, not yours! Get out of my sight. Go on."

She did not know why there was concern on the officer's face. Was this a trick he was playing on her? Where was the other officer? It seemed that he had vanished right in front of her. She should have expected this when she entered the house of the dragon. She could not have thought she would escape unscathed, when she was merely a woman with no weapon, family, or friends with influence.

The officer said, "You've made someone important angry, from what I can see. Poor thing. I want to help you. But I could be punished for kindness—please understand this."

He seated her on a couch, facing him.

"You will stay here until the morning when the office of public prosecutions summons you. But don't tell anyone. You were supposed to be put into isolation, but I can't do that with you. You are a mother. Forgive me, Umm . . ."

She said in a hoarse voice, "Umm Taha."

He sat on his desk. "Forgive me."

Gesturing with her hand, she asked, "Why am I here?"

He read from a paper: "Squandering your children's inheritance, selling land that you do not own, and forging land deeds."

She swallowed. "Who? Who accused me of this? My husband's family?"

"I can't tell you," he said uncomfortably. "Forgive me. Tomorrow you will know everything."

Seeing kindness in his face, she said, "I left my children alone, and my mother is in her eighties. I'm afraid for them."

He smiled and said, "I can call your son for you, if you like. I graduated last year, and this is my first year here. Believe me, Umm Taha, my hands are tied. I'm between a rock and a hard place. Again, forgive me."

He picked up the phone and said, "Here, call your son."

Her hand shook as she tried to call her son. There was no answer. She sat helpless, head in her hands.

Taha came in, and said in irritation, "Officer, sir, my mother has done nothing. The guard hit her and insulted her. That is illegal."

Then he went to his mother and said, hugging her and kissing her hand, "Mama . . ."

"You are the man of the house," she told him firmly. "Get a hold of yourself. You hear me?"

"Shall I call Uncle? Or the mayor? Or the commissioner?"

She said spontaneously, "Call Dr. Hazim. Maybe he will help us. Or maybe not. Probably not." She was silent a moment before continuing. "If you don't reach him, then call the lawyer. Go, don't leave your sister alone in the house at night. Go back now."

He looked at her, tears filling his eyes.

She turned her face away from him in shame. "Nothing happened," she said.

"There's blood on your face. Your nose is bleeding."

She wiped her face in irritation. "I told you, it's nothing. It happens sometimes when I'm tired. Go on, go home."

He nodded and moved to the door, his eyes fastened on her. She said sharply, "Go quickly. Or can't you obey me after you saw me hit? Do you have no respect for me anymore?"

He came to her again, sitting on the floor in front of her. He kissed her hand, saying, "As you wish."

She smiled. "Thank you."

He went out and left her. She wiped her cheek with the back of her hand, and remained silent.

Was it the captain? He had acted quickly, being a shrewd man, experienced in exterminating the flies that disturbed him. Did she expect Hazim to help her? What difference was there between the captain and Hazim? What did she really want from them, anyway? Should she ask for help from Karima?

A voice woke her suddenly: the officer's voice, and he was not talking to her. He was speaking gently.

When he saw her look at him, he ended the call. Smiling, he said apologetically, "I was talking with my wife."

Asma nodded without speaking.

The officer asked, "Would you like to eat something? I haven't had supper yet. My wife sent me some sandwiches."

She shook her head, suspicious about the officer's kind behavior. She had not expected it, and had never known such behavior before. She was always the one flattering and looking after everyone else.

He said, a little shyly, "You can use my bathroom if you need."

"I'm fine, thank you," she said automatically.

Encouraged, the officer said, "Umm Taha, why don't you wash your face? Come on . . ."

She stood and headed to the bathroom. She looked at her face; at the blood spattered around her nose. Without looking at herself in the mirror again, she washed her face and then wiped it with her skirt. She could not urinate. The urine was trapped within her in anxiety and tension. She went out, and returned to the couch.

Her mind revolved around one man. Would he do something? Why did she rely on him anyway, and what was their relationship? It was nothing, and never could be anything else. If only her emotions would stop overcoming her, she could think reasonably. She must prepare herself for getting out. If she got out, she would forget those people. And live in peace with her children. Then what? Marry her daughter off at the same age she had gotten married, and live with the patient nobodies who spent their whole lives without even the assurance of a grave. Her son would graduate from college, after studying for many years, and work as an employee for a salary insufficient even to pay his mobile phone bill. So he would work in the evening, in a café or driving a taxi. Her youngest son would suffer through public schools, coming home in tears. He would hate today, and tomorrow, and the future that was only too clearly marked out for him.

She would surrender, and forget all about selling the land, and the American University, and the diplomatic track, and the Royal Club. She would return to being a fellaha with a small parcel of land to farm. She would walk the small steps of the everyday with patience—a lot of patience; patience and peace were forever intertwined. She would call off the battle; she was defeated. We all give in eventually.

But no, she would not give in. Battle was inevitable. Dying without a grave now would be the death of a hero and martyr. Whereas death later, even with a grave, would be the death of a vanquished loser.

Silence reigned for hours, until the break of day.

"What is it now?" the officer called out to the guard. Then he said to her, "You will go to the prosecution. God willing, you'll be declared innocent or released on bail. Forgive me again, Hagga. You are a mother and a widow, and I've seen how you are with your children. All these accusations are false, I'm sure. My mother was a widow too. God willing, you're going to Paradise." Then he whispered something to the guard, and disappeared.

When she arrived at the building of the public prosecution office, her children were waiting for her. They all began to cry. They clung to her as if they had just left her womb—bundles of fresh flesh and fine bones.

She said forcefully, "Stop crying. Everything is going to be fine." She looked at Taha reproachfully. "You brought your little brother here? Is that a manly thing to do?"

The guard pushed her inside, along with the others. Taha defended himself: "He was crying all night, and needed to see you."

Hurrying alongside the guard, she asked, "Did you talk with Hazim?"

"I didn't call him yesterday," Taha replied. "I couldn't. I called him a little while ago, and the lawyer as well. Don't worry, Mother. Shall I call the captain?"

"No," she said with finality. Then she raised her voice, turning to look at Taha. "Go home with your siblings. I don't want them to see me now. Take good care of them. Don't worry about me, understand? Don't make any decisions without consulting me. And don't you dare talk to your father's family."

When she entered the attorney's office, she found her children's paternal uncle there. He looked at her in contempt. "That's her, the criminal. She's squandering my brother's money. She's dangerous for her fatherless children, believe me. No more than a thief. She stole our land. It's my land, mine and my siblings', and not this criminal's."

"I don't know what to say!" she told him in disgust. "You're exploiting your own brother. What can I say?"

He said angrily to the attorney, "I want to have the kids. They've been wronged. All of them. They should stay with me when she goes to prison as a convicted criminal forger."

"Get out of here, you bastard," she said with loathing.

The attorney of public prosecutions looked at her, a little annoyed and surprised. "This is not your house, Hagga. It's the prosecutor's office. You seem to think you can kick him out as if it's your own place, sister! Sit here, and I don't want to hear your voice until I begin the interrogation."

Shaking with fury, she replied, "First ask him who paid him to say this! It's my husband's land. He signed it over to me before he died, and when I refused to sell it . . . May God repay the one who set this devil upon me."

The attorney said indifferently, "Your land how? No deeds, nothing. And agricultural land turned into building land with no permission. Did you forge the deed to sell it?"

She sat down, saying, "I won't speak until my lawyer arrives."

The uncle made his statement, and then looked at her gloatingly. "You'll never get out of here. You're stuck. You can no longer control my late brother and his money."

She remained silent, fear creeping into her heart. What if Hazim knows about it? Suddenly, for the first time, tears fell from her eyes. She shivered, and despised herself and all those around her.

She heard his voice, and felt his presence fill the space. She looked up imploringly. Their eyes met. His eyes took in her swollen cheek and the traces of blood around her nose. He looked away. He began to speak with the attorney of public prosecutions, the lawyer at his side. She did not see his face, or know what he thought of her. But he had come. Hazim had come.

Her head remained in her hands while he spoke with the two men. Fresh tears gathered in her eyes. For the first time in her life, she felt that she was nothing but a poor, helpless woman. She bit her lip and looked at him again. This time he looked stumped. Then he whispered something to the lawyer he had brought. The lawyer whispered to the public attorney. He had come. It was no dream. Her emotions churned, and passed from longing to love, from pleading to tenderness. The public attorney, the lawyer, and her brother-in-law left the room. Hazim slowly sat next to her. He inclined his head to her without speaking.

Then he said, "Are you all right? Did anything happen to you yesterday? Who hit you?"

"I'm all right," she said hoarsely.

A strange atmosphere fell over them; an atmosphere of noise, rain, clouds, and silence. "Asma," he said softly.

She could not remember him ever calling her by name before. She was not sure if he was aware of that. She looked at him, her eyes full of tears, and then looked away in shame. He lifted his hand, only to let it drop thoughtlessly. He raised it again to the scarf that held her hair, which was in some disarray. Then he said, a little choked up, "You will be released today. I promise you."

She turned to him numbly, and impatiently wiped away the tears that were falling. He looked at his hand as if he had accidentally touched a hot iron. He looked at her in surprise, and then at his hand, staring at it. He said weakly, "Don't worry. You will be released." She nodded and shivered, and did not know what was happening.

He looked at her hands, intertwined in desperation, and at her legs. Then he placed his hand upon her hands, saying "Take heart. You will be fine. Everything will turn out well, and you will be home with your children today."

He patted her hand roughly, as if he were shaking hands with a colleague on a national plan of action. She bowed her head, regretting the weakness that overtook her in his presence.

He held her face in his hands and said, "Enough crying. Don't you believe me?"

Her eyes widened, and she could hardly believe what he was doing. She was not sure that he knew what he was doing.

She said simply, "Always."

His fingers paused a moment on her swollen cheek, as if he were assuring himself of her features and her presence; as if he were a doctor on the battlefield assessing the wounds and casualties. Then he removed his hand.

He stood calmly, and looked at his hands. He clasped them, as though to confirm that they were his own, and then left the room, leaving Asma all the more puzzled and disturbed.

Hazim went to his office, an idea slowly forming. There was only one person who knew where the contract was for the sale of the land. That person was his personal secretary, who he had discovered had been taking bribes all along from many of the people who came to Hazim's office with requests or projects. It had not concerned him as long as the man carried out his work, and caused no problems. Today, however, the situation was different. Asma was the collateral damage, a victim because of him . . . because she had sold him the land, instead of selling it to the captain.

He knew that was not the case. Asma had sold him the land because he had paid a fair price, and because it was in her interest to sell it. Disappointing the captain was not entirely linked to him. What did she have to do with him? What had happened to him? She was just a woman whom he neither knew nor wanted to know. . . . Had the situation muddled his thinking? Was he sympathizing with her situation? Pitying her? She was innocent. She had merely not given in to the captain. He must help her. She had chosen honor. But what is honor? She's a thief, isn't she? Is a woman's honor between her legs, or in her heart? For Hazim, the answer was easy: Asma was a victim. Even if she was a thief or a forger, she was still a victim, and he sympathized with her. He sympathized with her, just as he sometimes sympathized with Gaber, or Umm Ayman and all Egyptians. He wanted to help her, as he had helped her before. Nothing had changed. She would remain a fellaha in an embroidered gilbab and a tight headscarf, and he, Hazim . . .

But the secretary's betrayal must not go unpunished, for he despised betrayal. Today, especially. Everything had acquired a very distinct flavor; even pity seemed bitter. He would not think about the tenderness that overtook him, or the longing, or any of that. It was just sympathy for a poor fellaha, a widow raising her children. Hazim looked up his lawyer's number, and spoke with him for a few minutes.

When he entered his office, the secretary said, "Welcome back." He nodded, and looked at his watch. The police arrived within fifteen minutes, and a guard held the secretary, who protested desperately to Hazim that he had done nothing. He had never betrayed him, and had never stolen any papers from the office. The captain must have gotten the document some other way. He blubbered plaintively, the tears pouring from his eyes, and swore by his children, his mother, and his neighbors. It made no impression on Hazim. Indeed, he wanted the dramatic display to end as soon as possible. The day seemed too long.

Her body cringed as Asma remembered the blow, and the words that had accompanied it. How much had the captain paid the guard? Where had the police superintendent disappeared to? Had she really expected anything else? She touched her cheek, and was flooded with emotion. She did not know how the world would rebalance itself.

Her memory betrayed her sometimes, or perhaps it was her sole ally. She tried to remember the guard's face, but could not. She remembered only his words, and heard the smack of the blow. Memories do not follow the exact order of events. She shut her eyes, and the image of her father took over everything. He was smiling. His brown mustache and long lashes; she knew them well. He took her hand and walked with her, away from the train. She was twelve; it was her first visit to Cairo. He had chosen to take her, in particular, on some errand he had in Cairo. He took not her brother, not her sister, but her. She was hoping for three things that day: to buy a new dress, to go to the amusement park, and to eat a piece of French gâteau. Her father fulfilled all three of her dreams, and smiled at her with pride and tenderness. For a few moments, he was capable of everything. When she sat to wait for the train, he handed her a bottle of soda and said, "Here, Asma."

She took it and began to drink, with the whole world before her. The future was clear and simple, with everyone smiling and at ease.

Dr. Hazim. The name seared her throat, and the pain was not due to shame or to anger, but to tenderness. When tenderness appears, one's mind goes, more than it would from cruelty. She placed her shaking hand on her scarf, and stroked it as he had done. She had not dreamed it. She was certain, and of sound mind. He had held her face in his hands. And his hands were warm and strong. He pitied her, perhaps. Of course he did. Like the officer, and many other people, he had been moved by the sight of a helpless mother suffering in the office of public prosecutions. No . . . it had not moved him just as it had the officer. He had not seen her as a wretched mother, but as a woman, no more. To him, she was a woman, not a mother. She sensed that. Her feelings had not been wrong before, but they could be today. Of all days, today she was not thinking very realistically.

Why had Hazim paid her bail? She would have paid it. She had just been waiting for the lawyer. She had not expected that of him. All that generosity, decency, and gentleness. She grabbed her bag, and went out the door, sighing with a relief that was mixed with worry and fear.

She hailed a taxi to take to the train station and hurry home to her children, only to change her mind on the way. She asked the driver to take her instead to another place: Hazim's office.

His secretary was not waiting outside like he had been on other days. She was not sure he would be there. It was sunset, and the office appeared closed, but she knocked on the door. He opened it for her. He was clearly the only one in the office, since he was startled by her. He was nailed to the spot for a moment, at a total loss. Then he said, "Welcome back."

"I wanted to see you before I went home," she told him hoarsely.

Their eyes met, and he remained silent. She looked exhausted. There were dark circles under her eyes, and her loose black dress was wrinkled and covered in dust. She was shivering a little.

What distressed him most were her dull, lifeless eyes. Her pale face had been through so much. Her cheek was swollen. There were traces of blood below her nose. He sank into the chair in front of his desk. His hand gripped the desk, he knew not why.

She said hesitantly, shyly, "You think I'm a thief and a forger, right?"

His eyes leaving hers, he said heavily, "It doesn't matter."

"I want to explain things to you. I want to thank you. I want to . . ." She swallowed again and again. Her legs were shaking so much that the whole office shook. "I came to thank you . . ."

He nodded.

"You want me to explain. This is my right, and the right of my children. . . . I want a better future for them. . . . I dream of a better future. . . ."

He looked impatient and constrained. He did not know why he felt constricted. His hand gripped harder, until it hurt. There was silence. His eyes did not leave her face. He began to sense her, as if she were one with him, attached to his heart. He felt every pulse of her body. He began to feel his body quiver, tremble . . . yearn. It frightened him with a horror that he had never felt before. His body had never betrayed him like this.

She repeated, "I came to thank you. You've done so much for me . . . but I . . . I don't want to thank you . . ."

Her nervousness, agitation, and uneven breathing muddled his mind. Getting up from the desk, he walked to the door. He propped himself against it, needing the support of the wooden door in this confusing moment.

She too stood and walked to the door. She sighed. "I don't want to thank you. I know you never want to see me again. I don't want to sell the land. I don't want anything now. I know you probably hate me. You despise me, and what I've done. I'm a fellaha, a thief, and worthless to you . . . an opportunist . . . a nobody. Who am I to you? I want to . . ."

He propped his head against the door, sweat pouring from him, and a chill gnawing at him. He wished she would leave. Soon.

Hesitantly, she touched his hand. He shut his eyes for a second. Then he opened his eyes upon her face. Her eyes held his. She opened his hand, leaned forward a little, kissed his hand softly, and whispered, "I love you."

She lifted his hand to her face, and continued hoarsely: "You were merciful to me. . . . You were generous with me. . . .

But I don't want to thank you. . . . I wanted to say, even just once. . . . I love you. . . . That's all." She let his hand go, opened the door quickly, and ran.

She left Hazim a quivering heap of indecisiveness, longing, and confusion. She left him teetering between Egypt, India, and all the nations. He did not know whether he belonged to the age of the First Revolution, or the Second, Third, or Fourth. For if revolutions and feudalism both continued, and if the whole world turned upside down now, he could not care less. His world was shattered.

Nine

HE BRUSHED THE DUST OFF his face as he entered the crowded café, and looked about for the captain. He found him sitting in a corner, drinking an Egyptian beer. Beside him was a peach-flavored water pipe prepared and ready for use. On the table in front of him were dishes of clams and peanuts. As soon as the captain saw him, he waved him over heartily. Hazim approached, speechless indignation on his face. He sat in a chair facing the captain, and in renewed agitation said, "You will pay for what you did."

The captain smiled and took a swig of beer. "That's what I'm afraid of—the day I pay for all my deeds. That's why I need you to build the tomb."

"Murad, I'm not joking. You do not know me. To pay my employee to spy on me and steal documents from my office is a crime that I will not forget."

The captain slid the dish of peanuts toward him. "You punished him," he said. "It's over. According to my sources, he's now in the police station. He's facing several years in prison for stealing. He got his due."

"You play with people as if they were peanuts in your hands. Sometimes you swallow them or spit them out. Other times you just crush them."

Munching on peanuts, he replied: "First, I don't care for peanuts. Second, I don't do anything unjust. Ever. Sayyid stole, and he got what was coming to him. Now we're even.

As long as we're even, we can start to play together again, on the same team."

"I will not toy with people, and you and I are not on the same team. You screwed this country, and I am a scholar of it. There's a big difference."

There was a moment's silence. "Good analysis. I'm the thief, and the poor are the victims? We all steal from this country every day. I steal a big chunk, and they steal small chunks, but we're all equally liable. Hazim, we're all on a merry-go-round of sorts. The politicians toy with us, we go around endlessly, and we toy with the crumbs."

"You're quite the victim of the system," Hazim said sarcastically. "Every time I see you, you're whining and complaining. When will you grow up?"

"When they put me in charge."

"You can't be in charge of anything. Your strength is nothing but destruction. I told you that you will pay the price."

The captain picked up a clam and said, smiling, "All this because I attempted to spy on you? All this for Sayyid? Or is it for the fellaha who you didn't want? Like I said, we're even, one for one, like peanuts, as you say. I put her in prison, and you put Sayyid in prison. We're even, and now we can turn a new page. Build the tomb for me, and I'll forget the past. The memory of history is short. We can even rewrite the past. Did you know that? I tried to write a novel a while ago, but I never finished it. I must finish it before I die. It will be a pure, realist work of art. But we were talking about the tomb. A little skirmish, a maneuver, the victims of which were two thieves: a fellaha and a secretary. Now we can build the tomb on different land, and mend our wounded partnership."

"Then get her out of the disaster you caused her," Hazim told him.

He shook his head. "You misunderstand me. . . . She got herself into the disaster. I just helped to bring justice to the corruption that is ruining Egypt."

Hazim stood, and said in exasperation, "You want to thwart corruption?"

"Of course."

"Then consider the war not even started yet. Let's thwart corruption together."

The captain smiled. "Don't threaten me. I don't like it. I see that you've become attached to the fellaha. I wonder if you found that her arms could overwhelm you, as I predicted."

Hazim ignored his comment. "We will thwart corruption. We are agreed."

"A national campaign against corruption, with the victims being corrupt people."

"Don't tease me. You don't know me."

"Oh, but I know you well. I can't believe that my arrow hit the bull's-eye, and that Hazim concerns himself with the destiny of a fellaha—a nobody, and a widow to boot. Did she put a spell on you? They practice magic, you know. Or perhaps she lured you with her ample bosom, and her tush that can swallow a man until he melts into nothingness. I must admit, I envy you a bit. But not too much. Just a little. You're welcome to all the peasants of Egypt. Just build the tomb. That's all there is to it."

"I am building the tomb. But that's not all there is to it."

The captain grasped his hand. "Have a seat. If you're building the tomb, then there's no problem."

"I'm building it on the land of Asma al-Sharqawi."

He laughed. "It's not the land of Asma al-Sharqawi. The problem is that it's not Asma's land. I liked the girl you brought with you to Asma's house. Intelligent, highly educated, and . . . full of life. Go back to her and build a new tomb, and let's forget about the peanuts Asma and Sayyid."

"Who are you to tell me what to do?"

"You think you're the only one who gives orders?"

"I told you before, do not ever compare yourself with me."

"Of course not. Why would I compare myself with you? I am creative; I write stories and poetry. I weave history out of spiderwebs. You are an architect, working with measurements and supports. You understand nothing but arithmetic. Which one is better?"

Hazim came nearer, and said in a serious tone, "That is what we will see before long—who is better." Then he departed, his steps even, his eyes alert, and his heart astir.

For the first time in a long while, Hazim could not sleep, as if the day refused to end. He looked at his watch: midnight. He rose from his bed, needing to speak with a friend. His only friend was Rasha. She had no affiliations with the captain's mob. He picked up his phone and looked up her number, knowing that she would be still awake. When he said that he wanted to talk with her, she said, "I'll be there in a few minutes."

In less than a quarter of an hour, she was knocking on the door excitedly. When it opened, she found her usual place on the couch, sat straight-backed, and asked, "What's up? Tell me."

He smiled, sitting next to her. "It's been a hard day. You remember Asma?"

She scanned his face. "What about her?"

"The police arrested her, and she was sentenced today."

She nodded, trying to get to the bottom of what she was sensing. "And you?" she said.

As if he no longer saw her, he said, "She has an innocent face, like clear water. When she came to me, she was . . . strange."

"How?"

"She took my hand." He looked at his hands, and then said, "She said that she loved me. Can you believe it? I don't know what she wants, or what she expects."

"Then what?" she asked, a little enviously.

"She left."

"She needs your help, of course, and she's prepared to do anything to get it. It's normal. What do you expect from a woman like her? She has nothing—no education, nothing.

Even the highly educated in our universities today do not have enough to buy gas."

A little gruffly, he said, "She's different."

She looked at him again. "She's not the first woman to tell you that she loved you, Hazim, and she won't be the last. From what I know of you, it seems to be a fairly regular occurrence. Why this fellaha?"

Annoyed, he said, "What are you saying?"

"Do you want her?"

"Rasha. Please, try to understand."

She stood and said angrily, "Understand what? Of course she loves you. Why wouldn't she? You have everything she dreams of. For her, you are like a man she could read about, but never really know. Handsome, rich, educated, powerful, enchanting. It's natural for her to love you. But it's not natural . . . not natural, Hazim, for you to lose yourself in her presence like that. I've never seen you like this. If you want her—"

He cut her off. "You don't understand anything."

"I understand everything!" she replied aggressively. "If I told you right now that I loved you, what would you do?"

"Don't joke, Rasha."

"What would you do?"

"Rasha . . . seriously, stop joking."

"Your problem, my friend, is that you can't see the woman in front of you, and you don't pay attention to your feelings. You've been like this your whole life, as long as I've known you. You want to hear praise and feel superior, but you don't open your heart to anything more than that. If I told you that I loved you now . . . I did love you, and I still do, but I hate your arrogance and selfishness. The problem is that I'm seeing you lose control over a woman for the first time. You tremble, and want her, and hope, just like everybody else." She grimaced in disgust. "A mouse . . . a mouse beat the lion, and dropped him in the trap. Just a little mouse, not an armed hunter. What can I say? Good luck, my friend, with the people of the Nile Valley! But I don't think I want to see you ever again."

He watched her as she opened the door dazedly. She turned back to him, saying, "In any case, I'm fighting for the future of the Egypt I know. I don't want to see Egypt in the hands of extremists or ignorant people. That matters more to me than you or anything else."

He nodded as if hypnotized. Then he exhaled in fatigue, worry, and a great deal of confusion. He had thought that the day had ended, and that life had returned to order. He had thought that Rasha would help him toward a more balanced perspective, anticipating potential outcomes. Two confessions of love in one day were too much for a man to bear. But it was still the first confession that had overwhelmed all his faculties.

When Asma returned home, her children shot into her arms, tears in their eyes, and then they began preparing food, a bath, and anything else she wanted. On hearing Taha's cell phone ring, she looked at him curiously. He went to his room, and whispered to his girlfriend, "Please . . . It's over. I told you before. I can't explain. My mom needs me and my siblings. . . . Find another man who will make you happy."

She approached the door, listening quietly. Salma and Ahmed sat in silence.

Taha continued: "Listen, I told you to visit her, try to get to know her, but you didn't. I told you I would live with her, and you didn't agree. What do you want? Love? Where was love when I asked you to get to know my mother? She dedicates her whole life to me, and then I marry without her blessing . . . ? No. It's not a matter of obligation. You don't really love me. I understand that now. . . . Just forget about everything."

He hung up. Then he looked up and saw his mother. She smiled at him with pride. He took her hand and kissed it, and hugged her, saying, "I won't do anything that makes you angry."

She sat among her children like the stuffed duck in the center of the great table the day she invited the captain to lunch, and said proudly, "I should have gone to prison a long time ago so I could see all this love."

Her daughter said, "You didn't go to prison. It was slander, from Dad's family, of course."

"No, from the captain," Taha said. "He thinks we're his servants. I'm going to break his neck."

Asma said emphatically, "No, you must succeed, and become better than him. Salma, how is school these days? And you Ahmed?"

Her youngest son came close to her, resting his head on her chest, his hand reaching up to her face. He whispered, "I saw the blood coming out of your nose. How did it stop?"

She said, a little shortly, "It stopped."

"And that man who hit you," Ahmed asked, as if from casual interest. "Did the police arrest him? If Dad was here he would have killed him with his pistol, huh?"

Silence reigned. The blow was one of the forbidden topics that they had silently agreed to avoid discussing. Salma and Taha exchanged glances, and Salma looked guiltily at her younger brother. His mother patted his hand and whispered to him, "If your father were here . . . he would have cut him to pieces! Of course they arrested him, and I slapped him myself, three times! Your mother is worth a hundred men. You know, your mommy can do anything."

"Anything? Then why didn't you hit him here in front of us?"

"I didn't want to hit him in front of you."

He opened his mouth to ask another question, but she said wearily, "I want to sleep, Ahmed."

"I'll sleep next to you. They won't take you again, right?"

"Never," she said with certainty.

Her mother set a dish of dates in front of her, and said, "Eat, Asma. Eat, my girl. Dates make you strong. . . . They're mentioned in the Quran. If they could strengthen the Virgin Mary, then they can strengthen you, girl. Life is tough. Remember that. Say your mom said so."

She repeated, "My mom said so."

"What are you going to do now?"

"I'm going to sleep," Asma said, "and I won't leave al-Qalyubiya until the day I die."

She heard all three children say "God forbid" in unison, and then she closed her eyes and fell into a deep sleep.

There were days in Hazim's life that he would never forget. The day Shereen kidnapped his son. The day his father died. The day he decided to build the tomb. But none of those days changed Hazim. However, the day Asma confessed her love for him . . . that day changed him. Unfortunately, it changed him for the worse. Hazim's mind became scattered. His self-control weakened. Worse yet, God forbid, he began to find himself mired in the lives of the commoners: he began to get angry at them, and to sympathize with them. He began to feel like he knew them. For him, this was a great danger.

As for his strategic expectations for the behaviors of common people, they too fell into complete disorder. It was as if the French Revolution had risen again, complete with guillotines, and the disenfranchised had rebelled and spread terror in the hearts of kings. For on Friday, Gaber the driver did not steal the car as usual, and did not go to smoke a water pipe with his friends. On Thursday, Gaber's mother died, and Gaber called Hazim in tears, saying that he would spend several days at home.

"All right," Hazim said. "My condolences. Do you need anything?"

Like any Egyptian overwhelmed by a sense of noble generosity in times of crisis, Gaber said that it was meant to be, and that no money would ever replenish what he would lose with his mother's funeral.

Hazim took a breath, his attention shifting momentarily from Gaber to his conscience, which urged him to go to the funeral. He spent Thursday in confusion, caught up in a great internal struggle over whether to go. Going to the slum area of Saft al-Laban was, for him, like going to the planet Mercury. He did not know how to get there, or how to behave once he did. When Hazim called his son and asked how one might go to Saft al-Laban, Khalid laughed. He said that he would look it up on a map. Hazim closed his eyes and tried to sleep. Khalid called, and said, "I found it. Do you want to go?"

"No," Hazim replied in embarrassment, wishing he could set a good example for his son. "No, I don't think he wants to see anyone now. Maybe another time."

Khalid smiled. "Another time? Like when his wife dies?"

"What do you mean?"

"You said we had an obligation to others."

"Of course. I offered him assistance, and I know that he will need it."

Khalid asked interestedly, "Do you want me to go with you?"

"No need. Really."

"We'll just go for a few minutes. Gaber has worked for you for a long time."

Hazim hung up, exhaling in exasperation.

When his son arrived, Hazim was wearing a black suit with an elegant black tie. Khalid was wearing jeans and a black shirt.

"Want me to drive?" Khalid asked eagerly.

"No, I'll drive. But you know where it is, right?"

Khalid confirmed he did.

Hazim had not driven his car in more than five years. He did not realize how much Cairo's streets had changed. He did not know what it was like for a child to drive a toy car around in a small, tight circle as fast as possible, or how to close his eyes to meet a crash, or how to prevent the car from

135

flipping over. After driving for a few minutes, Hazim arrived at the kind of test that makes a boy into a man and a girl into a woman, and makes every human grow up and face the difficulties of life with composure and bravery. Hazim's test was very simple, and far less painful than circumcision. It took place when a microbus hit Hazim's car from behind because Hazim stopped at a red light.

The microbus driver got out and said angrily, "How could you stop in front of me so suddenly?"

Of course the greater fault in this situation was Hazim's, because he had stopped—no one stops at a red light. Red had become normal and pleasant. Cars stopped only when absolutely necessary, like England's policy in Egypt after the Revolution of 1919: intervene in internal affairs only when absolutely necessary.

When Hazim felt his car shake, he knew it was not just a friendly nudge, but an injury. Seeing his BMW, which was worth a quarter million pounds, at the mercy of a microbus driven by an obnoxious driver was too much to bear.

As he got out of his car, Khalid called out in alarm: "Leave it. Don't fight with him. He could be armed or something. You never know with these people."

Hazim did not hear him. He gave the driver a calculating look.

"It's your fault," the man said angrily. "What did you sud-denly stop for?"

The men who had gathered at the scene began to inter-vene, making calming comments and patting Hazim's hand. That got on Hazim's nerves.

The driver gestured sweepingly and said, "You think you bought the road with your money?" Hazim's fingers tightened into a fist, and he did something that he had not done since third grade: he punched the driver in the face.

For a second, the driver's mouth hung open in surprise. Then he curled his fingers, and punched Hazim in the face.

"Where are the police?" Khalid yelled.

When a guard came up, Hazim lifted his hand to halt him, and said roughly, "Nobody interfere."

After five minutes of exchanging blows, they were both panting. Hazim said contemptuously, "Thief! You're just a lowlife."

The microbus driver grimaced sarcastically, "Oh, we left all the honor for you guys. You stole this country, and sold it, you—" The guard grabbed him, and he resisted.

Getting into his car with new life in his face, Hazim told the guard: "Leave him. It was a fair fight."

He took off, driving aggressively. His son looked at him as if he did not recognize him. "Dad, do you want to go home?"

"I want to go to Saft al-Laban now. Do you know the way?"

His son looked at him. His eyes took in his father's torn shirt. He said nothing.

Hazim was speaking angrily. "He accuses *me* of stealing from this country! Of selling out! Idiot. If it wasn't for the likes of me, there wouldn't even *be* a country. People like me are this country's hope. We're the ones on whose shoulders rests the rebuilding of everything destroyed by the mob and the rulers. Fool."

"Don't worry about it, Dad."

"I should have left him to the guard. You know why I didn't leave him to the guard? Because he expected me to. He expects to be beaten for what he did, like in the days of feudalism. To be denigrated and humiliated, like in the days of Cromer. I wouldn't give him that satisfaction."

"You acted with the nobility of an educated man," his son said.

"Don't say that. I don't act with nobility. I don't want to act with nobility. Where is this Saft al-Laban? All I see ahead of me is a huge swamp, as if I were in sub-Saharan Africa, with jungles all around. What is this swamp?"

"It's a street, Dad."

"Do you think this car will run after today?"

"It's seen worse."

"Where are we, Khalid?"

"I think we're in Cairo. But I'm not sure."

"No. Really, I'm not joking. Where are we?"

"On the way to Saft al-Laban."

"Are we there yet?"

"We're close. Dad, watch out."

He drove the car quickly into the overflowing puddles, and the dirty water spattered across his clothes. He looked at the car window, then at his shirt, then at his son. He stopped the car and asked, "Who opened the window? I don't remember opening the window."

"I may have. I don't remember."

Hazim felt as if his spirit were wandering about in the air outside; as if his body were not his own. Looking at his suit, he said, "We must go to Saft al-Laban."

The garbage, piled everywhere like the Atlas Mountains, had no effect on Hazim. The dirt streets, unchanged since the days of the caliphate, could be considered evidence of pride in history and civilization, and the preservation of cultural heritage. What really caused him to lose his composure were the ramshackle buildings and the ubiquitous gray color. As women in mismatched clothes emerged from caves with doors on the verge of collapse and dilapidated steps, Hazim looked at his son and asked, "Is today Eid al-Adha?"

Khalid smiled. "No."

"Then why are they bringing us empty platters like this?"

"Maybe they expect us to bring them meat."

"All right. Next time."

"Dad, I think that's the house."

He stopped the car and got out, people crowding around him as if he were the centerpiece of a feast. Gaber approached them, calling, "Dr. Hazim! I don't know what to say. Your whole life you've been a good guy. Come in." He gestured for him to sit in the pavilion, and Hazim nodded mechanically.

Looking at Hazim's shirt, Gaber said, "I'm sorry. I'll get one of my shirts for you."

"No," Hazim said quickly. "We'll just stay a few minutes, and then go."

"Not at all. On my mother's soul, which hasn't even settled into the earth, you must wear a new shirt. I swear that it's clean. Umm Sami washed it with our Ideal washing machine, believe me."

Before he could reply, Gaber had ushered him inside. The smell of the house remained in Hazim's nostrils for weeks. It smelled like potatoes, garlic, tomatoes, and the residual scents of many children.

Eyes moist, Gaber said, "It's so good of you to come. On my mother's soul, you will wear the shirt. It's the best shirt I have, sir."

Khalid remained silent as he saw his father set to resist this tortuous operation that merited intervention from human rights organizations. America itself would have supported the mission to rescue Hazim from the trumped-up charges, freeing him to advocate for animal and human rights in Egypt.

Having closed himself in Gaber's room, Hazim took hold of the shirt suspiciously, sniffing it. He stood motionless. He heard the wails of three women with voices stronger than all the opera singers of Italy and all of Europe. He began to put on the shirt, which was patterned in red, yellow, and orange . . . a lot of orange.

He closed his eyes, and a shiver ran through his body as he buttoned the shirt. He went out of the room as if he were going to his execution, muttering to himself, "This will pass. It will pass."

Gaber grasped Hazim's hand and pulled him toward the pavilion, seating Hazim beside him. Every time someone from his street came up to Gaber, he introduced him to Hazim, who was obliged to drink coffee and stay a couple of hours. Hazim could not understand the brilliant light that emanated from the funerary tent, and from the faces of the living. It was a distracting light, reminding everyone that death was a blessing, and that life was a radiance for which there was no cure. He felt as if the buttons of his shirt were about to swallow him, or that he would shortly come down with an incurable skin disease. Who knew what might happen?

He made up his mind to excuse himself, and moved toward his car, sighing in relief. He said to his son, "We did our duty, right?"

Khalid declared, "Gaber is loyal, and he deserves that."

"I don't believe that Gaber is loyal so much as he is used to me, and I am used to him. Khalid, do you want to drive?"

Khalid smiled, opening a door for his father. "Yes."

Hazim rested his head on the seat, and checked that the window was closed. Then he said, "Let's go walk along the Nile awhile. I want to forget what I saw, and what I heard. The women's wails . . . how horrible. I wonder if they feel more sadness, or they just express it more."

Khalid said, as if he had not heard the question, "Death is terrible. There's no going back. It's scary, Dad."

"Yes, especially if you die without a grave."

Khalid parked the car in Zamalek, steps away from the house, and got out to walk with his father along the banks of the Nile, amid the lights of entertainment and restaurant boats, and the reflection of the lights on the deep, peaceful water. They were silent, Hazim lost in his thoughts and Khalid looking at the water. Finally Khalid asked, "Do you think they call Cairo 'Mother of the World' because of this?"

His father smiled. "Because of what? The death of Gaber's mother?"

"No. I mean all this difference and contrast, as if you're not in just one country, but in a whole world."

Hazim scrutinized his son. "Knowledge, Khalid. That's what I've given you, and that's what my father gave me. Knowledge lives on in every age and in every place."

"Sometimes I wonder who is happy and who is miserable. And I have no answer. I look at the people around us, and I see that they are completely miserable. And we . . ."

"You will be happy," his father assured him. "Of course you will be happy. Choose someone who suits you and is deserving of you, and have children, and do your work."

"What about you?" Khalid said bitterly. "Mom didn't suit you? Are you happy?"

He replied without hesitation, and not entirely honestly, "Yes, of course."

They were silent for a while. Then Hazim said, "Let's walk home. I haven't walked in Cairo for a long time. In a few years, we will move away from Cairo, and we might forget what the Nile looks like."

"Are you going to tell me about your problem with the captain?"

"I don't want to think about it right now."

"Dad, you know I'm not going to move with you to the villa you're building outside of Cairo. But I will come to visit often, believe me. And you will visit me too. You want me to be happy, right?"

Hazim looked at his son and smiled. "It was an interesting day. I'll see you tomorrow."

Khalid persisted. "And in case we don't talk, are you going to cancel my tickets, and the job that awaits me abroad? I know that I am your whole family, and I know that you think I'm neglecting my responsibility to my grandfather and my family, and I know that you're mad at me. But are you going to give me the chance to do what I want?"

Hazim smiled bitterly. He lifted his hand, only to drop it in surrender. "This day does not want to end! Your mother wants you to go, of course."

"Mom wants me to be happy."

"Rather she wants me to be miserable!"

"Dad . . ."

"You will spend tonight and tomorrow at her house, as we agreed."

"Dad . . ."

"We're not going to talk about that right now, and I don't want to know anything about your travel plans."

"I'm traveling in a week."

"Can you not hear what I'm saying?"

"Can't you hear anything of what I'm saying? Do you ever listen to anything that anyone says? Things are not always going to go the way you want them."

"Not one day has gone the way I'd like," Hazim said derisively.

"You can't draw the lines of fate too, your tools won't help you with this."

"What's with you, son? Have I ever interfered with your life?"

Khalid laughed, and retorted: "All the time! You love controlling everything and everyone you love."

"Are you going to criticize me all night?" Hazim said angrily. "You asked me if I wanted you to travel, if I would give you my permission. I said no. I don't support it. We each have our own position. The day you leave, what will remain for Egypt?"

Khalid answered, his anger doubled: "Egypt! Do you know anything about Egypt? Where is this Egypt of yours? The Egypt that's in your mind, and in your blood, or the Egypt that the rest of us are living in?"

"The Egypt in which my father grew up, and in which you grew up."

Khalid tried to sound calm. "Dad, that's not Egypt. We were raised in a locked cave, in the middle of the desert, that no Egyptians ever enter. Nobody knows about it but us. Dad,

142

I can't even read Arabic. Although, of course, neither can you . . ."

"You're full of clever metaphors these days. Will you be a poet or an engineer in America?"

"You're making fun of me. Why, when I'm trying to talk with you, do you make fun of me?"

Hazim replied severely: "Because I am your father. When I want to make fun of you, I make fun of you."

Khalid sighed. "Fine."

There was a moment's silence. Then he asked, "Are you listening to me?"

Hazim patted his hand. "I'm always listening."

"Don't be mad at me," Khalid pleaded. "You want me to be happy, right?"

Hazim embraced his son and said, trying to remain calm, "It's all right. It's all right."

"Can we talk now?"

"No. Let's not. I don't like fighting. I'm not in the habit of it. But you will do what you want. I can't stop you."

Khalid smiled hopelessly, and began to walk away. His father pointed at him, and called, "Khalid, I know Arabic well, reading and writing. You're the one who doesn't know Arabic!"

His son laughed, and did not answer. Hazim added: "But you are Egyptian. Even if you don't read Arabic. Whether you like it or not, you are Egyptian."

Hazim collapsed onto the bed, his mind working furiously: his son who was leaving in a matter of days; a cunning fellaha who had made an indelible impression on him; and his war with the captain. What would he do with the captain? He closed his eyes and fell into a deep sleep. When he woke at six in the morning, he looked at his arm as if he did not recognize it. He was still wearing Gaber's shirt. He quickly took it off, and walked toward the bathroom to bathe. He could not believe how, for hours on end, he had forgotten that he was wearing Gaber's shirt.

Hazim had ceased entirely to behave intelligently. He began to fear that he would turn out to be a commoner or a thief. He had changed so totally in only a short time. He had begun losing his temper over the most trivial provocations. He found himself wanting revenge, the rending of limbs from bodies, and the thrusting of daggers. He would not even try to think about the fellaha now.

The day that Hazim invited Major General Abdullah, his cousin's husband, to have lunch with him at a prestigious restaurant along the Nile, his cousin thought that Hazim must have a deadly disease, from which he would die in a matter of days. For Hazim had always avoided her husband. He had always visited her when Abdullah was at work. In twenty years, he had exchanged with him only simple, shallow words.

Major General Abdullah set to eating the shrimp with gusto. Hazim watched him silently, pondering the miracle of shrimp and Abdullah's prowess in removing the shell and getting at the meat. Abdullah asked the obligatory questions about Hazim's family, and congratulated Hazim on his notable achievements in his finances, his profession, and his family. Hazim listened patiently. "How are you?" Abdullah asked. "How is Khalid? Did you go to Marina this summer? I don't care for it myself. Crowded, and overflowing with corruption. The Amra al-Bahhar resort is better. After all, in the summer, you need peace and quiet. You don't want to see ostentatious wealth, and . . ."

Abdullah fell silent, looking in surprise at the key in front of him. "What's this, Hazim?"

Hazim said warmly, "The key to Marina, my friend. The villa is at your disposal this summer, and every summer after. We are family."

The major general grasped the key automatically. "What if you need it?"

Hazim replied without feeling: "I go for Khalid's sake, and Khalid is moving abroad. I won't go for at least a couple of years."

He knew that in Egypt, all things were possible. Every obstacle could be overcome. Inventing Marina was no less important than inventing penicillin.

Their conversation moved on. Hazim told Abdullah that he needed his help in stamping out corruption, and that corruption was centered on one individual. Captain Murad was taking advantage of this country, its resources, and its good people. Hazim never even mentioned Asma.

The major general looked uncomfortable, and told Hazim that he did not want to interfere in any financial or personal disagreements between him and the captain. He did not work for revenge.

Hazim assured him that this work was for the sake of the nation. It had no connection to any personal disagreement. On the contrary, he and the captain were friends. But the major general was not convinced. So Hazim pressured him with all the means at his disposal, both aboveboard and underhanded. Hazim told him that he would not die and be buried like an anonymous soldier's corpse in a main square, guarded by a miserable, skinny guard standing in the sun for hours, with no purpose or objective, cursing the soldier and whoever had killed the soldier, and whoever started the war in the first place. No. Instead, he would become the Unknown Soldier who had achieved all the honors and distinctions, including a tax exemption. Hazim said openly that he was prepared to help Abdullah, Abdullah's wife, and Abdullah's mistress, the famous dancer, and all of Abdullah's friends. Abdullah reluctantly agreed, and thus began his conferences with Hazim.

Hazim made his plans carefully, with precise order. As long as the captain had cargo ships, he must be paying bribes to more than one individual and to more than one quarter. An intelligent person anticipates implications and consequences, as in an engineering project. There were five people Hazim suspected after an official search and inspection, followed by discussion of the results with Major General Abdullah.

There was also the matter of taxes. A brief memo to the tax authorities could destroy the life of the captain and his family. Surely the captain had been evading taxes. If the captain had paid all the taxes he owed, then Egypt would not have had to accept financial assistance from the United States. Egypt's grain would have grown abundant and hardy. Egypt would have been enabled to make political decisions freely and unencumbered. If the captain had paid the taxes he owed, Egypt could have put an army of fifty million Egyptians in the Sinai just to stick out their tongues and taunt Israel. If the captain had paid his taxes, it would have changed the world, tamed fate, and opened the nation's doors with love, trust, and loyalty for its citizens. This meant war and it seemed to Hazim that he had the advantage. The captain had so many weaknesses.

Ten

AFTER SEVERAL DAYS, ASMA BEGAN to regain her bearings and think about her predicament. She felt overwhelmingly that her children would be taken from her, torn from her bosom. Then she would be flooded with another wave of feelings about her debt to a certain man. She longed for him like a teenager, without hope, experience, or even his presence. She began to regret her visit to him. Even though she had shown great hospitality in the past, and would do so again, she did not want to lose her dignity entirely in his presence. She had no idea what he thought of her. He might think she was a thief, a forger, and an exploiter, or a whore who wanted to take advantage of him. He probably thought that she had had a relationship with the captain, and that she had wanted to seduce him, and that she was worthless.

She would softly slap her cheek with remorse for all she had done to herself, her children, and everyone. Aspirations? Anger? Dreams? She did not know what had come over her and pushed her to act as she did. Was it love for her children, or the desire for self-affirmation? Or fear of the future? It had not been meant to happen—that she should meet a certain man, that he should rescue her multiple times, that he should buy her land, that he should build a tomb, or that anyone should notice a place called Benha, or the village in which Asma lived.

She had neither learned the meaning of happiness, nor become the person that she would like to be. Instead, she remained dangling in the wind by a mere thread, on the verge of disaster. No one came to visit her, as if she had a terrible infectious disease. She could hear women whispering behind her back. She saw the looks of mockery and smugness, as well as looks of censure from her mother and of sympathy from her children.

The people of the village were divided into three unequal camps. The first viewed the event of Asma's undoing, that had made her blood run in front of everyone, and even the guard's accusations of her perversion, as fair. Asma was a mysterious woman, difficult to deal with, who defied her husband's family. She might be an immoral woman. No one knew for sure. The government knew everything, however, and the guard must have known a lot about her. Otherwise he would not have disgraced her like that in front of her children. That her son was powerless in this situation could only indicate that Asma was walking a shady path, and that her family knew it, and so let go of her. And as Asma had never been one to believe in fate, or to obey any rules, she must not have any morals. Her husband had died over ten years ago. She had been only thirty, and it was only human nature. . . . We do not expect impeccable behavior from such a widow, cut off from her own brother. No doubt the path she had taken was the reason for their falling out. Thus relations with Asma were to be entirely severed. The commissioner's wife and the mayor's wife both belonged to this camp.

The second camp was more cynical, and sought to interpret the situation shrewdly. There must be a conspiracy, by an individual or even a foreign country, and Asma was its victim. Actually, it was Asma's son who must belong to an extremist group, but she had knowingly aided him. As we know, the police show no mercy to terrorists. Asma was a victim of the terrorist network, and we can only thank the government that Asma got out of prison with just one slap. Asma was taken in by this plot of some foreign country that wanted to undermine our nation and take advantage of its people. It was not over yet, and so it was best to avoid Asma and her children for the time being.

The third camp sucked its lips, blamed the police, and sympathized with the poor widow who suffered bitterly. They feared the violence of the government that could not separate friend from foe, innocent from guilty, widow from strumpet. It was best to avoid Asma in order to avoid undergoing the same fate that had befallen her.

Asma expected all this from the beginning, and did not rely overmuch on the people of her village. The sense of distrust between her and the other villagers was entirely mutual. She faced them in all her steadfast pride, going about her work and urging her children to succeed.

Yet as she sat on the flowered couch, looking at nothing in particular, the doorbell rang, and she heard the voice of a woman she did not know. She called to her daughter, "Who is it, Salma?"

In walked a woman in her twenties, wearing a white headscarf and blue ensemble. She smiled and extended her hand to Asma. "I'm Hanan, Umm Taha. I came to see how you were doing."

Asma scrutinized her, surprise in her eyes. "Thank you."

Hanan said gently, "My husband is the officer Muhammad, do you remember him?"

A little embarrassed, Asma said, "I remember him."

"Oh Lord, he feels so bad about that. He told me that he was so ashamed and he feels so bad for you and all you've been through. But what could he do? He is a civil servant."

"Have a seat, sister," Asma said warmly. "Have a seat."

Hanan sat, her eyes looking at Asma softly. "My mother-in-law is a widow too. She suffered bitterly, bringing up three children. But her son has become a good, caring man. We've been married three years."

"Do you have children, Hanan?"

"No, not yet," she answered uncomfortably.

Asma patted her shoulder, and said with conviction, "God will give you great kids. You can say 'Asma said so.'"

"God bless you, Umm Taha. Pray for me."

"I will pray for you, sister. Believe me. A kind heart like yours is hard to find these days."

Asma began asking her questions, and Hanan answered thoughtfully. She told Asma of their move to Benha after her husband was transferred from Alexandria, where he had been born, and where she and her husband had lived with their families. They hoped to be transferred back to Alexandria. Hanan avoided using her new furniture in her home in Benha, even in the bedroom. Her husband's meager salary was not sufficient for them, and so every month she received an allowance from her father. She had graduated from college, but her husband did not want her to work because he wanted to support her. She went to doctors to ask why she had not yet conceived, but they could find no reason.

Asma offered her advice and reassurances, heartened by the will and enthusiasm in this young woman. It seemed to Asma that there was still hope in Egypt, even in the government. This officer had such trust, and feelings like any human being, and his wife appreciated adversity and had faith. Hanan neither looked down on Asma, nor asked her for anything. She radiated a strange characteristic that Asma had never encountered: sincerity. It was not allegiance to the government or to any political objective, or commitment to any person in particular. It was sincere concern for a struggling mother, for a believing mother, and an attachment to the idea of spending one's life energy for the sake of others, and the giving of oneself for the sake of the whole. This was completely new to Asma.

As Hanan's visits continued, doubt began to enter Asma's heart. She feared that Hanan and her husband would be set upon her by her in-laws, or by the captain. But they never asked her about anything that she avoided discussing, and they always seemed somehow innocent and naive. God had sent her someone in the government. Yes, he was someone gentle and not yet ready, but nevertheless he had appeared.

It so happened that as Asma made up her mind to act, Hazim was also making up his mind to act. However, Asma's decision differed from Hazim's. A single thought had taken root within her: everyone was out to take advantage of her. A widow was alone like a newborn kitten that had lost its way, guided by fate to the middle of a road in the middle of the day. The cars pass over her without a thought, her mewling lost in the commonplace honking of car horns. One car after another hits her, until her bones are crushed to splinters and her body is ground into earth. Not one car stops. People do not take pity on her.

That is how Asma had lived for years. She had not expected much. She had known only that she wanted something, and so she must make an effort, giving of her hospitality and her time. Then a man came along and turned her life upside down with his gentleness, with his greatness, with all his being. But he was not like everyone else. He was unique and mysterious. However, the person who really shook her, like mulukhiya simmering in a great pot, the heat smiting her face, was someone quite simple. Someone ordinary. A nobody: Hanan, the officer's wife.

This gracious woman, with her familiar face and her kind words, neither looked down upon her nor requested anything of her. She felt for her, perhaps sympathizing with her situation, with a spontaneous sincerity that Asma had never seen in anyone else. The officer and his wife radiated mutual respect for her as if she were not merely a widow, but someone who represented the multitudes. She embodied everything that was innocent and beautiful: goodness, knowledge, and blessings. As if she had been a saint of some distant age, sent to bring justice to the world. For them, she was a mother, respected, valued. Just a mother, regardless of her femininity or her age, regardless of her place or time. An Egyptian mother, who dwindled away in humility, expecting and awaiting her own passing. One who did not begrudge the passing of time, or expect much. With time, a mother transforms from a woman to a symbol that we seek and create in the midst of all our pains.

What remains of a beautiful time?

What connects our unknown past to our foreordained future?

What holds us before we plunge into the details of this humdrum life?

Indeed, the morsels of kindness circulating in the heavy air reassured Asma that the future was not in the hands of the captain. Neither was it in the hands of Karima, nor the mayor, nor the commissioner. The future was, in part or in full, in the hands of whoever scattered around them these seeds of kindness—kindness with no particular objective or self-interest. Maybe she would never understand humankind.

Maybe this simple woman was wiser and more rational than Asma. . . . She had learned from Hanan in a matter of hours what she had not learned in her whole life. Perhaps she had wasted all that effort. And for what? To please rich people? To become one of them? So she would have a strong spine when the earthquakes came? To help her rise? What good did it do her? Rich people do not give for nothing. And no one can trade in life and death.

They ruled the world; they controlled life and death. They were a class that she did not know. Would she become one of them someday? Did she want that? What good did it do her? They toyed with her for a while, and then threw her in the wastebasket. Then they took her out of the basket, wiped her off, and toyed with her again.

Hazim was different. He was in his own class; she did not see many like him.

What good would it do if she became one of them? She looked down on them more than she would a mangy, feral dog that wandered about the village. She spit three times, and said to herself, "Moving between classes is costly, and it does no good. It probably does no good."

Asma met with the lawyer, asking him about the case. Sometimes he reassured her; at other times he frightened her. Hazim had sent his personal lawyer to her to ask her about certain details. She had not dared to thank him, or even to call him. He helped her as if she were his sister or his wife; as if it were his obligation to help her. She was too embarrassed even to thank him. One day the lawyer said flatly, "Umm Taha, Hazim wants to ensure that you are well. Your wellbeing concerns him very much. Do you understand what I mean?"

"I'm not sure I understand," she said in confusion.

"Let me explain, then. He spoke with a relative in the police force, an important major general. He spoke with me as well, and he wants to make sure that what happened does not recur. I can assure you of that. No officer or guard will ever touch you."

"I am grateful to Dr. Hazim," she said hoarsely. "He is a good man."

The lawyer said gravely, "But he cannot intervene in the justice system. If you are convicted of forgery, squandering, and the other accusations, then you will go to jail for six years or more."

"What should I do?" she asked hopelessly.

"Tell me the truth. Whatever I know, I will use to help you as much as I am able. Did you forge the land deed?"

"It's my land," she said stubbornly. "My husband wrote the deed over to me several days before his death."

"But was the deed forged? Did he have it recorded for you officially before his death, or was the deed forged?"

She did not answer immediately. Then she said, "He was concerned for his children, and he knew that he was dying. The land was his possession. He wrote me a preliminary deed, giving me full administrative rights."

"He trusted you!"

"Of course my husband trusted me."

The lawyer said, a little sarcastically, "It never occurred to him to doubt that you might take the land for yourself? If you remarried, for instance? The land would be in your name, so no one could claim that it was your kids', leaving you to squander the money on a new husband."

"Not at all."

The lawyer nodded. "He wrote out the land to you, and not to his children."

"The oldest of the children was nine at the time, and he did not trust his siblings, so . . ."

The lawyer smiled. "You persuaded him, didn't you? The first accusation they'll make is that you forced him. He was on his deathbed, and you persuaded him. You like to control everything."

"He was my husband," she said stiffly. "I forced him how? He trusted me. We had been married ten years. If he didn't trust me, then why did he stay with me? You speak of me as if I were a call girl overpowering an old man at the end of his life for some money."

"Forgive me, Umm Taha. That is how your husband's family will speak of you in court, and I want to see your reaction. I believe you: I believe that he wrote you a preliminary deed. How did you register the deed for land possession with the Land Registry Office?"

She remained silent.

The lawyer smiled and said, "You forged the deed after his death under an old date, with an agent? Is that it?"

"It was my land," she said, a little defensively. "He had written it in my name. I had no time, with him dying, to go register it. I registered it after his death, yes. What would you have done in my position? I didn't steal anything. It's my land."

"Your land, yes," the lawyer said calmly. "I told you, I agree with you there, but you did forge something. Do we agree on that too?"

She looked at him angrily, and did not answer.

He continued: "Don't get angry at me. When you lose your temper, you lose everything. You must control yourself."

Suddenly worried, she asked, "Are you going to tell Hazim what we did today? Are you going to tell him what you think about me being a forger?"

The lawyer smiled a little mockingly. "Madam, Hazim has known that from the moment he picked up a phone to call me when you were in the prosecution office. What did you think? He's no child."

She said sorrowfully, "He knew. He said nothing. He thinks I'm a thief? Could you tell him that I did not steal? It is my land. Could you tell him?"

This time the lawyer laughed. Then he said, "I can tell him. But even if he believes in your innocence, if the judge does not, then you will go to prison. Whose opinion matters more to you?"

"But he thinks I'm a thief."

"You did not listen to my question. You must stay calm and keep control of yourself. We can talk more some other time."

She nodded, and closed her eyes. It seemed that her life was coming to an end.

When her son informed her that Hazim would come to inspect the land and work on the tomb, she decided not to go out to meet him.

She could not sleep that night. She did not even try to sleep next to her children, as she usually did. Instead, she lay on the couch in the spacious main room, the breeze lightly touching her body. She squeezed her eyes shut, muttering to herself, "I will not go to see him tomorrow. . . . I will not speak with him. . . . I will not see him."

However, when morning dawned, she was prepared to meet him with longing, and without hesitation. She put on a red blouse and a black skirt. Wrapping a shawl around her shoulders, she went out at seven in the morning, heading toward the construction site. In the chill of the morning, she sat on the brown rubble, staring at the narrow stairway that led to the tomb.

When she heard the sound of a car approaching in the distance her heart fluttered. The more she remembered that she might meet her end in prison, the more she shivered. The more she recalled the strange, tense scene in the prosecutor's office, the more confused she grew. . . . What had he done? What had he said? Why had he helped her at all? It was better not to even ask.

As the car came into sight, a breeze lightly touched her eyes and she smiled with a sense of relief that she had not known since her release two weeks earlier.

He got out of his car, his eyes on the narrow stairway to the tomb. He was wearing his glasses, holding some papers. After a few moments, he noticed her presence. Their eyes met for an instant. He smiled warmly at her. "How are you?"

She lowered her head shyly. "Well, I don't know what to say or how to thank you. I want to . . ."

He did not speak. He turned to the worker beside him and asked him about the progress on the mausoleum. Then he looked at her again and said, "Don't thank me, Umm Taha."

She looked around, and declared: "I must thank you, and apologize for everything that I said. . . . You know, sir . . . at times of pressure, people say things they don't mean. . . . Don't think ill of me . . . please."

He looked away. "I don't know what you mean."

She opened her mouth to speak, but she was not sure that her voice would come out sounding natural, and a trembling was taking over mind, heart, and body. She remained silent, sitting on a pile of construction material, watching Hazim as he gestured with his hands, outlining the plaza and mausoleum. She did not move from her place for hours. Finally she returned home to check on things, but then she returned to the parcel of land. He did not look at her even once. But he felt her presence. He could feel her gaze grazing his back, his hand, his chest, and stroking his arms and legs. Her eyes followed him with an impossible longing. He found himself sighing heavily, frustrated for no clear reason.

When all the workers left, she had to return to her house. She looked at her watch. It was eight o'clock. Standing, she called to him as he walked to the stairway: "Dr. Hazim, I'm going back now."

Avoiding her eyes, he said, "How?"

She said with some confusion, "I'm walking home. It's just ten minutes."

He nodded.

Quickly, she asked, "What did the lawyer say about the case?"

"Is that what you have been wanting to say these past several hours?" he asked, a little stiffly. "I am not accustomed to circuitousness, and I don't care for it."

"I'm sorry," she said abruptly. "I was going to ask you. You—"

"He said that you did not have a good case," Hazim interjected, and had no idea why he sounded so cold. "I'm sure you know that. Perhaps you could come to some understanding with your husband's family."

Her voice contained tears. "That will never happen."

Suddenly he asked, "Have you seen the tomb?"

She shook her head, a little startled.

He walked in front of her, motioning that she should accompany him. There was a long staircase leading down into the earth. As she began to descend, Asma felt for a moment like she might fall, but he did not extend a hand to her. He walked ahead of her, briskly, as if avoiding her. She had never seen him so angry, and she had no idea what had aroused his anger. But what had she expected? He thought that she had no honor or dignity. He despised her. She entered through the small wooden door, engulfed by fear. The awesome terror of death surrounded her.

He closed the door, all of his attention on the wall of the tomb. "Close your eyes, and then open them after a second."

She did so, still fighting her tears, not knowing what he was doing or what he wanted.

Then he said with passion, "Do you see the light entering from the openings? Here, in the darkness, you can see it and feel it more strongly." He would have that door replaced, of course. It would be a heavy stone door. The supports in a tomb like this had to be very thick, but you could make them a little curved, and hollow on the inside, and look at the paintings on this wall . . .

The bewitchingly soft light poured over everything. Asma felt that she had died long ago. She touched the paintings with her fingers, and said breathlessly, "They're beautiful."

He stood behind her, breathing slowly. She could feel his breathing in her soul. Her body tingled, and a chasm within her cried out in longing. His chest could have just touched her back, but it did not. An atmosphere of magic, death, fear, desperation, and dread came over her. She swallowed, and bit her lip. Putting out her hand, she steadied herself against the wall.

He said, in a voice that he meant to sound strong, but which came out a little shaky, "Look at the openings in the ceiling of the tomb. You can see the weak light. Look up."

She lifted her head, and a tear fell from her eyes. "Am I going to prison?"

"For a crime that you did not commit?" he said carefully. "Or for a crime that you did commit?"

She said falteringly, "I have children. What will happen to them?"

"You didn't think of them before?"

"I've thought of nothing but them." She turned her face toward him, and wiped her eyes nervously, shyly. "Forgive me."

"Forgive you for what?" He was irritated, though he didn't know why. "Why are you always apologizing? I've never met such a woman. You apologize, you forge papers, and come to my office to confess your love. Maybe it would be best for you to go now, best for me not to see you again . . . and . . . stop crying. Why are you crying?"

"I'm not crying," she said hoarsely. "I'm not crying."

He came nearer to her. He laid her head on his chest and he held her there without a word. Her hand curved around his arm as he brushed his cheek against the top of her head. She stayed there in repose, in surprise. She did not embrace him. Nor did she resist. His grip tightened. Her chest melted into his. She instinctively clung to his hand, and murmured, "Don't leave me."

"I had no intention of leaving you," he whispered in her ear.

"Don't forsake me."

"I will not forsake you." She sighed, and held him. Then she held his face in her hands and kissed him warmly. A lifetime passed. And a lifetime had yet to arrive. Her body was trembling, and this same desire spread throughout his body, along with the instinctive knowledge that she wanted him within her, to become a part of her. Tears fell anew from her eyes as she scattered kisses along his neck, whispering between them, "What am I doing? I don't know what I'm doing. I love you. One time, perhaps . . . I want to just tell you for once, perhaps . . . If only—"

He cut her off with a long kiss, and then said haltingly, "I will marry you now . . . this very moment . . ."

She shook her head. "Don't say that," she told him, kissing his arm and chest passionately.

He threw back the headscarf from her hair, and began to undo the buttons of her blouse, but she held his hand fiercely, and said, "No."

He looked at her again, nearly losing his temper. He had never felt such desire for any woman. And no woman had ever toyed with him like this. Impatiently, he said, "Asma . . ."

She began opening his shirt greedily. "Please . . . I can't. . . . Don't ask for what I cannot do. I don't know what I'm doing. . . . I don't know. . . ." She took off his shirt, and for a second gazed at his chest as if she had discovered a treasure within a tomb. Then her shaky fingers moved across his chest, with trepidation and awe. She traced the curls of hair on his chest as if she were tracing the lines of the remainder of her life. She did not speak. Her fingers on his chest nearly made him burst. He closed his eyes. Her lips came close, kissing his neck and chest. Leaning forward, she kissed his stomach, whispering between kisses: "I have dreamed of you. I long for you . . . I would have given my life to touch you like this . . . to feel you . . ."

He whispered in excitement, and some confusion, "I will marry you now. If I marry you, all your dreams will come true."

"You don't know my dreams."

"Get rid of these clothes," he said impatiently.

She hugged him, surrendering to him and yet controlling him. "I can't. Please, I can't." Kissing his hand slowly, her lips brushing against his skin, she whispered, "I want you to have all my dreams today. . . . I have imagined you with me, in my arms. . . ." She kissed every part of him with desire and reverence.

She was a woman like no other. His experience with her was unlike any other. He was an ancient priest with a simple fellaha in his arms, full of hope and admiration. She loved him with an unmatched passion. And she would not allow him to take off her clothes. He penetrated her without even seeing her breasts. If it was a game, then she had mastered

160

it and won, and he had lost before he even began. Even if she had been an immortal jinni from the world of the jinn, she had fortified her attack well, and had aroused him as no woman ever had. She did not try to reach her own ecstasy. It seemed that she did not want to, as if she wanted only to please him, like a lady of the night or a consort just starting out. He did not know. She insisted that he climax quickly so that she would not. Doubt began to assail him: perhaps she would not come. Perhaps she could not. All he knew was that she longed for him, and wanted him, and that she felt such guilt that it could destroy her. When he had finished, she threw herself into his arms and wrapped her legs around him, trying to cling to him more tightly.

Breathlessly, sweat pouring from her, she said, "Don't see me again. Promise me you won't see me again."

He opened his mouth, and she clung to his neck, as if she would strangle him. "On your son's life, promise not to see me again. If I have any value in your heart, forget me."

He did not answer.

She stayed in his arms a few minutes more, and then stood. "Have I paid the price for your assistance?" she said hesitantly. "Now are we even?"

He said, with warmth and sarcasm, "I don't remember asking for any price."

"Everything has a price."

He smiled and said, "Then you have not paid the price yet."

A little hysterically, she said, "I have paid it. It's over. I am no prostitute. You think I . . . sell myself for money? You must think so. . . ." She waved her hand as if to ward off some unseen monster. "I won't see you. I am a mother who has dedicated her life to her children. We are from two different worlds, and—"

He interrupted her: "I understand. I know you, and I understand. Relax. Did you hear what I said? I'll marry you. Right now, if you like.

161

"You understand?" she said in confusion. "You mean to marry me?"

"Yes. I'm not lying, Asma."

"Dr. Hazim," she said with pride, "I must go."

He watched her wandering eyes as she looked for her things on the floor of the tomb, her hands shaking, muttering to herself in dismay. He came to her and took her hand. "Asma . . . I will marry you. . . . When I marry you, all your problems will end. Do you understand?"

"That's impossible," she said weakly. "I must go now."

He held her hand, and then kissed it, whispering, "Shall I come with you? Take you home?"

"No. Please don't."

He said impatiently, "I will see you tomorrow of course, for the last time, in the tomb."

"Why?" she asked fearfully. "I told you not to see me again."

He raised his voice vehemently. "I will see you tomorrow, Asma. In the mausoleum, and you will marry me, and we will talk tomorrow. Goodbye now. I have work to do. Thank you for the visit, and for everything."

"Don't do this to me!" she cried hysterically. "I trusted you."

He said nothing.

She went out, unseeing. She walked quickly home, thinking of nothing. The traces of his caresses were still on her warm body. She yelled at herself: "What have I done? What have I done?"

When she came through the door, her mother looked at her from the couch where she sat. "What's with you? Fall into a coalmine again?"

Asma did not answer. She went into her bedroom. She had avoided sleeping in it since her husband died. She threw herself onto the bed, burying her head in the pillow, holding the blanket and shaking. Death drives away one's reason. Tombs contain every treasure. There is no end to longing, and fate

162

does not grant us much time. Life is not in our hands, and good people are the first to be struck by magic. They lose their reason, and those who pass through tombs lose their identities, minds, and memories, and are scattered through the ether to the end of time.

She did not sleep or eat or talk with anyone. When her daughter called her, she whispered, "Close the door and leave me now. I'm not well."

"Do you need a doctor?"

"No. I need sleep."

She tried again to recall the image of her husband, with no success. She could not even remember his touch. When her memory stumbled upon the night that she lost her virginity, it was not even her husband and his face that she saw. She just saw herself, in the arms of a man who was not from this world but from another: from the world of immortality, the dead, and souls—both good and bad. She was in the arms of Hazim, a man who possessed the secrets of damnation and eternity, and the keys to all tombs and their contents. The moment he had penetrated her, his body pressing into hers, she gasped and felt him in the depths of her heart. The memory would shape the remainder of her days and nights. He pressed against her very arteries, and they gushed and flowed throughout her body. She gasped, as if she were a virgin with no experience; as if she had been sent from her pharaonic tomb to walk in the light of the sun. She rested her head in the crook of his arm, her fingers clinging to his neck. She could almost cry for a lifetime lost and another lifetime not yet arrived. She stopped breathing as if time could come to an end in that moment. He asked her, "Are you all right?"

She did not answer. He might have whispered her name. She did not answer, and clung closer. What could she do? She had no wiles left. In the dim light, in the bowels of the earth, with all the unseen beings and hellfire, a mortal had no recourse.

She held herself a little proudly. The one who had been in her arms that day was a man she would thank fate for if he even just turned to look at her. The one who had asked her to marry him that day was a man who built mausoleums and palaces, created civilizations, drove armies, and manufactured weapons.

From *The Book of the Dead and the Living*

THIEF . . .

I am not sure that I can't write poetry.
Why would a man write poetry?
My father told me nothing about writing poetry.
I do not know what I am saying.
Writing poetry is not expected, and does not rely on endless work.
Perhaps I do write poetry sometimes.
When my eyes are immersed in my country from every direction.
When I am overwhelmed by the spontaneity of things,
No matter how much I try to subjugate them to a particular design.
When the world around me shies away in confusion.
Sometimes, not always. I am still a rare Egyptian,
Like my father and grandfather.

Eleven

WHEN HAZIM RETURNED HOME to Zamalek, he laid his head on his pillow and gave a sigh of bliss, satisfaction, and relaxation. Asma was completely unlike other women. She gave liberally, and throbbed with life. Her touch was like fine white paper, without blemish, without words in mean ink. A white page in his hands to form, to fold in his hands and arms. She was a woman apart. She loved him as if he were a powerful spirit from another world, and she a mere mortal. Awe filled her eyes, and the trembling of her fingers was mixed with desire and submission.

He could not describe her as delicate. She was not slender, like his ex-wife Shereen. She was not a realist like Rasha. She did not expect anything. She was like one freed from her tomb for a matter of moments to live before dying forevermore. She was like one soaking up the sunlight between the shadows of heavy pillars and overbearing walls.

What had happened between them was not just love, and it was not a sexual relationship between a man and a woman. What had happened was different. Asma was an Egyptian who sacrificed herself, plunging her body between the folds of silt and heavy, warm water, filled with both death and life. She sacrificed herself, and yet also selfishly took from the powerful, treacherous river, knowing full well that she was drowning; that there was no escape. She was also everlasting, no matter what happened. She was dead, with no recourse, no way out.

Her longing would not cease with drowning. No, it was not a relationship between a man and a woman. It was not just between two beings at all. He could not understand it. He smiled, remembering the captain's words: "You'd be delirious in her arms!" He must be sure not to lose his head.

What made him delirious was her sincerity. He had never before encountered the sincerity of a woman. She was genuine, giving impulsively, as if time might end at any second. A sincerity he had never before seen in her. He associated with women frequently, and after his infamous divorce he had vowed that he would never marry again. For there was nothing better for a man than walking away with steady steps, knowing that it was over. That was what he did, with no strings or obligations. He selected his paramours carefully. After his divorce, he had had a relationship with a fellow architect for a number of years, then a relationship with Siham, then a relationship with one of his distant relatives. All of them had known the limitations and the future of each relationship. They were experienced, liberated, free women. They were not Asma al-Sharqawi. They did not make him delirious.

One time was not enough. Either he would marry her, or . . . He would think it over tomorrow. This was a day that he would not forget. He gave free rein to the unfamiliar emotions. They overwhelmed him, leaving him only more confused and desirous. He was not in the habit of analyzing his feelings and interpreting what his mind could not explain. There was nothing to analyze. He would want her forever. When, and how, and at what moment had this begun? He would not ask, let alone venture a guess.

In the morning, as was Hazim's habit, he went to his desk drawer with one hundred pounds. To his surprise, Umm Ayman had not stolen this week. There were three hundred-pound notes in the drawer. No one had touched them. The structured world that surrounded him had begun to fall apart distressingly quickly. His expectations of the masses were no longer carefully tabulated. The masses began to behave with frightening spontaneity. He too behaved, occasionally, like them. The structures by which reality was a shape with only four sides blew away in a wind scented by earthy tombs, airy shrouds, and corpses mummified with the precision of scholars. Even when he had worn Gaber's shirt, he had never dreamed that he would wake one day to find that he had become that person. He would change. Something would happen. He would scream. He would not accept this fate with enthusiasm. But nothing happened. Or so he thought.

So much had happened since he had put on Gaber's shirt. It was a magical shirt that ushered him into the underworld. He tasted their food and their words, became accustomed to their scent and their roughness. He grew used to colors not matching, and saw the splendor of colors mixing, colors throbbing, red bursting with the power of fire, orange lingering among the waves. Had he ever understood colors? Had he felt them? Umm Ayman did not steal on Thursday. That was reality, with no order or predictability.

He sat at the table, drinking his coffee, and awaited Umm Ayman. When she entered, she wished him a good morning, and began her work. She did not complain to him of her son or her husband. She did not say anything. So he said companionably, "How are you, Umm Ayman?"

She looked at him in surprise, and then said, "All right. What can we say? God be praised in every circumstance."

He sipped his coffee, and asked without betraying emotion, "Is your son well?"

She examined his face. Then she began to dust the couch and said, "Lousy! As usual, just like everyone. And Khalid—does he contact you? We miss him, sir, he used to light up our house. What a good son. He was like you in morals and learning. I swear, I never heard an ill word from him. Will he never return to us?"

He said calmly, "Yes, I miss him too."

"Children make the heart sore. We look forward to them so much, and then they take no notice of us. Really, it's like they come along just to break our hearts." She gestured to her heart, and finished, "What can I say? That's the way life is. They leave, and live, and don't think about anyone else. Are you going to visit him soon?"

He glared at his coffee cup. Then he said, "Perhaps. I prefer for him to visit me."

"Will he come soon?"

"In two years. No sooner than two years."

She said, with eerie intuition, "You're mad at him! I know you. When you're mad, you avoid speaking and you glare at your coffee cup like that. Don't be mad at him. If you had a son like mine, who comes home each day drunk, or sits about staring into space and asks for money, what would you do? My son's life is hard. He works night and day, and needs to be able to relax. Sometimes I wish that he would travel far away forever! If he moved, and just came to visit, that would be better. But he doesn't just roll away. Like a bad penny, he always comes back. And your son does not want to hurt you, so he must go away. Didn't I tell you that life was lousy?"

Hazim looked at her and asked, "Do you need money?"

Their eyes met, and she looked indecisive, so he said casually, "Are you sure you don't need money?"

"I don't understand. You're drowning me in kindness."

In the same casual tone, he said, "Today I found a hundred pounds in my desk drawer. Imagine that!"

She swallowed nervously, so he said quickly, "I don't know where it came from. Perhaps you could use it?"

"Your kindness is overwhelming," she said hurriedly. "I don't take other people's money. You know me. I've worked for you for years."

He smiled. "Yes, I know you."

She said defensively, "You don't believe me?"

"Of course I believe you, Umm Ayman. Go ahead with your work. I just wanted to know how you were doing."

She watched him in astonishment and alarm. He stood, leaving his coffee cup, and went to his room.

Major General Abdullah looked at him and said, "You look different. Are you all right?"

"How do I look different?"

"I don't know," he said noncommittally. "You're not the way you were. Actually, I prefer you this way . . . a human being. As if you were somebody's son, just like the rest of us." He laughed.

Hazim did not share the laugh. "You wanted me for something important?" he asked.

"Good news."

"What happened?"

"The captain . . ."

"Tell me quickly. Did the tax department get him?"

"No, he had been paying his taxes all along, or so it seems. However, we found an employee at the port who had been taking bribes from the captain, and they arrested him yesterday. He confessed, too. Can you believe our luck?"

Hazim gave a deep sigh. "We stamped out the corruption, then?"

"Some of the corruption remains, of course. Like seasoning in food, it gives a certain flavor. Anyway, do you need me for anything else?"

"No. Thank you, my friend."

When he arrived at the mausoleum, Asma was waiting for him on the rubble, her hands on her knees in surrender. She seemed to him hopeless, confused, and brimming with life. There was resignation in the slackness of her hands; a longing and resolve in her proud nose and her mouth, closed with precision. As soon as she saw him, she stood and spoke, her eyes avoiding his and casting around to make sure they were alone.

"Hello," she said.

He extended his hand, trying to meet her eyes. "Would you go in with me so we can talk?" he whispered.

She faltered. "I'd just as soon talk here."

"With the workers and people . . ."

She looked around. They were alone among the steel rods and dust, outside the deep tomb and the unfinished edifice of the mausoleum. She said decidedly, "There is no one here right now. Just don't sit next to me. Sit on another pile, and we'll talk."

He said impatiently, "Why all this masquerade and playing around? Didn't I tell you that I'd marry you?"

"It is an honor that I do not deserve," she said faintly.

"Asma, what do you want?" he asked.

"I came to find out what you want."

He wanted to say, "I want you," but he did not answer.

In a voice filled with sadness, she said, "You wouldn't marry a fellaha. Why would you marry a fellaha widow, with three kids to boot? I don't dare to even dream of marrying a man like you. I have forbidden myself to marry. What would I say to my son, who is even taller than me now? How . . . ? To sleep in your arms every day. . . . My daughter is nearly ready to marry. Would people say that her mother got married at the same time as her? After all that I have done?"

"I don't understand. Marriage was instituted by God, and yet you forbid yourself from it?"

"My son is taller than me. And . . . how would I face the village?"

"What village? We'll live away from the village."

"How could I face my children? I tell them that I sacrifice for them."

"You want to become a martyr?"

"I must live as a martyr."

"No one lives as a martyr, Asma. You can only die as a martyr."

"No, Dr. Hazim, I know lots of people who live as martyrs."

"Your words and sacrifice are lovely. So you don't want to marry me?"

"I can't. . . . I have no choice. I promised my husband before his death. He trusted me, and entrusted everything to me. I'm afraid. I don't know how to be like you. . . . I can't."

"What does it matter to me if you made a promise to your late husband ten years ago?" he said angrily. "Do you think I care about that? Do you think I understand or sympathize?"

She bowed her head, and did not reply.

Looking about, he said, "That's why I couldn't see you yesterday. You wouldn't take your clothes off because of your husband?"

She did not answer.

"Answer me!" he yelled. "You felt like you were betraying him, even though he's dead, right? You felt that only he could see you, and no other man."

She remained unspeaking, and shivered a little.

"All this weakness! You're getting on my nerves, you know. You get on my nerves like no woman ever has." He shouted again, hitting the heap of rubble with his fist, "Answer me! Don't stay silent."

She flinched, startled by his outburst. "I felt guilty," she said hoarsely. "Yes, I felt guilty, and . . ."

She fell silent, and he said, "Yes? Go on."

She looked around her, and then whispered plaintively, "Do we have to talk about this right now?"

"Now," he said firmly. "This minute."

She mumbled something that he could not hear, so he said, "Raise your voice, and say what you want."

With her eyes on some weeds that were waving in front of her, she said, "I didn't trust . . . I wasn't . . . I felt guilty, and I didn't know what you would think of me. I was afraid. I'm not like the women of your class, and I was afraid that maybe if you saw me . . . maybe you wouldn't find me pretty like them."

He exhaled in a huff. "Okay, okay. We won't talk about that now. I need to calm down first. I don't know what happens to me with you! I lose control. I normally never lose control. I don't act like an uncivilized savage. We won't speak of your husband. I don't want to talk about him."

"He died," she said weakly. "God have mercy on him."

"I know that he died. Did you love him?"

She said sorrowfully, "He was the father of my children. . . .What can I say?"

He raised his hands, and said to himself, "Yes. Of course. I don't know why I ask these questions. You don't answer."

She said mournfully, "He never mistreated me. He was good to me. . . .We would fight, of course, but he was good to me. I can't say any more than that."

Trying to remain calm, he said, "Yes. I understand." Then he said suddenly, "Would you rather have a relationship with me, instead of marriage?"

"I would, if only—"

He cut her off. "All right. Fine."

"Dr. Hazim . . ."

"Why do you call me 'Doctor' now? Don't you think that our relationship has moved beyond that stage?"

"It will never move beyond that."

"We will meet again tomorrow, at the tomb, at nine at night. Don't say anything. Hear me through. We will meet tomorrow. And I want to spend the whole night with you. Do you understand?"

She looked at him with a mixture of desire and reproof. Then she said, "I wanted . . . I hoped that you would help me to . . . to live honorably."

"I tried, and you refused."

"If . . . if you left me. . . . If I never saw you again. . . . If . . ." Her heart throbbed, and she whispered, "Will you help me?"

"No."

"And if I don't come tomorrow? What would you do?"

"Maybe nothing. Maybe a lot. I haven't thought about it. If I were you, I would come. I don't know what the consequences would be."

"I thought you were different from other men."

"I will see you tomorrow, Asma," he told her harshly.

The captain was not arrested. Instead, the employee at the pier and another employee of the captain were arrested. It seemed that his employee was paying bribes without the captain's knowledge. Or, in any case, that was how the captain was spared. Before two days had passed, the captain returned with another case of corruption. An architect, and recent graduate, claimed in front of reporters and the office of the prosecutor general that he himself had designed the famous hotel in Alexandria, and that Hazim had exploited and intimidated him. Furthermore, he claimed Hazim had earned his doctorate due to social connections and his father's influence. He, the poor architect, was a victim of the ruthless and unjust scholar, a product of the Third Revolution. The young architect had brought with him drawings of the hotel that he had designed. Misty-eyed, he told his story: how Hazim had taken advantage of the young man's love for the girl who lived next door, and his inability to provide for her financially; how he had been promised an apartment in Sixth of October City, but never got it; how he had been promised a Peugeot car, but never got it; how Hazim had even lusted after the young man's sweetheart, and gotten her pregnant, and she had aborted it; how Hazim belonged to a class of businessmen who were close to the government and hated by all Egyptians. In fact, he was descended from the Muhammad Ali Pasha family, and had thus evaded federal taxes seven times: twice in the premodern era and five times in the modern era. All of Egypt's disasters were the products of the injustice and decadence that Hazim promoted among the people surrounding him as easily as handing out pencils to his employees.

It became evident that they had reached all-out war, and breakneck maneuvers would double on both sides. Stamping out corruption involved many faces, most of them dubious.

Hazim began contacting lawyers furiously. The captain knew well how to strike at his most vulnerable spot. His discrediting of Hazim's skills and abilities was disturbing, but what really made him lose his temper was a phone call from the captain. As soon as he heard the captain's voice on his cell phone, he wanted to hang up. But the captain said quickly, "No, don't hang up."

"What do you want?" Hazim asked.

"Once again, we're even. Two to two. Let's start over. I'm giving you a chance to quit being obstinate and build the tomb."

"You think I will build you a tomb after all this? Are you kidding? Let the young architect who works for me build it for you!"

"You're not recording this call, are you?" the captain said.

"I've started recording right now," Hazim replied.

"We agreed to fight corruption in Egypt."

"Please, don't start. I don't have time for this."

"Hazim, I told you, we all love Egypt. Each in his own way. There are those of us who have not yet matured. There are those of us who don't know how to express their feelings. There are those of us who would exploit a poor girl, and those of us who . . . who long for the arms of Nile soil. Remember, it was my idea. The woman does not deserve our quarreling over her. Do you know why? Because a woman is like a cat in a boat. You think that she will eat the mice and save you from ruin. But she is merely playing with you. She has no fidelity. You think of her as bravery itself, but she is the most cowardly of creatures, and the most cunning."

"Spare me your ruminations."

"I'm almost done with the novel I'm writing."

"What do you want? Don't waste my time."

"Build me the mausoleum somewhere else. Not on Asma's land."

"I've almost completed it," Hazim told him.

"My tomb?"

"I'm not giving it to you."

"Does it have openings to let the sun in?"

"It is never dark."

"Let's start over."

"Our war is not over."

"You may be spoiled, selfish, and used to giving orders," the captain said. "And you may be talented, well-trained, and well-educated. But you're not seeing things clearly. You think, in a mechanical way, about expected outcomes. You don't realize that life is full of surprises."

"That's exactly what I was going to tell you. Life is full of surprises."

Asma did not sleep that night. She lay on the old bed alone, hugging her body in longing, in grief. All she wanted was him today, tomorrow, and for the rest of her life. She wanted to caress his chest with her fingertips. She wanted to gaze at him, to breathe his scent until the day she died. She did not trust herself around him. She could give in at any moment . . . and all would be lost. Her life and her children, and the role written for her since the beginning of time. What if her legs started running quickly, with no inhibitions, surpassing all limitations, only to hit electrified fences in shallow lakes—what would she do then? One time, one time only, she lapped up the light of the sun, from within a dim tomb.

Her body needed a lifetime, not one night. Even if she did give it her lifetime, what good would it do? She could not marry him, and she would not have a relationship outside of marriage. What difference was there between her and a floozy? She raised her head sharply. She *would* think about the love that had become a reality. She did not know how; it was a miracle. Because she was fortunate, or because she was entirely unfortunate. She did not know. Maybe both together. She would look to tomorrow, and to the yearning for his touches taking over all her senses.

Before Asma left the house, she said in a voice touched with emotion, "I'm going to visit the cemetery. I miss everyone there." Her children listened, openmouthed. She continued: "I'm going to spend the night there."

"Alone, Mom?" Taha asked

"I want to be alone with them. I need to be alone."

"But Mom, I'm afraid that—"

"Don't argue with me," she interrupted. "Don't call me or follow me. I have enough to worry about right now. I must go alone today."

She neared the tomb and looked around. Darkness covered everything.

As Asma descended into the tomb, her feet trembled, and her throat burned from yearning, expectancy, and fear.

She opened the small door, and he was inside on the floor, waiting for her. This time he had a small electric lantern in his hand. He seemed to be writing and drawing on a large panel in front of him. When he saw her, he put the pen on the ground.

She started nervously fiddling with her large handbag, waiting for him to speak. But he was looking at her as if he were a suspicious investigator. Then he said, with controlled anger, "You're late."

"All this darkness frightens me," she said fearfully. "What do you want from me?"

He answered in a serious tone, straightening his back from the floor of the tomb: "Today, I decide what I want from you. You said that you paid the price, but I say that you haven't paid anything yet."

Her eyes met his, and she said hopelessly, "Help me."

He grasped her hand and began unbuttoning her dress, saying, "I will help you. I want to see you, and touch you, and kiss you. . . . I want to kiss you."

She pushed his hand away. "No."

He took no notice of her refusal. He continued unbuttoning, and then he said firmly, kissing her cheeks, "One last time . . . that's what you want, right? Either you marry me, or else we never meet again after today, and I will do everything you want. Everything."

She opened her mouth, but he put his hand over it to prevent her speaking. He said, "We all fear the dark. It will come whether we like it or not. I love you." Her eyes widened in surprise. He took his hand from her mouth and held her to his chest.

She nestled her cheek in his neck and murmured, "I will lose my mind." The pain threatened to tear her apart. She shook, and whispered, "I never dreamed of hearing that from you, ever. Thank you."

Taking off all her clothes, he said gruffly, "I don't want you to thank me."

Tears pooled in her eyes, and she whispered, "One last time."

"I will sleep in your arms all night." He began kissing her whole body. She whispered, in something like agony, "I don't know how to thank you, Dr. Hazim."

He smiled, his body flowing over hers. "We don't need any formalities right now. Or words. Enough talking."

"What are you going to do?"

"Make love to you the way I want, and as you deserve." Longing for him filled her limbs. This one time . . . She let him have his way with her as he liked. She closed her eyes, and felt as if she were floating on a river, between trees . . .

She whispered suddenly, "What are you doing?"

She was urging him again to take care of himself, as if she would close the door on her feelings forever. But he was not perturbed by her words. When she could hardly think straight, she said weakly, "Why? Do you hear me?"

He did not answer. He did not give her the victory that she sought. He was patient with her to the end, although his social class was not known for its patience.

A new feeling swept over her for the first time ever. It came upon her all of a sudden. She did not understand it, and was not prepared for it. Like death, it came to take her on a great pharaonic ship, adorned with gold. Then it threw her into the warm river, and she did not know how to swim. It drowned her. It drowned her forever. It overtook her, and she shook in his hands. His control was complete. She collapsed in a heap, like the mud on the banks of the Nile. Did she lose consciousness? What could she say? What could she do?

His body remained on hers, and he whispered, "I love you."

She encircled his head with her arms and said nothing.

He stayed there perhaps an hour, perhaps more. Then he lay down beside her, and whispered, "Will you marry me?"

Closing her eyes, she said, "What do we do now?"

Then he said, reflectively, almost as if talking to himself, "You know what? I was jealous of your husband, very jealous. His image used to pursue me every day. But I'm not jealous of him anymore, because you never felt this with him."

She opened her mouth. She wanted to lie, to say that she had been completely satisfied by him. She felt that she should lie, but she could not, and so she remained silent.

He smiled victoriously. "Yes. You won't lie." He made love to her many times, and she slept in his arms all night, as if she had died and been buried in the tomb. Perhaps part of her wished she could die, and be buried with him.

When she awoke, she whispered from within his embrace, "You promised me."

He tightened his embrace, and said nothing.

She rose quietly, and said in a small voice, "Sometimes darkness is a blessing. Perhaps I will miss the darkness of tombs." She put on her dress and approached him hesitantly. Smoothing his hair, she said, "Forgive me for not being beautiful like the women you have known."

He protested, "You're not a woman I know. You're the woman I love, and the most beautiful woman to me."

She kissed his head. "Thank you."

He grimaced. "No woman I've made love to has ever thanked me. Who are you, Asma? What are you?"

She said mournfully, "No woman has ever cared for you like I do, and no woman ever will."

"Then marry me."

Her hand passed along his body, as he lay on the ground like a king nearing death and eternal life. She whispered, "If I see you again, I won't be able to quit . . . ever. I would destroy myself and my children. I would fail to live as a saint, and die as a martyr. I will not see you, no matter what it costs me."

With irritation, and some fear, he said, "You've lost your mind."

"I lost it the day I was born. And the day I met you, and since the day I came down these stairs."

"I will see you tomorrow, here."

Kissing his hand and wiping her cheek, she said, "I won't come tomorrow. I won't leave my house until the day I die. And I know that you won't do anything to hurt me. You love me. You said so. You told me that you love me."

He pulled his hand from hers, and said angrily, "Are you playing with me? You think you can play with me?"

"I beg you . . . to help me . . ."

He rose and said forcefully, "You will come tomorrow."

She bowed her head. Then she looked into his face, as if she were seeing him for the first—or last—time. She threw herself into his arms, pushing on his arms with all her strength and all her pent-up feelings, and shoved him to the ground—he lost his balance in surprise. He smiled and, circling her waist with his arms, with her hair dangling into his face, whispered: "You have forced my hand! In fifty years I have never met a woman like you! Stay for a while."

"A few minutes, no more."

An hour passed before Asma crept out of the mausoleum. She emerged into the light of the dawn, moving as quickly as possible.

Asma's mother searched her face, as if seeing her for the first time. Her daughter was different. Her cheeks were flushed and full. Her eyes shone with madness or victory or utter loss. Her body moved gracefully, as if the palm trees bowed to it in respect. She looked like a woman who had consorted with the jinn and had lived with spirits, as if she were still partly in that world.

"Where were you all night?" her mother asked.

She responded without hesitation: "In the graveyard. I told you that I was going to spend the night there, visiting my late husband. I needed to visit him, after all the stress and the chaos."

The mother nodded, and asked a little nervously, "What did you tell him? Did you talk with him? Did you complain about your fate?"

Asma answered on the way to her room, "How could I talk with a dead man?"

"And how could you spend all night in the graveyard, with all those spirits around? You're not the same. You consorted with a jinni, didn't you? You're not the Asma that I know."

Asma said solemnly, "When a woman goes to the graveyard and spends the night there, what happens to her?"

"Everything ends," her mother replied with finality.

Taking off her shoes, Asma said, "Everything ended, then."

Asma entered her room and closed the door. Her mother walked, a little unsteadily, over to Taha and Salma, saying, "Help me! Oh my God, oh my God! Your mother's touched in the head, kids!"

Asma gently caressed her body, the traces of his kisses lingering on every part of her. She sighed, the ecstasy overtaking her senses. Then her tears spilled over, and she said in a miserable voice, "Forgive me, Lord. You know I love him."

She had no choice in her situation. Fate had written her role: she was a mother—controlling, crazy, rough; and yet gentle, doing the impossible for her children. She was a mother who controlled everything. The day she married, she would lose her control and her holy status. The day she married, she would be a woman, not a saint. Her reason told her to remain on her throne, and not to give it up. Her mind told her that she was now a queen, and tomorrow she would be an empress. If any of her children angered her, she would still be able to say, "I gave up everything for you." How could she say that if she married? How many conscientious people fell victim to their desires? She was no different from the others. She wanted glory and grandeur. What had happened to her was dangerous. She had been under his control. Her husband had never done anything like that. She had not felt such a longing for her late husband. She had not trembled in his hands like that. She was a mother in her forties, with a son nearing marriage, and she had trembled in a man's hands, lost control in his arms. She had chosen glory, and was terrified by her new feelings. So she had felt it, then—the feeling that women around her discussed, and that ruled all men. She had felt it with a man.

She had not seduced him. She had not used her cunning or her wiles. She had not dominated his body, and nor had he hers. No, he was not like her late husband. With her husband, she had made love like she was making a delicious lunch. . . . It gave her strength and greatness; she did not lose control. She would evade, and hesitate, and she always won. Then when a certain man came along who caused her to give without condition, and to fall apart in his arms, what could she do? Had she ever dreamed of such a man? She had not even expected a few moments with him, although part of her wanted to spend her whole life in his arms. She touched her heart. Here he had kissed her, in the middle of her chest. Here he had preyed upon her like some preternatural spirit. There must be some way to preserve these marks forever. To carve them into her body, preparing it for burial and then for resurrection. Her body was still awake, on fire, full of life. For a time . . . Was there a way to hang on to this moment forever? To hang on to the effects of his fire for her, and her fire for him? She pressed on her belly, which also showed signs of him. . . . Her belly hurt. It was a warm pain, filled to overflowing with life. If only she could discover the secret of mummification. If only she could come up with a way of preserving these moments. . . .

When her daughter came into Asma's room, she looked concernedly at her mother, holding her body and shivering as if she were chilled. "Are you okay, Mom?" she asked.

Tears pooled in her eyes. "No, I'm not okay. . . . I'm not okay. . . . I feel cold. . . . I must have a fever. . . ."

Asma looked up at her mother, who had slipped in, and said, "Mom, something strange happened to me in the grave-yard."

"What happened?" her mother asked fearfully.

"I can't tell you. If I told you, I don't know what the jinn would do with you. I'm not okay. I don't want to see anyone—no one. Leave me alone."

From *The Book of the Dead and the Living*

FIRST THIEF,

Perhaps you want to know my experience within this tomb. . . . It's wonderful. Like a circle, at once light and dark. As deep as the earth's core. As pure as the woman I love. As honest as the honesty of death. As instinctive as wheat, corn, and the groans that emanate from the throat of the heavens. What has saddened me for some time, Thief, is that I possess very little of which I am proud. As I said, even the architects are imported from abroad. Our monuments are now built by others, by others' hands. This monument was made by the hands of an Egyptian. He knows Egypt, or he thinks he does.

Twelve

ASMA'S CONDITION ALTERED AFTER HER visit to the graveyard, as if the touch of the jinn was upon her. It was expected that this touch would overcome her. She muttered nonsense for days, her children looking on in alarm. She would embrace them strongly, and then close her eyes and slip into another world. She began crying frequently and glowing with more life. Between waves of guilt, love, and pride, she found herself lying on her bed, aimless and indecisive. Her back began to hurt her again, with intense pains. After two weeks, Asma decided to announce that she was paralyzed by pain. She would see no one and would do no work, and she needed a wheelchair. Her mother looked at her as if she were watching a show, part comedy and part tragedy. Hazim tried many times to call her at home with evidence for the case, but her children apologized to him, explaining that Asma was very ill.

After two weeks, he called her son again. "I must speak with her," he said firmly. "It's very important." Taha asked Hazim to tell him what it was, but Hazim insisted on speaking with Asma.

Taha walked into Asma's room and handed her the phone. It was a decisive moment. She sat on the bed, surrounded by her mother and Salma. Taha said, "Dr. Hazim wants to talk with you about something important. You must try to speak with him, Mother. It's about the case."

Her hand trembled, and she said nothing. She grasped the phone, holding it to her ear, and did not ask anyone to leave the room. "Hello . . . ?" she said shakily.

He replied, in anger as well as longing: "I want to see you, soon. What are you doing with yourself?"

All eyes were upon her, scrutinizing her. The eyes moved to her chest, which rose and fell haltingly, as if she were on the verge of dying—or, indeed, of living. Her tears began silently falling. She cried out within herself: "I need him. I won't leave him now. Perhaps after a period of time . . . It is my right to be with him. I should have . . . just one more time . . . meet with him again . . . a week . . . to be with him, and then leave him . . . perhaps one time . . ." The words pursued her from every direction.

When she heard his voice again, it was filled with concern. "Asma? Do you hear me?"

Her mother held her cold hand, and said firmly, "Take the phone from your mother, Salma. . . . She can't talk."

Salma took the phone, while Asma stared into space. Salma spoke briefly with Hazim, and took the phone out of the room.

Asma clutched at her throat as if she were choking. All eyes were still upon her. Her tears continued to fall silently. Then her mother said, "Leave her be."

"Should we bring a doctor?" Salma asked. "We shouldn't leave her like this."

"The doctor won't do any good," Asma's mother replied.

The children went out, and Asma's mother walked slowly to close the door after them. Then she sat beside Asma and whispered, "Who is Dr. Hazim? Have I seen him? I must have seen him. Oh yes, I remember him. He looks like he just stepped out of the television. There aren't any men like him in our village. I don't know how they make them like that. Is it the food? The water? It must be the water. They drink imported water."

Her mother closed her eyes, and continued in a wheezing voice, "I never did understand you, my girl. You had so many questions, so many. And I don't like girls who ask questions. Your father would answer patiently. He's the reason you turned out like you did, God have mercy on him. When I had my first son, he died after three months. I didn't ask why. When I had my second son, he died after a year. I didn't ask. You don't ask about things that don't concern you or benefit you. Then I had your brother, and he didn't die. And I didn't ask. Then you came. And you started asking about everything. You were as annoying then as you are now. I put up with you. What could I do? Then your little sister came along. She was such a blessing compared to you. Then your little brother came. And died. May he rest in peace. And you asked why. You annoyed and tormented me, and I said to you, 'He got sick and died.' You asked, 'What made him sick?' I said again, 'He got sick and died, nobody knows from what. Why ask, after he already died?' And you said, 'What did he die from?' Do you remember?"

Asma said nothing.

So her mother asked again, "Do you remember?"

"I remember," Asma answered wanly.

Her mother leaned forward and back, and said with finality, "There isn't an answer for every question, and life isn't in our hands. . . . If I ask you now what's wrong with you, will you answer?"

Asma shook her head.

Her mother said smugly, "I won't ask you. I won't ask, girl. Plenty of questions have no answers. The problem is when we ask about things that don't concern us. Then we make other people angry, and we make them sad. I won't take revenge and ask you now, as you did with me. No, Asma. I never really forgave you. Did you blame me for his death? That's all right. You're my daughter. You've put up with me all these years. What can I say? When we visit the grave, there's no going back. No going back. Everything ends."

Asma closed her eyes and said nothing.

Her mother said with finality, "Stop your questions and your aspirations. Leave it all to fate. Your children's fate will take care of them. What are you running after? If death comes to claim them, it will have them. If fate decrees that your son be rich, then he will be rich. If fate decrees he be poor, then he will be poor. There's nothing you can do. Do you hear me?"

"They will be happy. They will be better off than me."

Her mother said hopelessly, "Don't you understand anything of what I'm saying?"

Asma shook her head, her tears falling in silence.

A week later, Ahmed clung to her, gluing himself to her legs, and fearfully whispered to her not to die like his father. The scene made Salma tremble with emotion. She studied day and night for her sick mother who might end up in prison. Taha sat next to his mother for hours in bewilderment. Asma even refused to see Hanan, the officer's wife. She asked her daughter to see her and take care of her and make her welcome. No one knew if Asma was just acting for some purpose known only to her, as usual, or not. It seemed that not even Asma knew for certain.

One day, Asma reached out to her son, beckoning him to come closer. "Come here, Taha. I can't get up."

"You want a doctor, Mother?"

"No. There's no medicine for this. Tell me, how is the land?"

"Good."

"Do you see Dr. Hazim?"

"I haven't seen him in a while."

"You must check on him."

"All right. I'll call him tomorrow."

"No. Don't call him. This headache has nearly destroyed my mind. Is your sister studying in her room?"

"Yes."

"And your brother? Did he go outside to play without my permission?"

"No. He's watching TV."

"And my mother?"

"She's watching with him. Do you want to leave your room?"

"I won't leave this room until the day I die. Do you hear me, son?"

"If only you hadn't visited the graveyard. I'm worried about you."

"God be praised that I visited the graveyard. When you visit the graveyard, you see the world in a different light. It's like I am seeing it for the first time, son."

"What do you see?"

"I'm not going to tell you. That's enough for today. Leave me be. My back is killing me; this headache . . ."

Asma's relationship with Hazim was one of a kind. She trusted him more than she did any other person. Asma sensed that Hazim would remain by her side always, even if he received nothing in return. This made her love him—a painful, desperate, wild love. She knew that he would probably try to see her, but he would never endanger her reputation, especially in front of her children. He would not behave in any way to arouse suspicions. So he would not come to visit her in her home. For if he came, and simply looked at her, everyone would know. They would read the gentleness in the creases at the edges of her eyes. As long as she kept the door closed forever to her house, her room, and her life, he would never reach her. If she wished to live in darkness, as if in a tomb, then she would do so. She used a staff to support herself after she simultaneously stopped living and running about. Her decision to bury herself in this new, gloomy tomb ensured that he would not reach her. No one dares to excavate tombs and expose their corpses in full daylight.

But people's questions did not cease. Indeed, Asma was more popular than all the Arabic soap operas put together. Her story about the graveyard reached all of Egypt, from the Said region in the south to the Nile Delta in the north, and from the desert to the elite, the endowers to the endowed, the next generations and the past generations, to the point that everyone would entreat Asma daily to tell them what exactly happened to her in the graveyard. Hanan the officer's wife came every day to ask her what had happened in the graveyard. Even the mayor's wife asked her plaintively: "What did you see in the graveyard?" Asma's name came to inspire fear mixed with awe of her great knowledge.

Based on everyone's requests, when a month had passed, Asma decided to talk about what she had seen in the graveyard. But preparing for the fateful day was not easy. Inviting everyone concerned was obligatory, so Asma decided to limit the invitation to women only, which naturally roused everyone's curiosity even more. All the neighbors and relatives who had already signed a peace treaty with Asma were permitted to attend. With a pure heart and a soul as transparent as cellophane, Asma invited the commissioner's wife, and seated her next to her own mother. She invited her Christian neighbors Maryann Tadros and her sister Mervat, and seated them between Hanan and her sister Fawziya. She decided that, in light of the number of guests, the gathering would take place in the spacious courtyard of the house, following the evening prayer.

Since the weather was still cold, with rain falling sometimes, during which the spirits and pure souls moved about, everyone brought along shawls, blankets, and wool coats. Taha also lit a fire in the center of the courtyard, arranging chairs around it. When everyone had taken their seats, Taha took his mother's hand and led her out among the guests. She was not strong enough to walk alone, of course. As soon as everyone saw her poor condition, they sucked their lips, some whispering to one another of the power of spirits and jinn.

Asma sat in a chair near the fire, and motioned to her son to depart. Then she whispered in a hoarse voice, "Fate . . . What can we do with fate . . . ?"

The women nodded.

"Tell us what happened to you," Hanan said.

Asma nodded wearily. Then she said, "Sister, never go to the graveyard at night, and definitely do not go alone."

She heard a voice ask: "What happened there?"

"Did you see—God forbid—jinn?"

"Did you see jinn or ghosts?"

"Did the ghost of your husband come to you?"

"Did you hear his voice?"

"Did the jinn come in the form of a black cat, with long ears, and red square-shaped eyes? My mother saw one of them once."

Gazing at the dark smoke coming off the fire, Asma said weakly, "I was walking slowly. Life had me reeling. The injustice of this world had torn me into little pieces. . . ."

Hanan nodded in sadness and sympathy.

Asma continued: "A woman alone, with no support. . . . They humiliate her, and imprison her. . . . They had threatened to take my children from me, to tear them from my arms. I never remarried or squandered their inheritance. I wanted a better future for them. I just wanted a better future for them."

The mayor's wife spoke: "Asma, enough complaining. We know your story, dear."

Ignoring her, Asma continued: "I sat in front of my father's grave, and I felt this light . . . coming from afar . . . round and golden . . . I was crying and complaining to him about fate. . . . My whole body shook. I started to shiver, and the light came closer. . . . I closed my eyes. . . . It still came closer. It pierced me, so I rose from my place in confusion. . . ."

Maryann made the sign of the cross. Mervat did the same. The commissioner's wife began reciting verses from the Quran.

Asma continued: "It pierced me, every part of my body. . . . It penetrated me. . . ."

Someone whispered, "It sounds like her soul is haunted by spirits!"

Asma gestured to the smoke, saying, "This darkness . . . in front of me . . . it moves like a woman embracing a man . . . melting into him . . . mixing, dispersing, disappearing . . . disappearing . . ." Tears rose in her eyes, and she sighed. Then she said, "I opened my eyes, and I was trembling. I focused my vision on the tombstone. Then I grabbed at it in fear, and I couldn't move my feet. . . . The wall was very cold . . . and rough to the touch. I hurt my finger, and a drop of blood welled up. I looked at my finger. It was white like snow. I thought I'd died and come alive again. The drop of blood was red, and it moved by itself on my finger. It moved all the way to my heart. . . . In front of my very eyes . . . it stayed there. Then I looked for it, but I couldn't find it. Suddenly, I heard a sound . . . like a chicken searching for food . . . I looked in front of me, and he was standing! He was standing right before my eyes!"

Hanan gasped in alarm, and passed out, falling across the legs of the commissioner's wife, who looked at her in consternation. Maryann began shaking. Fawziya calmed her, patting her hand, and saying, "God is great, in the name of God, God is great."

Maryann mumbled, "She had a revelation. She's touched by spirits." Their eyes did not leave Asma.

Asma was quiet. Then she said hoarsely, "He was standing in front of me just like you all now."

"What was it?"

"Him."

"Who was he?"

"He . . ."

"Human or jinn?"

"I don't know."

"In the form of an animal or a person?"

"I don't know."

"Did he have goat's legs, or a cat's face?"

Apprehensively, Asma said, "Two yellow eyes stared at me from the darkness, with long lashes and a strange look. I don't

194

know. It came out of the darkness. I saw a shadow . . . like the shadow of a fox, maybe. But all I saw were the eyes. Whenever I tried to close my eyes, I felt a hand turn my head and open my eyes. Whenever I turned my head away, the hand slapped me. And the yellow eyes never left my face. They engulfed me. I almost lost consciousness. . . . I held on to the tombstone, and begged the creature to go away."

"Did it go?"

"Did it take advantage of you? Did it prey on you? Did it say anything?"

Asma held her head, and said, "I don't know how long I stayed, or what happened. Those round yellow eyes . . . They don't leave me . . . and I felt like I heard their voices together."

"The dead?"

"My father and my husband . . . They were laughing. . . . Their voices were calm, and inhuman. They spoke quickly. I didn't understand what they said. I just heard my name. . . . They were talking about me . . . saying that I must die . . ."

"Don't say that!" they all cried with sympathy in their eyes. "God forbid!"

By the end of the evening, everyone bemoaned Asma's condition, and was afraid of Asma, and believed her.

That day, Hazim was different. His condition had begun changing rapidly every day. The major general looked at him suspiciously, not knowing whether Hazim had already lost his mind, or if he had yet to do so.

Two other people were certain that Hazim had lost his mind. Umm Ayman and Gaber knew Hazim's moods by heart. Umm Ayman saw the details of both his private and his public lives. Despite the distance between her and Hazim, she could see his madness and his weakness. She heard all his telephone conversations, attended all his family gatherings, and knew him better than she knew her own husband and son. The distance allowed her to see him better up close.

She considered him both kind and strange. She expected a man who lived alone to live differently: to go out more often; to drink alcohol or smoke pot, or do both; to bring women home day and night; watch racy films on television; not read much; dim the lights; listen to music. When his son was with him, he spent a long time talking with him. When his son left, Hazim's life did not change much. He had no friends, and no girlfriends. He did have a lot of acquaintances. But lately, something had changed in Hazim.

He no longer woke early, or sipped his decaffeinated Nescafé. He did not leave one hundred pounds every Thursday. He would bury his face in his pillow, and would not answer if she called for him. His face was downcast; his eyes looked baffled. It seemed to her as if Hazim must have lost his mother, or gotten involved in some shady business, or undergone some financial disaster, and it was her duty to help him. So Umm Ayman decided not to steal the hundred pounds for three weeks in a row, giving Hazim time to return to his usual self. She was not heartless. She was a mother and a wife, and was sensitive to others. Before all else, she was a human being, a part of the world, and of her country. She had to do her national duty. She still had no national identity number, even with all the government's great efforts. If nothing else, she could fulfill her duty to this poor man. Three weeks passed like a gust of wind. After that, she needed to think of her children, her husband, and herself.

Gaber saw Hazim more than anyone else did. He always went with him to Benha, even the infamous day of the graveyard, when Hazim had decided to spend the night in the mausoleum because he had work to do there. He had asked Gaber to return in the morning. Gaber had not understood what Hazim was making—perhaps a subterranean vault in which to hide treasure, or maybe drugs or something.

He finally decided that Hazim must be dealing in antiquities, and the captain was his partner in crime. He was the one who had bullied Hazim into this unscrupulous line of work. When they had differed, Hazim had decided to carry out the work alone. What got on Gaber's nerves was that he was still earning the same meager wages, while Hazim would soon be drowning in money. Every day, Gaber was tempted to confront the thief Hazim, who hid behind his veneer of education. No doubt the police had begun to suspect Hazim. Otherwise he would not look the way he did. He had begun to utter "Good morning" as if it cost him more than the cell phone companies make. At least these companies followed their motto, "Talk on your mobile as much as you want," but Hazim never even spoke. His downcast face and cold eyes never looked up from behind his book.

Actually, Gaber had one particular suspicion, although it was completely unconfirmed: Hazim had begun smoking weed, or maybe something worse. If this was the case, things were looking up. Hazim ought to know that smoking was an equalizer among people. A driver could sit with a doctor, for instance. In the presence of fresh hashish, all classes disappeared. What confirmed Gaber's suspicions was the night Hazim spent in the mausoleum in Benha. Gaber returned in the morning to take Hazim to Cairo, and Hazim's face was full of warmth and ease. He was smiling and relaxed, his eyes shining like car windows that have just been cleaned by an innocent street urchin holding a towel dripping with water.

Hazim had leaned back in his seat that day and closed his eyes, as if he were having a beautiful dream. He neither read nor asked for anything. He covered his eyes with his hand so as not to awaken from his dreams into the sunlight. From Gaber's limited experience with hashish, which had recently become very expensive, he knew its effects. He could remember the first time he had tried it. It was his wedding day, and his friends had advised him to take his time with his new wife. They told him that hashish would help him last longer. Beyond that, he remembered almost nothing of that night. Gaber smiled as he watched the owner of the car at rest, seemingly out of his senses, pleasant in a way completely foreign to him. It seemed to Gaber that that the smoking would not last long. Hazim must be entering the worst days of his life, at least since Gaber had started working for him. Gaber concluded that Hazim must be a desperate thief. Gaber could not keep from hinting to Hazim that he knew some things. So he said casually, "Dr. Hazim, did you smoke a cigarette today?"

Hazim looked at him in surprise. "No."

A little stiffly, Gaber said, "Excuse me, sir, if I disturbed you."

Hazim nodded, letting the conversation pass.

Gaber fell silent, and thought to himself, "What a thief."

The major general was looking at Hazim amusedly, saying, "Who is she, who got the best of you, my friend?"

"Excuse me?" Hazim said in surprise.

"The woman. A man always loses his reserve over a woman. Tell me about her and I'll help you."

Hazim said sharply, "We were talking about the captain."

"If she's leading you on, then forget her. These days, there's no time for playing around. Your battle with the captain is sufficient. You don't need a civil war too."

Hazim ignored the major general's comment. "He has a son in high school," he said, "from his second wife. He married her secretly twenty years ago."

"I don't understand. We were talking about the woman who's leading you on. They're all the same—white, yellow, blonde . . ."

Hazim said, "I'm talking about the captain. You are making me very uncomfortable."

"We're friends."

"He has a son in high school, up for his high school exam. I remember those days. The children of the elite, like you my friend, would be visited by the superintendent during the exam. He would come over to them and whisper a few answers in their ears, in a subtle and vaguely guilty way. Today, the superintendents don't even feel guilty anymore. The children of the elite no longer need any whispering from the superintendent, with the accompanying looks of envy from the rest of the students. These days, my friend, they give the whole test to the students a day, sometimes even months, before the exam. We've come a long way in the past several decades. We have all become greedier, and fairer. With the captain's son in high school, I have some thoughts of my own . . ."

"Just a minute! Are you also implying that my son cheated in the high school exam?"

"That's not the point."

"It *is* the point. I help you because I don't like corruption. Not because I'm like the captain."

Hazim sighed. "All I said was that your son was a child of the elite."

"Child of the elite, yes, but he never cheated once."

"But the captain's son will doubtless buy a test. The question is, which one? What is the most difficult exam these days?"

"If he doesn't just buy them all . . ."

"You are my best friend. You deserve a Mercedes."

"I don't like your attitude anymore. You've changed."

"A little. Not much."

Change? Hazim had never considered it. He had to continue the battle. She had to remain safe. The sound of Asma's weak voice had mobilized him. He understood her position, for he was the cause of her suffering.

Her daughter had said, in a sad voice, that her mother was sick and could not move. She was not well. She cried night and day.

Self-control was a trait of nobles. Power was a trait of ancient priests. In this woman's presence, he was not sure that he could control himself, and he possessed almost nothing. He wanted to slap her ten times, and then kiss her ten times. He wanted to wring her out until she swore that she was his forever. He wanted to torture her with no mercy until she regretted the day that she thought to bury her body in the little tomb. He would open the tomb and turn it inside out in broad daylight. He did not care. He would pass his hand over her whole body, as he had before, and she would tremble and fall apart before his eyes.

She did love him.

She adored him, and fell to pieces before his eyes.

She was neither disloyal nor a liar.

Sincere.

He trusted the dead.

She loved him passionately, like a thief loves treasure.

For her to remain in the tomb was as impossible as his coming days.

Compassion floated to the surface. All the mightiness faded.

His disaster was like no other. His life was lost, but not like other lives. He would not leave her. The day his hands closed around her heart, and it had quaked between his palms, he knew that she was hidden in his depths . . . in his substance . . . in his longing and in his grave. Her eyes pleaded, cried, and grew to encompass history, and all the dead and the living. The problem was that he had never lived a day until he spent a night in the tomb. All the awakening of death and the desire of life had poured from his arteries. The moment of penetration, when their bodies clung together, she had stopped breathing and closed her eyes. She held on to him as if she hoped that he would be part of her forever. Her body engulfed him, as if it would take him in. She was like no other woman. The moment she reached her climax in his arms, she shivered and moaned as if she were a mage from another world. She did not ask for anything. She expected nothing. She basked in his presence. Every touch of his set her voraciously afire. In his arms, she transformed into a woman. She melted and took form, as if her life had just begun.

She did a lot of murmuring. She begged, and dreamed, and hoped. He did not understand all her words. He did not need to understand them. Her murmurs still whispered in his ears. They made him feel that he was penetrating the impossible; that he was not like everyone else. Does a man need more than that? Does one dream of anything more than that? The night that he spent with her, he came to know how a woman could give and expect nothing in return. And how her feelings poured forth endlessly. And how emotions could overcome all sins.

Time is always passing. Before he could ask her about her life, talk with her for hours, laugh and quarrel, anger and forgive . . . it passed . . . before his arms could encircle her head like the pillars of his mausoleum. He understood. Unfortunately, he knew . . . She was afraid, of him and of herself. She did not want to destroy her palace with her own hands. He might understand how she thought, but he did not feel the same way. He was not able to tear down her palace with his hands. There must be a way out. He wanted her, and he did not want to destroy her. Fear for her overcame him. It overcame the anger, the longing, and the memory of a day or two. The earth leveled on its supports again, and all his pains ceased. If something happened to her, what would he do? Why must love conquer all?

The dirty secret came to light, and it appeared that the captain would purchase only two tests. It was unclear whether he had attempted to purchase more tests, and failed, or if he had not even attempted it. The police arrested the teachers, and the captain's second wife, who claimed that the captain's secretary had purchased the tests, and that she had known nothing about it. The secretary was also arrested, and the captain went to the police station several times. His blood boiled, and he resolved that Hazim's remaining days would be red— the color of hell—and that he would deal the next blow at Hazim's most vulnerable spot.

*

While Hazim analyzed his latest victory against the captain and those of influence, he received a call from his lawyer, who seemed tense, and asked to meet with him as soon as possible. What occurred to Hazim at that moment was a certain woman who had become part of his life and his being. The thought seeped into his veins, and through his body, spontaneously and smoothly. All the way there, he agonized about what had happened to her. What had the captain done to her? Imprisoned her? Killed her? Tortured her? And what would he do? What did he want?

Inside the car, he closed his eyes and said to the driver, "Go as quickly as possible."

Gaber nodded.

Hazim arrived at the lawyer's, entered the office, sat down, and asked, "What did he do with her?"

Surprised, the lawyer asked, "With who? The lady from Benha?"

"Did he do something to her?"

Giving Hazim a long look, the lawyer answered: "No."

The lawyer did not ask about the reason for Hazim's concern. He did not ask once about the nature of Hazim's relationship with Asma, or why he sacrificed time and money for her sake. Mr. Munir, the lawyer, was in his seventies, and had seen a lot of life. Nothing could move him or astonish him. He had grown accustomed to not asking about things that did not concern or interest him. He was practical to the highest degree. He carried out every action efficiently and discreetly. For twenty years, he had been the central figure of Hazim's company. Without him, nothing could be accomplished. Hazim had neither the time nor the talent to deal with the masses, and he did not need them.

The lawyer said calmly, "I know there is a personal difference between you and the captain, and I want to help you as much as I can."

"It's not a personal difference," Hazim replied angrily. "It's a matter of principle. He is a man who irritates me on more than one level. Corruption pours out of him."

"Hazim," the lawyer said casually, "we've been friends a long time. I don't believe that we ever agreed to fight corruption in Egypt. Indeed, my work with you prevents me from that."

Hazim opened his mouth, but the lawyer continued: "Sorry. Perhaps I am interfering in something that does not concern me. . . . Forgive me. I am old enough to be your father, and today I find myself in a crisis because of the captain."

"What do you mean?"

"I mean that a lawyer who works for me is under investigation. He's supporting his siblings and his parents. Because of the captain, they arrested him today for bribery. Evidently he will spend years in prison because of the captain."

"I don't understand. If the employee was found guilty of giving bribes, then he deserves to go to prison. I don't understand what that has to do with me."

"If the employee was giving an envelope containing a thousand pounds to a government employee, as he always does in order to secure new building permits for your company, then he deserves to spend years in prison? He and the government employee concerned?"

"You mean that you give bribes in my name? To fulfill the needs of the company? Did you ever ask me about this?"

The lawyer smiled. "Hazim, your company has run like this for years, since it was established. And you know it. Don't tell me you don't. You pay me to take care of your dirty work. If I didn't do this, then you'd have to close down today. Do you understand? If I didn't give a thousand pounds to the government employee, then he would not issue the permits. I am not doing anything against the law. It's a very complex situation. There are two kinds of corruption: clean corruption and dirty corruption. We all partake in clean corruption, every day. With every breath we take, we lie, we give a bribe, we treat with respect someone who is undeserving. But dirty corruption is the corruption of the captain. Now a young lawyer has lost his future because of your idea to stamp out corruption. In the end, it is a personal battle between you and the captain over a fellaha you both wanted. I have no issue with that in and of itself. My issue is with the innocent victims."

Hazim said, "Mr. Munir, I think that's enough."

"Yes, it is enough. A young man has lost his future because he wanted to do his job as thoroughly as possible, and secure a permit for you. For you."

"I understand what you mean."

There was a moment's silence as Hazim tried to process the lawyer's words. Clean corruption and dirty corruption, a bribe to a government employee who counted on it to get by, from a young lawyer whose job was to secure building permits. Had he really been ignorant of this? Had he been ignorant of it, or had he ignored it? How fate played with humanity through corruption, until one did not know whether to take pity on it or punish it, fear it or respect it.

He put his hand to his forehead.

The lawyer said gently, "Hazim . . ."

"I'm listening."

"I'm sorry. Forgive me. I had to talk with you."

"I know. What will happen to the young lawyer? Might they release him with a fine, perhaps? How can I help him?"

"This is a case of bribery. We can try to help him, but I'm not optimistic."

"And his family," Hazim said, a little painfully. "His monthly wages must reach them regularly. I will pay them myself. And we must try to help him as much as we can. Will he be released?"

"You understand me now? Your war with the captain . . . Perhaps a winner will emerge from it, but I'm not sure that it would be worth winning that fight."

"He's despicable. A savage thief of the first degree."

"In this day and age, those who are caught for bribery are the small fry who have no influence. Hazim, if you wanted to oppose corruption, then you'd have to arrest everyone, from the smallest to the largest. It grows in us, my friend, with the fog of Cairo, and the rust that leaves its taste in our mouths when we drink the pure water of the Nile. . . ."

"I must think."

"Of course. I sympathize with your position. Asma's position in this case is also ambiguous. She may be sent to prison, and she may not. But there is a difference between the young lawyer's case and Asma's case."

"What do you mean?"

"We cannot interfere in the young lawyer's case. It's a clear case of bribery. As for Asma's case, ultimately it's a case of inheritance, and a family dispute over land. It might be resolved or it might not. Her husband's family does not want to negotiate because they already made an agreement with the captain, as you know. Do you see what I'm getting at?"

"I believe so."

"What do you intend to do?"

"Let me think about it."

When Hazim stretched out on his bed that night, he had no intention of sleeping, or resting, or reading. He felt like the general of an army who had lost his soldiers for no cause or benefit. The corpses accumulated in front of him, and under his feet. He was left standing tall, holding a flag of victory, but there was no one to cheer and rejoice. No one to salute the flag. Everyone had died. It seemed to him that most of his army had not even known the reason for the battle, or the nobility of its cause. The soldiers had fulfilled their service against their own desires. They made their promises, leaving behind children, women, elders, destroyed homes, and ruined reputations.

An oddly niggling, disturbing thought came to him: there was not much difference between him and the captain. Indeed, he and the captain were two faces of the same coin. Perhaps his father had been mistaken. Maybe the social class of scholars was not really his. Maybe the real class of scholars was the wretched, belittled one that stretched its few pounds, and did not know the route to Marina, and did not have a car like his, and had never once eaten in an American restaurant, and never entered his social circle, his building, his street, his country.

His country.

The country that was in his mind was pure, glorious, with no traces of ancient woodworms, no decay of mummified corpses, no scent of musty air. The statues of great ancients had no effect on his world. Nor all the slaves through the ages, nor the turnover of nations. Naive imaginings for those who had enough comfort to allow them to ponder, judge, design, build, fight, love, dream, give, take; to hire the masses and the poets, to observe the valley from above, astride their white horses.

His country . . .

No. Gaber and Umm Ayman, and everyone who crossed his path, morning and evening, did not concern him. The captain was none of his business. Neither the lawyer, nor his bribing secretary, nor his unfaithful wife, nor . . .

His country . . .

One woman did concern him, though. She approached him from afar, wearing a long, loose gilbab; with a warm heart, an innocent body, and a bundle of well-used clothing mixed with alluvial soil; with desperation, hope, fear, and overwhelming ruthlessness and strength.

Usually everything comes to an end in the morning. And when morning arrived, Hazim would have to come to a decision. War or peace.

There was not yet time for Asma.

But there would be soon.

The young lawyer came to his mind. He had seen him before. Dark skinned, short, slender. He had a shy smile. His words were few, and full of admiration. He was the victim of whom? Of Hazim? This pain in his heart was not only from love. It was more than passion for a woman. It was a nagging feeling of guilt.

When the phone rang, he was not at all sure that he wanted to answer. Hearing his son's voice, he remained silent to contain his longing. Khalid began speaking in a weak voice: "I'm fine . . . I miss you. Everything here is easy and new. There are so many conveniences and machines, and . . . I'm probably a little lonely. I work day and night. . . . I'll try to come in the summer. . . . Dad, you know what I miss in Egypt?"

"What?"

"Sugarcane juice from the juice shop in Mohandiseen. You know which one I mean? I can still taste it. That green, dry taste, like you're drinking plants from the ground, or jungle leaves. Totally sweet, and totally green."

His father was silent a minute. Then he said, "You never told me that you drink sugarcane juice."

"Is it not allowed now?"

His father smiled. "No. I remember the last time I had some. We should have drunk it together. It will give you a reason to come this summer."

Khalid was quiet a moment. Then he said, "I think that I've lived in Cairo more than you."

"And yet you left it."

"I miss it, and I miss you," Khalid said decidedly. "It's beautiful when you see it from a distance."

"The colors go together," Hazim said.

"Dad . . . are you all right?"

"Why do you ask?"

"I can always tell with you. You don't sound good."

Hazim smiled bitterly. "I'll be good tomorrow. Don't worry."

It was three in the morning when Hazim dressed and went out. Cairo was, of course, still wide awake. He felt a strong desire to do something he had never done in all his life. He decided to buy a carton of yogurt from the supermarket. He did not ask the concierge of his building to purchase it, and he did not order in. He did not ask Umm Ayman to get it. He did not stop the car and ask Gaber to get out and buy it.

He saw ahead of him the European-style supermarket that was only a short walk from his home, and was open twenty-four hours per day. He went inside briskly, looking for yogurt. He heard a woman yelling at a cashier. She looked middle-aged, and was fashionably dressed, with blond hair and eyes that looked like they owned the whole world. She was clearly angry, and probably drunk. Instead of punching her pillow with her fist, she had decided to buy shampoo and take out her frustration on the young employee. He lowered his head in embarrassment, and did not respond. She yelled, "Answer me, or I'll slap you in the face! Such insolence! They pay you to work, not to talk to me like that! What kind of man are you?"

After she huffed in exasperation, and left the store, the clerk looked at his co-worker and said, "Whore!"

Hazim smiled sorrowfully, and said to himself, "Father—may you rest in peace—you must have been wrong. Excuse me, but we do not know one another here. We don't know each other at all."

He grabbed his yogurt and left the supermarket. He studied it, touching the white surface. "Asma," he whispered. "You're going to be well. And you will be mine." Even after he finished the whole container, the bitterness had not left his throat. He was worried that it would never go away in his lifetime.

He spent a restless night, remembering the few hours with her, afraid of forgetting them. Hours in which the world was as clear as light and grief was defeated. When he seemed to control the whole world, building an entire civilization. Asma was in his arms, brimming with life, in a dark tomb amid the heaviness of death. She was a corpse come to life to eat food from pharaonic dishes, sip refreshing milk, and listen to music. In her coming to life, she also brought him to life. Life was complete, lightning appeared in the sky, and he disintegrated.

The little freckles remained on her cheeks, as well as the creases around her eyes when she looked into the sun. He must have loved her from the moment his eyes fell on those little freckles. That very moment. There was no controlling his heart. The echo of her voice when she told him that she loved him made his eyes sting. Her moist, tender lips never left his hand.

In the morning, he took matters firmly in hand. He had decided that a truce would not be just at this point. The day that he surrendered, he would have the leverage to impose his conditions on the captain. At that moment, negotiation would be impossible. In any case, though, there would be casualties. Every war has its casualties.

He spoke first with the major general, then with the lawyer. It seemed to him that nuclear deterrence was the best strategy in this situation. He would begin studying his weapons now. He wanted everything prepared for the decisive blow. Perhaps he could avoid it if he began by negotiating. He spent two weeks exhaustively researching the captain's life, his family, and his many connections.

From *The Book of the Dead and the Living*

FIRST THIEF,

Those big eyes will follow me forever. A look of longing and hope-lessness, pleading and haughtiness, her fingertips on my body—delicate, hesitant, nervous. When I startle at night, it is because I am frightened for her, and long for her. She must be kept safe forever. For her fingers are in the depths of my heart.

These writings are about my country, not about me. I wanted a book all about me. I wanted something to immortalize myself. Like every Egyptian, I wanted my name recorded in history. I was obsessed with history, not with the present or the future. Every nation has its strength, and every nation has its magic. Every nation has its concealed corner from which one sees things clearly. I am not sure of my history. The past has begun to grow obscure. The future does not yet concern me. As for the present, it is contained in those frightened, shy, adoring eyes.

We were talking about Egypt, O Despicable Thief. It turns out that my Arabic is not so poor. I am certain it is better than yours. Are you Egyptian too? I hope you are Egyptian. I do not like the idea of foreigners robbing our tombs. If you are Egyptian, then at least, as my father used to say, "I'll come to an understanding with you"! Poor Father. If you are Egyptian, then I will call you Fellow Thief, and if you are not Egyptian, then I will call you Lowly Thief.

Thirteen

HAZIM SMILED WITH SATISFACTION. Then he looked up the captain's number. He looked at the lawyer sitting across from him, and the major general at his side, and waited for the captain to answer. When the captain picked up the phone, Hazim began recounting, in the undeniable excitement of revolution, Captain Murad's long history.

"Murad, or should I say Sir Murad, you were in Port Said in '76. You were a nationalist who loved Egypt. I don't know when you gave this up, my friend. . . ."

"Are you joking? You call me to waste my time?"

"Where shall I begin? There is so much I could say, so much. Details of smuggling hashish in '78. Cannabis was illegal at that time, was it not? A man in your precarious position, with your wide network of contacts, should be cautious."

"One more second and I'm hanging up. I had no idea you were this tasteless."

"Are you recording this call?"

"I am now."

"Captain, in 1995, a relationship was discovered between your daughter and a failing student. He got her pregnant. You traveled with her to London, where you forced the young man to marry her. You gave him what he demanded. Don't say anything. I won't use this against you. These things happen. I just want to inform you that I have just as capable a hand as you do. What I could use against you, my friend, is your young son's involvement in a homicide case in 2000, when he stole your revolver and took it to Marina. After he got drunk with his friends, he asked one of them to go down to the ocean. Do you remember? His friend refused, and your son threatened him. He said that it was a game, and that he should follow him. His drunk friend went down to the ocean. They found his body floating on the surface in the morning. The blame was placed on an unknown party. But the party was not unknown. None of the friends spoke up. They were all drunk, playing with life and death, just as their parents do. I could assist in reopening the case, or at least in refreshing people's memories of the scandals of the wealthy. The media these days will talk about anything. They have complete freedom."

"You've lost your mind. You must be crazy—you dare to threaten me?"

"I dare to do more than that," Hazim said.

"I haven't even gotten started! When I do, you're gonna see bodies dropping all around you. And the first thing I'm going to do, pal—and I am recording this—is to make sure that miserable, thieving fellaha spends the rest of her life behind bars. I promise you that. Enough with your stealing and coveting."

"I don't know who you're talking about. There is no fellaha who is any concern of mine!"

"Don't provoke me, Hazim. I'm beginning to lose patience."

"Do you still want a tomb? Or have you ensured you will be damned in this life and the next?"

There was a moment of silence while the captain thought. Then he said, "I don't know what you're getting at."

"Do you want to negotiate?"

They were silent for a while. Then the captain said, "May I invite you to dinner in my new house?"

"I accept."

In the days of the war between Hazim and Captain Murad, many thieves and scoundrels were arrested. Unfortunately, not all corruption was brought to justice, as Hazim had hoped. Instead, Egypt's jails filled with bribing employees, double-talking architects, and greedy teachers. Hazim sensed that the war could continue for years, claiming the lives of many. He might remain alive, but losing troops and ammunition would do no good. Of course what he truly feared was the arrest of a single thief whom he loved passionately, and for whom he cared deeply: Asma. As long as she was held hostage in the enemy camp, then he must exchange hostages, no matter what it cost him.

Having established his advantage, he was able to call for negotiations. As long as he negotiated for and by himself, and as long as Asma was the only one who needed rescuing, the negotiations would be easy. However, Hazim had come to see people from a different perspective. He began asking himself who was stealing, and who would likely steal one day? Who was disenfranchised, and who would be? Who had lost his dignity in all the commotion? And who would be altogether lost? For whom would tombs be built in this day and age? Who was worthy of immortality? Who deserved death by thrown stones and tomatoes? He had gotten mixed up in a variety of circumstances, but had not lost himself between the commoners and the elite. He remained himself. He created history and a legacy, weaving together art and engineering from death and fire. Maybe he had lost himself a little . . . just a little.

When the captain opened the door for Hazim, he was wearing red pajamas. His hair was dyed a deep black, and he was meticulously groomed. The captain embraced Hazim warmly and patted his forearm. He led him in graciously, seated him on the couch, and sat down beside him. Then he said, "We were just playing games. It wasn't really a war."

"Perhaps you're right," Hazim replied.

"I told you before, nothing binds the friendship of two men like a woman they both want."

Hazim opened his mouth to disagree. The captain smiled, and said, "The fellaha's yours, my friend. I can't handle her cunning and sorcery, and I don't need anyone burdening me at this time of life. You know what I really need, and what I've left worldly things for?"

Hazim did not understand, and promptly replied, "What do you mean?"

"What, your friend the major general didn't tell you? Don't you see? If this was a war, no one would ever win. But it was a game. Each of us set his animals on the other, the animals perished, and we're left laughing at the end. Egypt is still all right, as long as it still has men like you."

"Pardon me, but I cannot say the same about you."

"I started telling you about the novel I'm writing," the captain said, "and about my poetry, but you didn't show any interest. Want to hear some more? Or have *you* taken up writing poetry and novels?"

"Have you remarried?"

"To a woman who likes my poetry, and likes my novel. Every day she reads to me of a world that I have seen but not felt. It made no impression on me, nor I on it. Land that my feet would cover hundreds of times every day, but the soil never stuck to my shoes. Its polluted air never seared my eyes, awakening me and bringing me back to life."

"So that is poetry. Please, don't tell me you love Egypt, when every one of your children has an American passport!"

"No more than a passport. Like a bank card, or a ration card from the old days, just to make life easier. Belonging is not a card, or a language, or any *thing*. It's dirty water, the taste of which never leaves your throat. Sorry, I'm talking too much. I've missed our conversations. Would you be mad if I told you that I've gotten married?"

"Why would I be mad?"

"Because I married a certain university professor named Rasha."

Hazim burst out laughing. Then he said, "Are you kidding?"

"You're in love with a peasant, but you can't believe I'd marry a scholar like you?"

"Why?"

"Why did I remarry, or why are you in love with a fellaha?"

"She's not from . . . I mean, she's different. I don't know what to say."

"Congratulations. Say 'Congratulations.' She reads my poetry, and she needs me, and I need her. She doesn't want my money, and she's not overly needy. She has her life and I have mine. Most important, she's a free-spirited woman. She doesn't have a closeted heart and eyes like other women. There's a shortage of smart women. She and I both feel the danger of the unknown. Her unknown may differ from my unknown, but either way it's the unknown. Egypt is slipping through our fingers like a silk ribbon. That's what frightens me. I don't understand this generation. I don't know if I've been living in an illusion, or living a lie of my own making. Like me, she fears the unknown. It comes from distant lands, foreign to us. They call it extremism, conservatism, revolution, and I don't even know what else. Maybe terrorism. Maybe ignorance. They're all rubbish. Even the students in her university ascribe to these ideologies—can you believe it? They criticize her clothing, and her philosophical talk. When the day comes in which the students think they know more than the teachers, what do you do? I used to love my country of the pharaohs; we were all brothers. But now I dream of another time. Perhaps it has not yet arrived. She and I hate the unknown. We met, we came to an agreement, we find comfort in looking forward to another age. And freedom that no one comprehends. So much freedom. Women laughing without inhibition, giving liberally of themselves. A bottle of wine inspiring merriment, not burning in hell. Or do you think that I will be burned no matter what, and a mausoleum will do me no good? No, don't say anything."

Hazim smiled, and remained silent.

After reflection, the captain said, "You know what I think?"

"I'm not sure I want to know."

"I think our country is not slipping through our fingers like a silk ribbon after all. It's time that's slipping through our fingers. If fate would grant me some time, I would do so much."

"More than you have already?" Hazim asked sarcastically.

"I need to understand, and see, and enjoy. I've had no time for enjoyment."

"So you're greedy, and don't want to leave the women of the world until you've tried them all out?"

"I haven't tried them all."

"And Rasha is happy with you?"

"She's what I always wanted. She is the hope that sustains me now."

"And for her?"

"What's that to me? Do you ask Asma what makes her happy? We all think of ourselves. But I will answer your question. Yes, she is very happy with me. We talk for hours. We drink coffee. We listen to music. We read poetry. Ah, I'm finally at ease. I wish you could come across a woman like her. Ah, but I forgot. She *was* yours at one time. That doesn't bother me at all. Are you going to marry the fellaha?"

Hazim did not answer. It was the captain's turn to laugh. He laughed until his eyes filled with tears. Then he said, "All right, I'll get her out of the lawsuit. But I have one condition."

"What is it? Don't tell me that you want a mausoleum built somewhere else."

"You came to negotiate," the captain said, "and I want to negotiate. I will get Asma out of the lawsuit, and I will buy the land and the mausoleum from you. I won't pay more for the land than you did. I will pay the full value of the mausoleum, but I have one condition."

"I agree."

"Don't be too hasty."

"I agree."

"Do you know what it is?"

"I think I can guess."

"What is it, then?"

"You want me to change the color red."

"Will you do it?"

"Immediately."

"You're starting to understand me, and I'm starting to like you. I always liked you, but now I consider you a real friend."

The captain extended his hand, and said with emotion, "It was quite a game, wasn't it?"

Hazim agreed: "It wasn't war, and there were no winners. We are friends, and we were all along."

The strange shift in Asma's condition over the past several days worried her children. Her mother watched her, and sucked on her lips. It was clear to everyone that Asma was not well—that she had been through difficult times, flipped on both sides like a fried fish. She sat in her room for hours, looking out the window at the fields of pale corn. Her mother said with finality, "My prediction came true. You've lost your mind."

Tears gathering in her eyes, Asma replied: "I've accomplished everything that I desire. I sold the land, and I accomplished everything I wanted to do."

"Your whole life you've circled around yourself like a frantically hungry nanny goat. You make me sick."

"I will go on Hajj this year," Asma said steadily, eyes brimming. "But before I go . . ." She fell silent. She rose, and dressed herself. As she walked, she recited Quranic verses, her tears pouring, her hand wiping them away. She arrived at the home of Umm al-Madamir, and went in. She said weakly, "I want your help."

Umm al-Madamir looked at her, her eyes steady. "Ask, my daughter."

She trembled, remembering him. "A man . . ."

"I know. There's always a man upsetting our lives. Fate, my daughter. Did you come to ask me to bind him? I knew you would."

Asma trembled, and said bitterly, "I want him to wander his whole life, never seeing another woman, ever. Don't just bind him. Blind him. Stop up his ears. You understand?"

"We all wander our whole lives, apple of my eye. No one sees or hears. Ask for something that I can refer to my spirit partner, that won't make him angry with me."

Asma's fingertips passed over her neck and chest, and she whispered, "That he will never love someone else. That he will be for no one else. I couldn't bear it. That he will be just as deprived as I am. It's inevitable that he will meet someone new, that he will lie in her arms, and close his eyes, ecstasy on his face." She was silent a moment, remembering what he had looked like with her. Then she continued: "His eyelashes move a little, and his grasp tightens on my arm. I would die before seeing him with another woman. I mean, in my imagination, of course."

Umm al-Madamir replied with compassion: "You don't need to tell me about it. They know it already."

"He's a man in my imagination. I mean . . ." Asma fell into a miserable silence. Then she continued: "So bind him."

Umm al-Madamir said slowly, "There is no reversing this."

"Is there any reversing a love like mine?" Asma replied fiercely. "They say that love purifies one's heart, blotting out selfishness. But it's the very essence of selfishness. Do you understand?"

"I may not understand, but he will. Don't worry."

Asma's health showed some improvement after her visit to Umm al-Madamir. She began talking with her children more, reviewing the accounts for the land, and facing her unknown future. The legal victory came, who knew from where, or because of whom. Or did she know? For her . . . had he done it for her? Should she celebrate, or kill herself from sadness? She had so much to put in order. People expected so much from her. There were friends who came to her daily, bearing offerings in fear and awe. Her children clung to her. Their fear that their mother could have ended up with six years in prison prompted them to flood her with their obedience, gentleness, and sympathy.

As Asma slept in her bed, holding her back as usual, the phone rang. Her daughter answered. Salma approached Asma's room softly, her eyes shining. She said, "Mama . . . Do you want to talk with someone who's calling for you?"

"Who is it?" Asma asked hoarsely.

"Karima!"

Asma paused. "What did you tell her?"

Salma answered confidently. "I told her that you were here, of course. Mom, you have to talk with her. Tell her that we're better than her now, and that I got into the College of Engineering, and that we have plenty of money . . ."

Asma cut her off. "Tell her that I'm sick and sleeping."

"Talk to her for my sake," Salma persisted. "She treated us like servants! Please, Mom."

Asma took the phone, and said weakly, "Hello, Madam Karima."

"What's up?" Karima asked warmly. "Have you forgotten your friends? I haven't heard your voice for so long! What are you up to? Are you going to come visit me sometime soon? I want you tomorrow, and bring some of your kaak cookies. I have guests, and they want to try some country-style kaak."

"It would be an honor, Madam Karima," Asma answered weakly. "But I'm sick, and not leaving my house."

"Sick? With what?"

"My back is bothering me."

"Then come the day after tomorrow."

"I can't. Believe me, I'm not going to be going out. You and your friends can come here any time. My house is your house, but I won't be coming to Cairo again."

"Are you crazy? You won't be coming to Cairo! Ah, I understand. You got into trouble with my ex-husband, Murad. It's over at last! I threw him out, the low-down good-for-nothing! I got rid of him for good. But we're still friends, honey, right?"

"Of course," Asma said. "But I can't, believe me. Ask anyone."

"Come in a wheelchair then! You have to come tomorrow. I want to talk with you about so many things."

Asma persisted. "I won't be able to."

"Don't be so silly! What sort of fellahi trick is this?" She hung up.

Asma gave the phone to her daughter, saying, "She won't call again."

"Why didn't you chew her out?" Salma said angrily. "Why didn't you insult her? Mom, I don't understand."

Asma gestured for Salma to sit down, saying, "Women like Karima are foolish and conceited, but we don't know the future. It's better to keep the powerful within reach."

"And our hospitality? And your graciousness?"

"Status, Salma, is like the seasons. Grapes don't come out in winter, and guavas are green in May. Status is like guavas, my girl. It needs the summer sun. When you're rich and powerful, and married to an officer, and your brother's a diplomat, and you have a villa and a car, then your status will ripen and be ready for picking. Until that season arrives, you must be patient. If you pick a guava now, it will never ripen. Its season will come, my dear."

"Why doesn't the season ever arrive for you?"

Asma smiled bleakly. "Like my mother says, because I'm Asma-the-Nobody. And perhaps the season did come, and I let it go bad so that you could pick the guava. Real status is very rare, my dear."

"But you're better than her."

"Come on, Salma. My back's hurting me again."

"But dignity doesn't have seasons. We either have it or we don't."

"Indeed it does have seasons, and the season has not yet come. Don't fight with me. My back hurts."

Hazim leaned his cheek on his palm as he looked at Taha. He resembled his mother, and had her large eyes and delicate mouth. He smiled warmly and asked, "How are you? Have a seat, Taha."

Taha sat, a little shyly, and said, "I came to thank you for everything you've done for us, Dr. Hazim."

Hazim picked up a card from his desk, and wrote on it some words in English. He gave it to Taha, saying, "Take this card to Ambassador Mohsin al-Rajhi in the State Department. I've spoken with him about you, and he wants you to intern in his office. You're going to be a diplomat someday, right?"

Taha took the card joyfully and exclaimed, "I don't know how to thank you!"

Hazim took some smaller cards from his pocket. He said, "Here's a membership in the Ahli Club for you and your family. A diplomat like you has to be a member of a club in Cairo. Also," Hazim continued calmly, "the British School will accept your brother Ahmed whenever he is ready."

Taha said quickly, "My mother does not want that any-more. She says that she's staying in Benha forever, and she wants him nearby. But she's going to have him learn English."

Hazim picked up the phone and called his secretary. "Isn't there a private English school in Benha? I want to know who owns it."

Then he turned back to Taha, saying, "And Salma?"

"She didn't make it into the American University. Mom says that her scores are good enough for the College of Engineering, and that the College of Engineering is better." Taha sipped his orange juice shyly and nodded toward Hazim.

The phone rang, and Hazim jotted down some information. He hung up and said, "You can consider Ahmed accepted into the English school in Benha. Its head is a friend of mine. Don't pay him anything."

Taha's jaw dropped. He said, "Dr. Hazim—"

"No need to thank me," Hazim said casually. "You already did." He smiled. After a moment, he asked, "How is your mother doing?"

Taha said automatically, "Not well."

A slight shiver passed through Hazim. "What's wrong with her?"

"We don't know exactly," Taha replied, his voice suffused with emotion. "Ever since she spent a night in the graveyard, she's been different. We think that she's touched by spirits, or something like that. We've tried everything with her. Sometimes when people pass by graves at night, they go insane. Did you know that? We're worried about her. God be with her. My grandmother reads to her every day from the Quran. Sometimes, when she's with us, she just withdraws and disappears, as if she's in another world. She doesn't see us or hear us, and her eyes fill with tears. We're all worried about her. She's going on Hajj this year. We all hope that she'll come back well. She must be touched, because her heart is as pure as an angel's. My mother has never hurt anyone. The jinn like to humiliate people who have kind souls. She shouldn't have gone alone at night to the graveyard. Dr. Hazim, are you listening?"

Hazim was gazing toward the window, as though he did not see Taha. Then he said, with deliberation, "Taha, I want to give you a piece of advice."

"Anything."

"Don't talk about jinn in front of the ambassador. It gives a poor impression of you, and you want to give a good impression in your workplace."

"But it's the truth," Taha said. "My mother's been touched by the jinn. You don't know her. She was never like this."

Hazim said reflectively, "Yes . . . perhaps I don't know her. She was never like that." Then he asked suddenly, "Is she in pain?"

"She's in lots of pain. She suffers like a saint, believe me."

Hazim said decidedly, "I believe you."

Taha continued: "She's such a blessing. Really. She blesses everything she touches. She's sacrificed so much for us; she's suffered so much. But when she touches my forehead in the morning and murmurs a short prayer, I feel comforted. There's no one like her in the whole world."

"She is one of a kind," Hazim said slowly.

Taha spoke with enthusiasm. Extolling his mother always animated him. "She never married after my father. Everyone told her to, but she didn't. I was nine, and she was my father and my mother. Even if she put a knife to my throat now, I would obey her. Her word is my command. Whenever she wears white, she looks like she's from another world. . . . I'm worried about her, but she'll get better eventually. Right?"

"Yes."

"I'm sorry. I'm taking up too much of your time, but you are my mentor and my model. Mom respects you so much, and she prays all the time that I'll be like you one day."

Taha extended his hand to Hazim, who shook it warmly and said, "I hope to see you often, and hear all your news. Give my regards to your mother."

"I'll do that."

When Hazim descended the stairs, he felt his mind wandering. His heart was full of worry and sorrow. He had never felt so sad. It was a heavy sadness that weighed down his heart and clouded his eyes like fog.

He got into his car, and Gaber started the engine. Cairo seemed extra foggy that day. There were the clouds of pollution that hung on the horizon, as if the city was always on the verge of drowning. Yet it never drowned. Or as if it was on the verge of expiring between flames. But it never burned. And then there was the fog of sadness, helplessness, love, longing, dreaming, the past and the future, and a life of both ease and misery at the same time.

As soon as Gaber began driving, he pushed a button to close all the windows, as usual. He turned off the radio and ceased to talk.

Hazim smiled sorrowfully, and said, "Gaber, open the window."

Surprised, Gaber opened the window with relish. "And the dust, the pollution, the noise . . ."

Hazim said softly, "Don't open it all the way. Just part way. A little dust is healthy and necessary." His eyes strayed to the window. "What is this area called?"

"Shubra, sir."

"Yes. You've told me that before. And what about you, Gaber? How are you doing?"

Gaber opened his mouth to respond, but Hazim continued: "Is it possible for you to answer the question in only three words?"

Gaber began internally ridiculing Hazim's eccentricity and arrogance, as always. Aloud, he said, "I don't know, sir. Sorry, I never studied grammar much."

"All right, go ahead and talk. But I'd also like to read, so I might stop you at some point, okay?"

"Whatever you want, sir. My mother-in-law is going on the Umra pilgrimage this week. Poor thing—you know her story. Have I told it to you? Her son lost the fingers of his right hand. He was a blacksmith. Her second son lost his right leg in the same accident. Since then, she's been in shock or something. She told my wife and me to have lots of kids. In case one of them loses a leg, the others could still work. I give her money, and her second daughter's husband works in a customization factory. He lost his job . . ."

"Gaber . . ."

"I understand. I'll stop now."

Hazim leaned back in his seat. "You can open the window more, just five centimeters. What's this area called?"

From *The Book of the Dead and the Living*

In my country, Intelligent Thief, we venerate mothers. We bow and scrape to them like so many ancient goddesses. A mother's hands contain goodness. By her hand, she spreads blessing. From her hand, when her displeasure falls, famine, drought, and poverty spread. I know an Egyptian mother. She dazzled and enchanted me, and ensured her control over my soul. She showered her children with her gentleness, and her severity horrified them. Sometimes, Thief—you coward, robbing dead people and tombs—we fear women as if they were devils who ruled over every weed and piece of greenery. Like locusts, inundating life and burying hope.

Asma Muhammad al-Sharqawi is an unknown mother who crowned herself Queen of the Age. She succeeded in elevating her children and achieving her aim of equality in Egypt. Asma succeeded in realizing the goals of the 1919 Revolution, the Red Cross and the Red Crescent, the July Revolution, the Revisionary Revolution, the Privatization Revolution, the revolution of those who went never to return, the Religious Revolution, the Industrial Revolution, the revolution of the four financiers who monopolize all of Egypt, the revolution of the ancients and the moderns, the revolution of open markets and closed markets, the revolution of team spirit and of dissolution, the revolution of private schools and wiping out the low-income bracket, and incomes altogether. Asma Muhammad al-Sharqawi decided that she wanted a better future for her children, and that she wanted to renew and restore the principle of equal opportunities. Unfortunately, no one informed her that trying to revive a corpse that never even existed is very difficult. Or that humans are born with their fate in their hands already: a farmer's child is a farmer, a baker's child is a baker, the child of the wealthy is wealthy, the child of the poor . . . Or that everyone has a foreordained place, and that whoever tries to cross those borders ends up in a mental institution. In any case, Asma the mother, Umm Taha, in all her innocence and naïveté, fought the fire-breathing dragon, and she won. Her eldest son will enter the Diplomatic Institute. Her youngest son will attend a private school and learn English. Her daughter will study in the College of Engineering. Asma is still a fellaha. She realized, while fighting the dragon, that the fire it breathes is no match for the power of floodwater, flood soil, and our longing for floods. Nevertheless, Asma will not outwit me, even if she overcomes all of Egypt. For I am a scholar, and I hold the secrets of civilization. She will be mine whether she believes it or not. Perhaps the age of peasants and soothsayers has come to an end, friend, and we have entered a new age. I do not know what to call it: The Age of . . . do you know? I will search for the word I need in the dictionary, and then return to writing on this wall. . . . Or maybe I will invent a new word. In any case, Asma will be mine. Record that in your memory. As for describing this age, allow me to look up the word.

Fourteen

ASMA, WITH HER WHITE GOWN and her calm, patient face, was seated in the courtyard of the house. Beside her was the walking stick upon which she leaned these days, due to her agonizing back pains for which no one had any explanation. No one knew whether they were real or not. When Asma went on Hajj with Hanan and her husband the officer, Hanan was pregnant in her sixth month. She would look at Asma with reverence because Asma, in her uncanny intuition, had predicted that Hanan would conceive. She even told her, during the Hajj pilgrimage, that she would give birth to a beautiful boy. During the Hajj, Asma rushed about in complete health. It seemed like such a miracle that Hanan the officer's wife trembled, and said with feeling, "God be praised. Oh, God be praised!"

When Asma returned from the Hajj, she decided to return to her walking stick. It seemed to everyone that it was magical, with a head like an ancient Egyptian snake, or a wise scarab granting harmony to all it touched. The staff was part of an extraordinary power that did not work by force.

A staff endowed with knowledge of the unseen.

A staff endowed with the pain of days past and patience for the days ahead.

A staff endowed with honor maintained and widespread graciousness.

A staff endowed with the ability to spread curses or destroy a home.

A staff endowed with spirits from the graveyard, a darkness that could captivate a soul, and a light that could bring pain or hope.

A staff endowed with the longing that never leaves hearts, and the peace that gleams from between gusts of cold wind.

A staff she gripped gently . . . It stifled her, stimulated her, and weighed on her like a heart beating endlessly.

With her loose white gown, her sweet, winning smile, and her eyes filled with sadness, compassion, and strength, she would whisper to her children, "May God bless me through you."

Everyone, from child to grown-up, approached her with reverence, and bent toward her. And she would lay her hand on each head, reciting some words from the Quran. She would pat the head gently, saying, "May you be blessed, God willing. From a mother's heart, I pray for you." A boy might smile; a girl might get misty-eyed. Thus the graveyard incident, and Asma's victory over the devils due to her deep faith and her forbearance in the face of pain, multiplied her charisma beyond comparison, providing the sort of power few possess. Even the people of the village revered her. For she had communed with the jinn, and had become one of those rare people with supernatural knowledge. If they angered her, it would surely be their undoing.

No one but Asma touched her chair in the middle of the courtyard. When, following three years without children, Hanan gave birth to her first son—as Asma had anticipated— Hanan gathered him up in her arms to go to Asma's courtyard. He was not even two days old, and Hanan took him to visit Asma, for her to bless him with her innocence and purity. As soon as Asma saw him, she took him gladly and laid him across her lap. He nearly disappeared in her flowing white garment. She extended her hand to Hanan, saying, "Give me a date." Then she took the date, chewed it, mashed it in her hand, and put it in the baby's mouth. He remained serene, watching her with curiosity. He opened and closed his mouth, chewing the mashed date in surprise, and its tart flavor was the first thing to shock him in this world. It roused him and taught him.

Asma murmured some Quranic verses, softly stroking his head. She whispered to Hanan, "God will bless you through him, inshallah."

Hanan replied with feeling: "You choose a name for him, Hagga. Please. Give us your blessing."

Asma said confidently, "He is Yusuf. For his beauty and his honesty."

"His name is Yusuf then," Hanan agreed.

Asma's eyes wandered momentarily to the window. She whispered to her son, "Is the mausoleum finished?"

"Yes, mother."

She nodded. Then she smiled sadly, and said, "There is nothing better than a son in whom God blesses you. He will support you, like my son has supported me."

Taha patted her on the back, and said nothing.

Then she whispered, a little hopefully, "When are Hazim and the captain coming?"

"Today at seven. For some reason, Hazim wanted to see the sunset. I don't understand, Mom. Who needs a palace, just to die?"

"Maybe the one who never knew how to live."

"Yeah," Taha said admiringly. "You have a beautiful way with words, Mom."

She leaned on her walking stick, saying, "I want to see the mausoleum today, from afar. . . ."

Hazim gestured to the space around the mausoleum, saying to the captain, "In less than two years, I created all this. You see the marble on the floor of the plaza? High-quality marble gives the place a sense of peace. One must select really excellent marble for a place like this. If we imagine, for instance, that those who come here will be your children visiting after you have passed away, sadness will overwhelm them for the first year, and perhaps the second as well. After that, they may grow bored, and cease to make visits. That is why we need a design that will draw them to the mausoleum."

The captain frowned. "Your words always were like bullets."

Entering the plaza, Hazim replied: "If my words are bullets, then you are the pistol itself."

"Rasha dumped me," the captain said, looking around the plaza. "Did you know that?"

Hazim whistled appreciatively. "Why doesn't that surprise me? I heard the same thing about your first wife. What was her name?"

The captain waved his arm, saying, "Don't remind me of her. What a disaster that was."

Hazim smiled. "You've been dumped twice. An honor few Egyptians attain. Why did Rasha dump you? I thought she was your soul mate."

"She's complicated and crazy!" the captain told him glumly. "How were you ever able to be with her? She screamed at me—can you believe it?—and she wouldn't listen to my poetry. I married her so that she'd listen to my poetry. When she quit, I left."

"Didn't you say that she dumped you, or did I misunderstand?"

The captain fumed. "Enough talk about women. I've written my will. When I die, I don't want any woman buried next to me—especially not my wives! This mausoleum is just for me and my children."

Hazim continued with enthusiasm: "Look at the tall pillars and the giant windows, the way light fills the place, as if you were beginning your life . . ."

"This plaza is for them. I won't see it."

"Look at the mausoleum," Hazim said swiftly. "Tell me briefly what you think. A lofty tower, stretching to the horizon. Do you see the way the arrangement of stones is like a rainbow?"

"I'll tell you what I think at the end."

"You must tell me now. Come on, have you ever, in your long life and in all your travels, seen anything more beautiful than this?"

The captain looked at him and said, "First let's see the tomb. That's what concerns me."

Asma gripped the head of her staff, yearning for his face and eyes. She could feel her fingers tracing over his face, his chest, and his entire body. She closed her eyes and opened them repeatedly to assure herself that she was really seeing him. He was approaching with the captain, walking toward the mausoleum, talking confidently, gesturing toward the edifice, his design, his glory.

Most of her body was hidden behind the wall that Hazim built. She forgot all about her walking stick, and it fell to the ground. Her hand fluttered automatically to her throat, touching her neck as though making sure that she was alive, or as if she wished for death and the grave. In a split second, her breath floated through the place, and Hazim sensed her presence, he knew not how. He knew she was near. He broke off speaking, and his gaze moved toward the wall behind which Asma was hidden, her eyes forlorn and wistful.

His hand squeezed into a fist. He closed his eyes, and reopened them. The edge of his vision took in the fingers that were pressing into the wall so hard that they turned white. They were hesitant yet tenacious fingers. He knew them well. Asma's fingers.

The captain looked over at Hazim as if he could see them both together, here and now in the plaza. He smiled, saying, "You go delirious in her arms, don't you?"

Hazim did not answer. His eyes wandered to where Asma was hiding, his face solemn and stony, as if he had just made a new decision.

The captain said, with boyish delight, "Where is she, the owner of this green land? Will she meet with us today, or do you think she's still mad at me?" He pitched his voice louder. "Umm Taha!"

Asma looked around for her walking stick. As soon as she found it, she leaned on it, hiding entirely behind the wall. She breathed quickly and fearfully. She dreaded Hazim's approach at that moment because she would fall to pieces in a second in his presence, throwing her stick into the river and burying her fear in the graveyard. The wall was thick, protecting from the sun's rays, rain, revolutions, enemies, poverty, oppression, wasting one's life, gaining possessions, and the great lethargy that overcomes all the miserable survivors. Asma muttered to herself incoherently. His scent and the touch of his hands never left her lips, or her hands, or her soul.

Her son grasped her hand, and she said energetically, "Let's go—take me home—I don't like tombs." Her son guided her, bewilderment showing on his face. His mother's new energy was another of her miracles. She spoke decisively, striding beside him: "I want to meet with the land supervisor. Don't discuss anything with him, or come to any agreements with him. We're going to sell the harvest differently this year. Taha, did you meet with your aunt yesterday?"

Her question took him by surprise. He said defensively, "She called me. She's the one who called me."

"She should call your mother first, then you. If someone hates your mother, then they hate you too, son, right?"

He nodded.

"What about the mayor?" she continued. "Why didn't he come to congratulate me on completing the Hajj? I hope the low-down bastard rots! When you become a diplomat, people will take us seriously. I want you to prepare to take your siblings to Cairo on Friday. Buy Salma some clothes from there for college, and take her to the club. Take good care of her. You're not just her brother. You have to protect her as her father would."

He said solemnly, "I understand, Mother."

"And Ahmed has no self-esteem," she went on. "He's as happy as can be at his new school, but he must be more confident. Talk with him, and teach him some English."

Suddenly she stopped. Taha looked at her, awaiting more orders, or wise words. She said thoughtfully, "They buy life and death. And both their lives and their tombs are robbed. We're not like them, son, but I would like you to find us all a clean piece of land that gets a nice breeze and dew over night."

"Why, Mother?"

"I want it to be appropriate for a simple tomb, so that death will not part us. We safeguard our beginnings and our endings, my dear. But we won't build a great mausoleum. Dewdrops and breezes will suffice for us."

"Don't talk like that, Mom. It makes me worry about you."

"Taha, the place where your father was buried is full, and it gets inundated with water. We must find a good place. Death has certain claims on us, son."

The captain laughed, a little hysterically and a little excitedly, since he felt Hazim's emotion and Asma's presence somewhere nearby. Suddenly he said, "I don't know who ended up winning in the deal of the mausoleum—me, you, or Asma."

Hazim replied, still distracted, his eyes boring into the wall: "Must there be a winner?"

"There's always a winner. I'm sorry to say that my intuition tells me neither of us won. Asma's won."

Hazim inclined his head sadly, a little broken, and said nothing. The captain continued: "The future's in her hands, not mine or yours. I'm from a past age. . . . And you? An unusual priest, and she . . . always is."

Hazim wanted to tell him that he had not despaired or given up, that Asma was his, that he had complete control over her desires. If he wanted her—and he did want her, as he had never wanted any woman. He did not know for certain if he would ever win her. If only he were sure, or even almost sure. No expectations, or contingency plans, or any order at all. Even with all his distaste for randomness, his very existence had become haphazard.

"You want to enter the mausoleum now?" he asked. "This time, if you don't tell me what you think, I'll leave you here and go home."

The captain was walking next to Hazim, and watching him. "Tell me first," he said. "Is it beautiful? Do you like it?"

Hazim answered proudly: "Stunning. An artistic wonder. See?"

The captain descended the steps greedily, his eyes devouring the tomb.

"What do you see?" Hazim asked confidently.

The captain whistled appreciatively. "I see wonderful things."

Hazim said excitedly, "Look at the colors, at the symmetry of the walls, at the fine carvings at the corners of the wall, as if they were the corners of time and of one's lifetime. See the beauty? Look at the little openings that timidly soak up the sun. I'm going to add a few more words here on this wall. . . . Captain?"

The captain did not answer. Hazim looked around for him. The captain was sitting on the steps, his head leaning against the wall. He had left this world. Hazim dropped down beside him, and said irritably, "You try my patience to the very end. Now you die before praising this great work! Oh well. It's a really beautiful mausoleum. See the little openings that lap up the sun?"

From *The Book of the Dead and the Living*

FIRST THIEF, THE ONE WHO hastens to take the first step, we are surrounded on every side by real enemies, but they have been present forever. Doubtless you know them: the Persians and the Romans.

The Persians—I do not know much about them. I have not read Egyptian history. Did they once colonize us? Perhaps. They try to penetrate the borders from every direction, though in this age they enter through the heart instead of the borderlands. And the Romans? They colonized us, and still do to this day. We have neither gained independence from the Romans, nor prevailed against the Persians.

Our hope, First Thief—and you may know the future that I do not, and maybe you are laughing at me—our hope is for victory to come from within. For Asma to soak up the Persians and the Romans as the sands soak up dirty and clean water alike. We have few weapons, but our army is great. Patience is the key to survival, as it is also the place of expiration.

Forgive me for waylaying you when you are on your way to rob a tomb. I have bothered you with words that you may never understand. Here lies the tomb, waiting for you—untouched, overflowing with treasures. Plunder as you like.

Modern Arabic Literature

The American University in Cairo Press is the world s leading publisher of Arabic literature in translation.

For a full list of available titles, please go to:

mal.aucpress.com